The Other Side of Darkness

Linda Wood Rondeau

The Other Side of Darkness

Contact Information: titleadmin@pelicanbookgroup.com

Cover Art by Nicola Martinez

Harbourlight Books, a division of Pelican Ventures, LLC
www.pelicanbookgroup.com PO Box 1738 *Aztec, NM * 87410

Harbourlight Books sail and mast logo is a trademark of Pelican Ventures, LLC

Publishing History
First Harbourlight Edition, 2011
Print Edition ISBN 978-1-61116-138-0
Electronic Edition ISBN 978-1-61116-137-3
Published in the United States of America

Dedication

To Steve: Thank you for your years of understanding and making life anything but boring.
The road we've traveled has rarely been smooth. Yet, you have stayed beside me through every twist and bend, even a few detours. Thank you for being my friend and constant companion.

Prologue

He stilled the storm to a whisper; the waves of the sea were hushed…and He guided them to their desired haven.
Psalm 107:29-30

Spaghetti legs, Daddy called them, spindly appendages that kinked when stressed—like now.

Samantha Knowles leaned against the table for support as Bailiff Don Hunter came to the front of the courtroom. "All rise." Judge Normandy entered, his limp necessitating a much longer plod from his chamber to the bench. Soon, the wait would end—three years of sleepless nights, endless days of preparation, postponements, and courtroom theatrics by defense attorneys. After three interminable years, Justice would now show its face.

As the judge took his bench, the crowd silenced to await his summation. Sam glanced at the defendant's table where a calm Harlan Styles sat, a wart on the cheek of humanity, an insulated icicle against the rising heat, tried and convicted—the rest up to Normandy's guillotine.

She fingered her notes, though she didn't need to see them—the image of Kiley's tiny, battered body tattooed on Sam's brain, a brazen scar, indelibly etched on her heart.

Judge Normandy spewed his rhetoric—penal codes entwined with case facts, cold, distanced from the victim, yet succulent to Sam's ears. In spite of their dry, unflavored essence, she feasted on his words—each pursuant finding heaped upon the other and topped with the last morsel, "The court can find no other just rendering than life imprisonment."

Victory should taste better, like syrup over pancakes—not this metallic aftertaste.

A woman's scream silenced the murmurings, and Sam turned with the rest of the throng toward the source. Kiley's mother, Brenda Smith, had leaned over the rail and grabbed Styles's sleeve while Don Hunter ordered her to step back.

Brenda was weak—just like Mama was weak. Brenda Smith deserved the same fate as Styles. Too bad stupidity wasn't a felony.

The DA stood in the back of the courtroom. Without a word, Abe Hilderman, her boss and second chair, abandoned Sam to shake the DA's hand. A simple, "Good job, Counselor," would have been nice, even a slap on the back. Nice, but not necessary. Abe often said that Justice was its own reward.

Emboldened, Sam stepped closer as the deputy handcuffed Styles. He saw her, pulled free, put his shackled hands on the prosecutor's table and leaned into Sam's face, his cologne lethal… a designer blend—suede, water, and moss—like Daddy's. Sam fixed her stare into steel-gray eyes, magnets that drew her headlong toward a spinning saw—Styles's demeanor, a calloused calm…except for his lips… parched, purple–tinged lips that formed his threat. "Keep your light on, Miss Knowles."

Her spaghetti legs wobbled. Three years of lamp-lit nights had failed to chase away the recurring dreams—dreams Sam kept secreted from everyone, *especially Justine,* Sam's best friend. How, then, did Styles know she kept a light on all night?

1

Three Months Later

Sam searched Bob's Bistro for Justine. A short ball of fire like her shouldn't be that hard to find in an empty diner. Sam spotted Justine's wave from the back of the restaurant, her perky demeanor hardly indicative of her frenzied call, begging Sam to meet for lunch.

Justine shoved the basket of greasy fries in Sam's direction. "Sit down long enough to eat and hear me out."

Sam's stomach flip-flopped. "I'm not hungry."

"You're never hungry. Don't argue. I thought we could split the fries, but I ordered you a hamburger…no bread and Swiss cheese. Good grief, Sam, you need to eat more or you'll waste away to a vapor. I thought after the Styles case—"

Everyone thought Sam would return to normal after the sentencing. Normal, by whose standard? Normal was a word prosecutors found hard to describe. "This case will never go away, Justine. Scum always rises to the surface." Sam grabbed a fry, took one bite and put it down on a napkin.

"You have to let go, Sam."

"Are you talking as my friend or as Abe Hildernan's new paralegal?"

"Both."

"Which one first?"

"Friend—look, Abe's had some private conversations with the DA, lots of them. That's all I know."

Abe's chats with the DA were nothing new, only their frequency caused alarm. "What did I tell you? Sometimes I wish I could curl up on my bed and sleep into next week—that I'll wake up and this whole ugly mess will be over."

"That's the other thing I have to talk to you about."

"This is Abe's assistant talking now?"

"Have you looked in a mirror lately? When's the last time you had a day off?"

"College, maybe? So what? Vacations are overrated. For a friend, you sound a lot like Abe."

Justine chomped on a handful of fries, took a sip of her root beer, then swallowed. "Abe has arranged for you to take a three week vacation—his orders…his treat…his itinerary."

"You have *got* to be kidding. Not now—not when Styles has filed another appeal."

"Abe's worried about you, and he thought maybe you'd listen to me better than you listen to him. You haven't slept in weeks."

True enough…sleep was a rare luxury over the past three years. Might as well let Justine think Sam's sleeplessness had been caused by case worries. If Justine knew about the nightmares, she'd tell Abe, and he'd drag a shrink into the whole mess.

Justine leaned in like a period at the end of the sentence. "Besides, you know how slow Justice is. Chances are nothing will happen for months."

"Yeah. Slow, all right…in Kiley Smith's case it crawls. She would have been five years old today."

Rest in peace little girl.

"Abe thinks you've become obsessed, and frankly, I agree. You need to take a break."

"I don't—"

Justine glowered, and when she glowered, it meant only one thing—the fat lady had sung her last aria.

"Fine. I can't fight both you and Abe. So where am I going?"

"Vermont. It's all arranged."

Vermont? The other ADAs described the state like a wilderness ready to be discovered. Not for Sam. Vermont meant nature, and the closest to nature she ever came was a walk in Central Park to mull over her latest strategy against Styles's petitions. "What am I supposed to do in Vermont?"

"Ski. Your instructor will be Alonzo Altamont. Handsome and available, I expect."

"With my luck, gay or married. Besides, I don't have time for romance. I'd prefer to catch up on my reading."

"Read or ski. Whatever."

Skiing…not a chance, not even if Mr. America waited for her at the end of the trail. "What if I refuse?"

"You can't."

Abe wasn't God, he was only her boss. "What does that mean?"

"It means you either go on this vacation, or Abe's writing you up for insubordination. He thinks you need perspective. You could pack your whole wardrobe in those bags under your eyes."

"That obvious?"

"Makeup stopped covering them about two years ago. Three weeks of fresh air will do wonders for your complexion, too. You're looking more like my great-grandmother every week."

Sam searched Justine's face for a hint of a smile or a flicker of amusement in her blue eyes. Nothing. Maybe she meant it, that Sam's face pickled in a brine of zealousness. Oh, well, Justice demanded its ounce of flesh, and if Sam wasted her bloom on its pursuit, so be it. "Thanks for the morale booster."

"I'm serious, Sam."

"Vermont, eh? Where?"

"Three weeks at the Top Notch hotel."

"The Top Notch? Isn't that the Niagara Falls of Vermont? Sounds like a place for couples, not a hot spot for single, available men."

"And skiers, don't forget."

A cruise would have been more opportunistic, restful and would have been cheaper, too.

"If everyone thinks I need rest, why can't I stay home in bed?"

Justine pushed the fries back in Sam's direction. "You shouldn't be so unappreciative. Abe went to a lot of trouble to arrange this for you. Sounds to me like you need a lesson in gratitude."

"I don't need a sermon."

"Wouldn't hurt for you to go to church while you're on vacation, either."

Sam sighed again, this time with resignation. "If you weren't my dearest friend in the whole world, I'd walk out right now."

"Well?"

"Well, I haven't been to church because I've been busy with the Styles case."

"See? You *are* obsessed."

Sam stood. "I'm not obsessed—I'm merely doing

my job. Special Victims prosecutors speak for those who can't speak for themselves, like Kiley Smith."

Justine leaned back in her chair, her posture like a *tsk.* "You're as noble as they come, Sam, but if you're not careful, nobility will hang you."

"Abe said that, didn't he?"

"Not in so many words—"

Sam laughed. She couldn't be angry at Justine any more than a buzzing fly. They both did what they had to do—flies annoyed and Justine preached. "If it means I won't have to listen to your sermons for three weeks, then I guess I'll accept Abe's offer and go. When am I supposed to leave?"

"Saturday morning."

"What about Styles's latest appeal?"

"Already done. Abe and I worked on the brief last night. Sam, you have to step down on this case, let Abe handle things for a while."

Justine called Sam obsessed. Maybe she was, but not over one case. She couldn't let go, not while children still suffered at the hands of abusers, and perpetrators went free. Like the rocks in a riverbed, every time she removed one, a dozen more fell in. "I can't promise I will, I can only promise to try."

"Call me when you get there. And tell me all about Alonzo."

"You've got no business tracking any man, no matter how good looking. Your wedding's in six weeks, or did you forget?"

Justine fondled her engagement ring. "I haven't forgotten my wonderful Robert Ferrari."

"I know… every bit as wonderful as the car."

"I'm not looking. You're the one who needs to ogle once in a while."

Sam Knowles didn't ogle. Men were a distraction she could not afford. "I'll go on this stupid vacation, but that doesn't mean I have to be on the lookout for Alonzo the Beautiful, or anyone else for that matter."

"Methinks you need a new life, Miss Knowles—one where you curl up with a living, breathing male-type person—not the latest bestseller. I hardly need a calculator to add the number of dates you've had since you broke up with Johnny Miller after high school."

All were the crowning arguments of why Sam should never date again. Like Eric who was a cross-dresser, or Phil who forgot to mention his wife. Wild-eyed Jason rode a motorcycle into a department store window after downing a bottle of whiskey. Steve preferred his women in threes. And Tom...well, Tom seemed nice, but had an operation and became Teresa. Romance no longer rode the crests of Samantha Knowles's future—that ship had sailed right past the port of opportunity.

The hamburgers arrived, and Sam took three bites before setting it next to her half-eaten French fry. She pondered as she chewed. Maybe a vacation wouldn't be so bad. Only three weeks. The world wouldn't change in that short a time.

Harlan Styles paced his dormitory room while his cellmate met with a therapist. Three months in this hole, and still no word from Brenda. This prison scene unwound like a bad dream, one where he never woke up. When they brought him here, he thought he could manage a month or two on a misdemeanor, for Brenda's sake, but not life, not for her, not for anyone.

Prison pummeled a man's spirit to a frothing blob. Promises…that's all his lawyers gave him—promises that stung as much as his foster mother's belt while she spouted scripture with every lash, promises as useful as meatless bones tossed to a starving dog. First, they said he'd get out on a technicality, something about a mistake on the ME's autopsy report, a typo, wrong time of death.

Darnell Washington promised he'd figure out an alibi for the both of them at the corrected TOD. Whatever that over-paid excuse for a lawyer manufactured had to work soon so he and Brenda could go on with their childless lives. Too bad about the kid, but that brat should have known the difference between his coke and sugar for her tea party.

Brenda understood Harlan's rage when he found Kiley serving his stash to her stuffed animals. At least Brenda said she understood, and promised to stand by her man. More promises, three years and three months of hot air, full of sound and fury that signified nothing, Brenda's words as rehearsed as a grade-school poem.

The guard rapped on his cell. "Styles, you got company. Follow me."

Couldn't be Brenda…not regular visitation hours. Though he hoped against hope, even if her visit meant listening to her nasally whining. He'd shut out her unpleasant rasps and leer at what he most enjoyed about her. He'd been crazy to tell her to stay away until this mess straightened out. Three months without so much as a whiff of her White Jasmine perfume, which he bought at a hundred dollars a pop.

His face drooped as the officer opened the door to the private visitation room. Not Brenda…only Washington, who lifted his head toward the guard in a yank of authority. "I'll need ten minutes with my client."

The guard stepped outside.

Harlan blinked away his hatred for all things legal, even this mound of flesh disguised as a friend, the proverbial wolf in sheep's clothing and Harlan's only hope. "What's up? I didn't expect you until tomorrow."

"I had an inspiration, Harlan. The private eye we hired handed me our best out, yet. I'm filing a motion for mistrial, maybe even a civil suit against the city."

"Don't mess with me, Darnell." Harlan put his hands on his head, squeezing until he winced from the pain. "If you don't get me out of here, I swear, I'll kill myself. What have you got?"

"The ME angle isn't going to fly. Judge Normandy hasn't budged one iota, and the cops have punctured every alibi I've been able to come up with. I could go to appeals court, but I don't know if I can prove harmful error." Washington held up a folder. "But, this… this is a gem. How does prosecutorial prejudice sound?"

"Prejudice? Is Knowles a racist?"

"Not racism, Harlan. Gender."

"She some kind of man-hater or something?"

"It's a stretch, but eventually I could prove her psychologically unfit to try your case."

Harlan cringed at the word, *eventually*, a word that smacked of more stalls, more hearings, more thin promises. He swiped a trembling hand over his brow. "Do whatever you gotta do, Darnell. Just get me out of here."

Prosecutorial Prejudice. Pretty words, whatever they signified, and the way they slipped off Washington's tongue jump-started Harlan's hopes. Like kindling, the phrase ignited new purpose; Samantha Knowles would regret the day she signed on for the case. She'd pay, one way or another, an eye for an eye, tooth for a tooth.

The more maddening thing, the thing that wrung him inside out, wasn't so much the thought of losing Brenda, as hard a pill to swallow as any—only a matter of time before she found another golden goose, regardless if Harlan was in or out of prison. But for three years, he'd been Knowles's target—a scarecrow holding a wafer-board shield while she slung her thousand arrows.

Like Lot's wife, fire and brimstone turned his life to a living hell—all because of Knowles.

She had to pay for killing his soul, suffer as he had suffered—a death for a death.

2

Sam turned on the car wipers and drove the next hour to a rhythmic *clip, clap* in sync with her off-key rendition of "Me and Bobby McGee." Lucille, her Cavalier, didn't mind a few sour notes now and again. All the assistant district attorneys scoffed at her refusal to trade the old girl in. But how does one sell a friend—a first car—Sam's only car. The day she turned eighteen, she walked on to the car lot, said that she wanted to buy a Cavalier and that she didn't care what color. And that was that. Never asked questions, paid in cash, named it Lucille and drove her off the lot. Something powerful in that experience...like she'd become a grownup.

She patted Lucille's dashboard. "You're still a right smart-looking car, as good as the day I bought you."

Sam avoided singing in public places, only daring to let loose when in the shower or the car, and she never sang in church. She supposed God didn't need to hear her voice to know her heart. Besides, Justine sang loud enough for the two of them. Though she never bragged about her short-lived professional singing career as a Christian rocker, she showed off her talent at every chance, ripping into harmony and hitting high notes challenging any diva. Who dared to render their sour notes when standing next to perfection?

Sam snapped on the radio, filling the air with a

mix of oldies while the morning mist thickened into torrents, rendering visibility to near zero. Common sense told her to pull over, not try to push her way through to Vermont in this weather. Common sense said that Stowe Mountain could wait a few more hours. For thirty-one years, Sam obeyed common sense, but what was a vacation for if not to escape the dictate of common sense?

Common sense aside, Lucille would not run without gas. Sam scrunched herself forward; the road signs still no easier to read. Logic, common sense's sister, said there should be an exit ramp soon—a fill-up for Lucille, a bite to eat, and a cup of coffee, prudent objectives even for the weather-resistant driver.

Or—

She could use the weather as an excuse to turn around and go back to Manhattan, tell Abe thanks, but the rain melted all the snow and that maybe she could go skiing next year. She'd tried one more debate with Abe last night, but his ultimatum punctured her thoughtful rebuttals. "You're going, Sam, or you won't have a job to come back to tomorrow."

Justine had to get one more sermon in, too. "Don't look a gift horse…"

Horses were something else Sam avoided.

There had to be better places to go in April other than the Green Mountains. Shivering with the sudden drop in temperature, Sam hit the defrost button and wiped the window with her sleeve, swerving to the right slightly when she saw the sign. "Ah. There. Haven—two miles."

The icon underneath the exit sign indicated only one hotel and one gas station. Where there was gas, there had to be coffee, although she could try to push on through to Whitehall. Or, maybe there'd be better choices on I-89. She couldn't be far from the junction. Her stomach groaned like a disgruntled defendant. Sam glanced at her gas gauge—Lucille was running on fumes.

She turned on her directional. "Haven, it is."

Merging onto a two-lane thoroughfare, she followed the white lines until she came to an intersection. The sign said to turn right onto a narrower road, more like a cow path, a tarmac trail through the forest. What next, a dirt road leading to Ma and Pa's Boarding House? Wilderness stretched to the right and to the left, as far as she could see through the downpour, anyway.

Logic could not be silenced as easily as common sense. Something had to be wrong. Even a town she'd never heard of couldn't be that isolated. She should turn around now and chance it to Whitehall.

The mountainous mammal came from nowhere, a mammoth brown blur that stood directly in front of her. Sam screamed and braked, but too late. The wheels locked, and Lucille screeched forward, a two-ton bullet. Metal crunched and glass blasted. Sam's head snapped forward then backward, a limp appendage as Lucille slid down the embankment, the crumbled, blood-spattered moose stuck to her hood. Car, driver, and beast came to a rest at the bottom of a ditch in the middle of God-only-knows-where-I-am-ville.

Fingered antlers pressed against Sam's right shoulder.

She could do nothing except mentally assess the damage and raise her left hand to the hole that was once a window. A sharp pain shot up her leg, and Sam noticed a large piece of glass jutting from her upper thigh. Instead of emitting a scream, she squealed with delight. "Yahoo. I can feel! And you can talk, too. Though no one's going to hear you except that thing on your hood. Hey you, if you're alive, say something."

Dead eyes glared back.

A warm trickle slid down her left cheek…too warm to be rain. She lifted her only moving body part, her arm, up to her head—more protruding shards on her scalp, right arm, and forehead.

She tried the door handle.

Jammed.

Wind-driven, icy rain slashed her face, freezing onto the carcass, a crystallized shroud. Water lapped at her ankles. "Great, Sam. You'll either drown, or freeze to death."

Where on earth was she? Justine had warned her to buy a GPS. "It'll direct you to restaurants, gas stations, hotels, and everything. Some of them have buttons you can push if you're in an accident," she'd said. All well and good, for Justine, who bought every techno gadget that hit the market. Not Sam. She owned a laptop, carried a cell phone, and knew how to shoot a gun, essential skills required of every officer of the court. Beyond that, she left technology to the geeks of this world and Justine.

Maybe, by some miracle, the area had cell service. Sam groped for her cell phone, remembering Justine's not so gentle edict. "Cell phones and diamonds are a girl's two best friends, Sam."

"Rats." She'd thrown her cell into the back seat next to her purse and laptop. "Now what?"

Pray.

"Is that you, God?"

Been awhile, but I'm still here.

"I know. I'm sorry. I got so wrapped up in the Styles case that I haven't had time to even go to church."

Or read your Bible or talk to Me. Not one prayer in three years.

Once upon a fairytale, she believed in prayer—in the seventh grade, after Daddy and Mama died, after she'd moved in with Great Aunt Susan, met Justine, and started going to church with her. Those early days played back, a movie trailer of memories—how Justine and the other people of her church prayed for one another, mostly about doctor visits, blood tests, and x-rays, but for other things, too, like Amy Defort's estranged husband. And then there was a prayer for five-year-old Kiersten Newell, in a coma following a car accident. Justine said people needed to pray in one accord, explaining that meant they had to have the same mindset. Thirteen-year-old Sam feared she might distract God if she stopped coming to church, and ruin Kiersten's chances of getting better. Kiersten came out of her coma, and by that time church became a habit—one Sam managed for over seventeen years, until the Styles case came across Abe's desk and Sam begged him to give her first chair.

Maybe she deserved this fate; a just punishment if God abandoned her. She'd always imagined she'd die young but at forty, not thirty-three, and in the line of duty, not by killing a wayward moose. Abe had laughed when he filed Styles's threat with the police. "Only five years in the District Attorney's office and already your hate file is thicker than Will Ipslick's, and he's been here forty years. Zeal can be a dangerous, thing, Sam."

Sam laughed with the memory. "Well, Abe, so's taking a side trip into a country paradise."

She struggled once more to move her legs.

Nothing.

A fierce gust scraped its frigid claws across her face; rain beat inside and out. "Close your eyes, Sam. Wish it away like when Mama and Daddy argued."

She opened her eyes again and glared at the remains. "Didn't work any better then, pal."

Round, glazed moose eyes peered straight at her. Sam averted her gaze. "Don't look at me like that. It's not like I killed you on purpose."

If these were to be her last moments on earth, she should at least attempt a plea bargain with the Almighty. "God, I know You and I haven't talked in awhile. I'm sorry about that. The thing is, I'm not ready to die, but I don't have much to bargain with. So, I guess I'm throwing myself on the mercy of Your court. If You let me know You heard me and that I'm going to live, I'd sure be appreciative."

Before the concluding arguments, a familiar fragrance, one that simmered from long ago days, rode on another gust of wind. Sam sucked in the hyacinth scent then drifted into unconsciousness.

She stirred from some deep hole; a bright light shone in her eyes. Had she died and gone to Heaven, or did God come to render deserved judgment?

"You OK, miss?" The masculine voice sounded nearby, but where?

"Am I dead? Are you God?"

"No, ma'am. I'm Trooper Cummings. We've got a

team out here to help you. Try to stay awake. Trooper Mitchell is going to talk to you while we get you out of here."

A yellow-slickered sleeve appeared and removed glass fragments from the crooked window casing while a distant voice bellowed, "Bring those oversized pliers here."

The rain had stopped, but rivers still streamed off the moose's remains.

"Ma'am, I'm Trooper Mitchell. Are you Samantha Knowles?"

The female trooper's broad-rimmed hat covered most of her tiny face, but she seemed pretty in an athletic sort of way, as much as Sam could tell in the darkness. She willed her head to nod, but her neck rebelled. "Yes. But how—"

"We ran a make on the license plate. You're an ADA with the District Attorney's office in New York City?"

"Yes."

"Is there someone you'd like us to contact? We couldn't find any info on next of kin."

"My boss, Abe Hilderman."

"We'll notify him as soon as we can. We'll have you free and on your way to a hospital in short order, but first, we need to be certain of your condition before we go yanking on anything. OK?"

"I hardly think I'm in a position to put up a fight."

Another male voice, younger than the first, filtered through the window, "Miss Knowles, I'm Zack Bordeaux. I'm an EMT. We're going to get you out of here, but I need to make sure there's nothing holding you down except Bullwinkle, here."

So they'd sent a comedian. Sam laughed, and pain

zipped along her right side. Abe used to say he got through the tough times by seeing humor in turmoil. Maybe she should consider all this as a minor setback, hardly a tragedy. Her vacation *had* started off with a literal bang and a story to be remembered, one that should bring a smile to Abe's face. Maybe she'd buy a stuffed moose to put on his desk as a thank-you present for her vacation.

"Well, Zack Bordeaux, EMT, I don't think anything else is holding me down. Mind where you put those hands."

Melodious twangs highlighted his snorts, then quiet.

"Zack? You still there?"

"Yes."

"Do you believe in God?"

"Sure do."

"That's good. Would you pray for me?"

"Of course." Masculine fingers pressed against her neck. Maybe she couldn't move, but at least she could feel—she wasn't paralyzed.

Hope.

Had God heard her?

Justine believed accidents were ill-named and called them providential interference, that these episodes people called accidents were God's way of getting one's attention. If God were trying to get her attention, couldn't He have sent an angel instead of a moose? Since she was alive and help had arrived, maybe she shouldn't second guess God, right now.

Zack leaned through Sam's window and offered a comforting smile. "We'll get you out of here as fast as we can." Then he seemed to vanish. "Whoa!"

Trooper Mitchell half-yelled and half-laughed.

"You OK, Zack?"

"I'm good," Zack's response muffled and distant. "Tripped is all. Pretty slick on this incline."

Great. Her rescuer was not only a comedian, but clumsy, too. Alonzo would have swished his way to a damsel's distress.

Shuffling feet and a groan, then Zack's face reappeared. "Your car must've slid at least fifty feet. Nearly out of sight from the road. There's a path on this property that leads to a private lake used by the local fishermen. One of them spotted your car, and hiked back to the main house to call us."

"I thought everyone had a cell phone these days."

"Most folks around here don't bother to carry one—service is non-existent in these hills," Zack said.

"Did you get the fisherman's name?"

"Haven's town justice, Aaron Golden."

"Please thank him for me, will you Zack?"

"I will. He's my uncle."

Trooper Mitchell stuck her head inside the window and handed Sam a sheet resembling a summons. "You can thank him yourself, Miss Knowles. You've got a date in court on Thursday. Speed imprudent."

"You have got to be kidding."

"Sorry, ma'am. We have to give you the ticket."

"No, you have to pay taxes and you have to die, but you don't have to give me a ticket."

Trooper Mitchell didn't offer as much as a smile. "Judge Golden's a fair man—"

"You already know I'm an attorney."

"Still have to write the ticket, ma'am."

Trooper Mitchell left and Zack reappeared, a stethoscope dangling around his neck. Sam dropped the summons and slipped off the stethoscope. "I'll place it on my chest myself, if you don't mind."

"OK." He contorted his face into a serious profile. "I need to take your vitals." His warm fingers against her cold wrist tickled. In the misty night, pearly whites flashed as Sam returned his stethoscope with a smile of her own. If only she could see him better. She imagined him to be as handsome as his smile, a Justine-approved hunk, Haven's Alonzo. "Your BP is a little low, but your lungs seem clear. We're doing everything we can to get you out of the car as quickly as possible, but it's going to be a little tricky freeing you from your hood ornament. Are you impaled?"

"I don't think so."

"Rather than tug Bullwinkle off your hood, we're clipping the antlers."

"Sounds like a good plan—caution is always a prudent course."

A sea of yellow blended into the night. *Snip…snap* and her victim slid off, landing to the earth with a quaking thud. Sam rotated her right shoulder and winced—full range of motion, but at a price. She sucked in the first of several deep breaths, while her rescuers' movements flickered in the flashing lights.

A half-dozen slickers hovered near her left door.

A sudden *pop.*

Another gust blew against her whole left side.

"What was that?"

A new voice answered. "We just took the door off."

Zack leaned through where a door used to be, lifted her arms and checked her shoulder.

"Ouch. That hurts, you know."

"Sorry. Hard to examine at this angle. But nothing

seems broken." He fingered a piece of antler stuck in the seat next to her left side. "Looks like Bullwinkle tore your seat, not your shoulder. Though, you might end up with one huge bruise. That was nearly a half ton against your chest and shoulder. Lucky your ribs weren't crushed. Anything else pinning you down?"

"I don't think so."

He aimed a flashlight toward the floorboard. "Dashboard's pretty crumbled up, but it looks like we can get you out. Can you move your feet?"

Sam wriggled her waterlogged toes. "Some."

Zack turned toward two men in orange vests. "Better work her from the back, fellows. Don't want to go tugging on her legs until we're sure nothing's broken." He reached across to unhook the seatbelt, and a whiff of musk mingled with man smell, like Abe after his noon workout. Strong arms repositioned her, and Trooper Mitchell spoke from the other side of Lucille. "You're going to be fine, Miss Knowles. Zack will ride with you in the back of the ambulance."

"Where are you taking me?"

"Gladstone Memorial Hospital," Zack said.

"Haven has a hospital? Doesn't even have a decent road."

Zack laughed, a tiny snort as if not to offend."Yes, ma'am. Small, but it'll do. As for the road, you took a wrong turn. You should've hitched a left off the exit ramp onto 9N."

"But the sign—"

"Probably some kids messed with that sign again. They think it's funny to switch the road markers. Now, take a deep breath so it won't hurt so much when we move you."

"What do you want us to do with your

possessions?" Zack asked.

"What possessions?"

"The police found your phone, purse, and laptop in the backseat. Not much hope for the electronics, I'm afraid, but I thought you'd probably want your purse."

"Thanks. What about my pilot case...in the trunk?"

"No can do at this moment. It'll take a demolition team to open that trunk. The frame appears bent. Our first priority is getting you to the hospital. You'll have to get it later."

Weakness came over her, a vague sense of being present, yet somewhere else, too.

Lifted.

Now lowered.

She knew she was lying on a stretcher, yet, she felt above it, as if swimming in the air. She gazed upward into Zack's concerned hazel eyes as he covered her with a thermal blanket. "This should warm you up a little." He snapped a buckle. "The incline to the road is pretty steep. We'll be as gentle as we can. Ready?"

"Like I have a choice?"

"Don't worry. We won't drop you."

"Be sure you don't. Remember, I'm a lawyer."

As they loaded her into the ambulance, Sam sighted the North Star, a twinkle of good will. "What time is it?"

"Eight-thirty, ma'am," Trooper Mitchell said, and closed the ambulance door as Zack wrapped a blood pressure cuff around her arm and pressed his stethoscope against it.

In the light, she could finally see his face, cherub handsome, firm, round cheeks, and a pouf of curly blond hair sticking out from underneath his Orioles baseball cap, hazel eyes that met hers with dead-pan seriousness. Alonzo…move over. Sam liked hazel eyes, although she didn't trust them. Daddy had hazel eyes.

Moving.

Unshackled.

Floating.

She could see her body, Zack holding her wrist, checking her pulse, and his worried face. He rapped on the window and shouted into an intercom. "We're losing her…hurry."

Sirens.

"Sam. Sam, don't leave us."

Zack's call commanded her to return to the living. She felt sucked into her body and opened her eyes.

"You're back." He pumped the blood pressure cup again. "That's better. Your color's returning. You scared me there for a minute. Don't you die on me, Sam…you're too pretty to die."

A slight veer to the right, and the ambulance came to a stop. Doors opened, more pulling and lifting, wheels dropping, moving toward opened doors. Zack clipped beside her. "We're at the hospital, Miss Knowles."

"*You* may call me Sam."

"They'll take good care of you here, I promise. A relative of mine works the ER. Her name's Tracey."

More strangers emerged, this time in scrubs, and ushered her into a room.

Unbuckling.

Lifting.

Zack's disembodied voice. "Sam, we're moving you onto a hospital gurney." He came into view, his smile like a tether, willing her to live. Twinkling eyes set off a five-o'clock shadow, a tower of virility. Not rugged, mountain-man handsome but definitely worth staying alive for, if living meant seeing his face again.

Zack set a bouquet of hyacinths on her chest.

"How…where did you get these? Are you a magician, too?"

"Hardly. The owner has a lot of them growing by his lake. I picked these while they were loading you unto the stretcher."

"Hyacinths don't grow in the wild in North America."

"Maybe not in most places. But at Dawn's Hope, they're plentiful. A friend of mine, Jonathan Gladstone, lives there."

Don't debate a gift, Sam, or maybe you should. Look what a mess the last gift got you into.

She sniffed them, their scent spiriting her to another time and place…Westchester. Mama snipped a bouquet and handed them to her. "Go put these in a vase, Samantha. Your father's always in a better mood when I put these flowers on the table."

"Thank you, Zack. Hyacinths are my favorite." Sam drank in their scent, nature's laudanum.

"I'll put these in a vase. They'll be in your room waiting for you," Zack said.

She hated her fondness of hyacinths since Daddy had liked them, too. Why couldn't she love roses or even lilacs, Mama's favorites? Daddy used to stomp on the roses and cut the lilac bushes so far back, they died. For some reason, he spared the hyacinths. Sam never let Daddy know how much she liked them, so he wouldn't hurt them like he did all the other flowers. She never told Justine or Abe about the hyacinths, how their scent came to her whenever she felt afraid, late at night, alone in her apartment, after a bad dream.

She sniffed them again, and blessed sleep took her to oblivion.

3

Zack paced the hospital corridor, torn between wanting to leave, a zillion and one other things he had to do, like grading papers and going over lesson plans, and wanting to stay to be certain Sam was out of danger. He chose the latter, preferred option. He wondered if he should call Jonathan with an apology for not showing up to watch the Red Sox-Orioles game.

No loss for Zack. Lately, Jonathan Gladstone had been as sour as the fox's grapes, his dour moods nothing unusual in and of themselves, especially since his wife and son died. Morose was too tame a word to describe him. His mood was darker now, five years later, then when the divers brought their bodies out of the lake.

Christian duty demanded Zack visit Jonathan tomorrow, but sometimes Christian duty took a man so far out of his comfort zone, he landed in a foreign country. He'd tired of Christian duty. The more time he spent with Jonathan, the more Zack's own moods deepened. Who'd have thought depression could be so contagious?

It was a mystery how some people cocooned their grief and others sprouted wings through tragedy. Sam had a reason to let despair get the better of her, but there was strength in her sass. Her humor seemed sensual in a way. No relatives…probably alone in the world except for her work. He imagined somewhere, or at sometime, life had pushed her down, yet she'd sprung back up, determined to bloom without the sun.

Like Jonathan's hyacinths.

For Zack, faith made a difference when disappointment came. Then again, he never had to cope with losing a wife and child. Grief sometimes ate people inside out, like cancer, and Zack feared Jonathan's grief would devour him. Aunt Sadie had more confidence. "Quit playing shrink to Jonathan's sorrow and leave the boy alone," she'd said every time Zack complained about Jonathan's dark moods. "He'll rout himself out, eventually." Maybe so, but an afternoon with Jonathan drained Zack more than pitching nine straight innings.

His beeper vibrated. Now what? Another accident? He checked the hail. Jonathan—probably wanted to brag about the Red Sox's win tonight. At least the interruption brought him out of his well of thoughts. Good thing. "Much too deep in there to dawdle," Aunt Sadie would say.

Zack went to the nurse's station and dialed Jonathan's home phone. "I heard the recap on the radio. You didn't have to beep me to rub it in. Besides, I was about to call you."

"Not why I beeped you, but for your information, the Orioles got smashed, not beat. Anyway, what happened to you? It's not like you to blow me off."

"I had to go out on that 911 to your property."

"Odd thing about that moose. Aaron told me a few days ago he thought he'd seen one hanging around the lake. I thought he was joking. She's not going to sue me, is she?"

One never knew when Jonathan told a joke, even if you stared him in the face—his vibrato as constant as a fog horn. "Don't be so paranoid, although, she is an attorney."

"I knew it. I don't need to be sued right now. I've got too much on my plate as it is."

"Yeah, right. Like what?"

"I started a new landscape, I'll have you know."

His art might be the very thing to rout Jonathan out, like Aunt Sadie said. "Good for you. As for that lawyer, don't worry, she's not a litigator. I think she's an ADA in New York City, although, you didn't hear that from me."

"Is she OK?"

"Banged up quite a bit, and she went into shock. She's stable now. Thought I'd visit her before I bag it tonight."

Jonathan hedged.

"Why did you call?"

"Can you stop over tomorrow?"

"Probably. Why?"

"Got a question to ask. Nothing serious."

"You can't ask it over the phone?"

"No."

Hesitation. Could be Jonathan didn't want to talk anymore. He generally ended his conversations with a rude disconnect. Sometimes he'd put the phone down and walk away in the middle of the caller's sentence.

Zack heard deep breaths. At least he hadn't disappeared. "Is she pretty? The lawyer lady, I mean. Must be a looker if you're hanging around."

"Not her looks that interest me, although she's pretty enough."

"What, then?"

"She's different."

"In comparison to what?"

A philosophical argument Zack would debate another day. "When I handed her a bunch of your hyacinths, you'd think I'd given her a million dollars. She's like this little girl trapped inside a glass coffin of distrust."

"Stop analyzing, Zack. People aren't puzzles to be solved. Nobody really knows anybody, not even after a lifetime together. Seems like you'd have learned that by now, after Ellie—"

"I told you never to mention her name again." Zack's cheeks burned.

Dennis Faubert stuck his head out the door. "Your passenger's awake, Zack. We're going to move her up to the floor in a few minutes."

Zack nodded an acknowledgement. "Sorry, Jonathan. Gotta go. I suppose you won't change your mind about church tomorrow?"

"You know I don't go to church. Not since Angelica—"

"I'll stop by after services, then. Do you want to fish at the lake?"

Disconnected.

A blonde girl in pink scrubs held Sam's hand. "Miss Knowles, you're in the emergency room. Can you hear me?"

The past few hours rushed in on her... a run-in with a moose...she lived...the moose died...the crumpled car...a handsome EMT...sirens. "Yes. I remember coming in here, now."

The walls and ceilings had stopped their concaves, allowing Sam to focus on the myriad of scrubs that bustled about her. She raised her arm, wrapped snuggly in a sling. "What's this for?"

"The doctor wants you to rest your arm for a few days."

"Is it broken?"

"No. But, you do have significant bruising on your upper torso."

"You talk like a nurse."

"I am."

Sam strained to read the name tag when the nurse checked Sam's IV port. "Tracey Golden. You're Zack's relative?"

"Cousins." Tracey stroked Sam's hand. "Dennis will be in to talk to you shortly."

"Dennis?"

"Dennis Faubert, the physician's assistant. He's almost a doctor…will be as soon as he finishes his studies at Albany Medical Center."

Another reason to never leave the city, real doctors twenty-four-seven. "When in a pinch…"

"You've been in and out of lucidity for the past hour. Glad to see you coming around."

"My head hurts."

"You banged it against the driver's window…hard enough to break the glass. Dennis will explain everything. He's ordered pain medicine, if you'd like something for your headache."

Pills? Should she? Mama took pills the night she died.

"No, thank you. It'll go away, eventually. My clothes, my purse?"

Tracey bent underneath the gurney and put Sam's soggy purse by her feet. "As for your clothes, I'm afraid we had to cut them off. They were stuck to your skin."

A bearded man in green scrubs walked in. "Miss Knowles?"

"You know me. Now who are you?"

He smiled. "Dennis Faubert."

"Ah. Yes. Almost a doctor. So what's the verdict?"

"We ran some tests and did blood work. You obviously hit your head, so we needed to rule out a concussion. Zack said your blood pressure bottomed out, too, although it's stable, now. Nothing's broken, but your shoulder's sprained. We sewed up that gash on your forehead and disinfected the other lacerations…they're small so they didn't need anything else…more like paper cuts...a lot of them. They'll heal quickly. I'm afraid you're going to be very sore for a few days, and the larger laceration on your forehead might leave a scar, but it might not show with bangs. "

Bangs? She'd never worn bangs in her life. She'd worn the same hairdo since grade school, letting her straight red hair fall slightly over her shoulders. How else was this crazy accident going to change her life? Sam stretched her brows and blinked her eyes. "My neck is sore."

"That'll go away. Only minor injuries. You were lucky."

"Luckier than that moose, anyway."

Dennis and Tracey laughed as Tracey took Sam's blood pressure. "That was quirky, all right. Last January we had a confused bear walk down Main Street during a mid-winter warm spell. Poor animal thought it was spring and came out of hibernation. Crazy how that moose decided to take a stroll down the road."

"So what now, almost Dr. Faubert?"

"Dr. Brandon wants you admitted for observation and respiratory treatment. You had about 800 pounds pressing against your chest, a miracle your ribs weren't crushed. You could have easily been impaled. Somebody up there must've been watching out for you. I want you to wear that sling for a couple of days to give your shoulder a rest. Your oxygen levels are a little low, which could be from hypothermia. You're dehydrated, too, so I want to keep that IV in overnight."

"I don't remember you running all those tests."

"You pretty much slept through everything, although I don't believe all your fatigue is attributable to the accident. Some of what we're seeing could be exhaustion."

Could be, at that.

"Does anyone have a cell phone I can borrow?"

Tracey clicked. "Haven's one gigantic dead spot, I'm afraid."

Some vacation, Abe. No phone, no laptop, no clothes. Stuck in the wilderness where wild beasts roam, and they don't have a real doctor.

Another nurse sashayed in, a curly-headed, petite blonde, too young to be a full-fledged nurse, or else she got her degree while still in high school. "Miss Knowles, your friend Mr. Hilderman called. He said if you wanted to go home, he'd come pick you up, but that he thought you'd be better off staying here to recuperate."

Common sense said she should order Abe to bring her home, blame him for her injuries and milk his sympathy for all she could—the sensible thing to do—the Samantha Knowles, ADA thing to do, the woman-who-wore-flats-and-a-black-pantsuit thing to do. The practical thing would be to go back to her apartment or bunk in with Justine, watch chick flicks, and feast on pizza and Dunkin' Donuts.

Moose eyes haunted her.

Dennis said *Somebody* was watching out for her, if so, the accident couldn't have been a coincidence. If God used a moose to get her attention, maybe she should stay and find out what the Almighty was trying to tell her. Besides, if she bunked with Justine, she'd sing hymns or preach all night long.

"Tell Mr. Hilderman I'll give him a call tomorrow."

The yellow-haired Shirley Temple bit her lip, then spoke. "I don't mean to butt in, Miss Knowles, but if I were you, I'd stay a couple of days. You shouldn't be jostling around in a car right away."

"Sound advice. I'll see what I can work out. Then you can tell Mr. Hilderman that I'll be staying in Haven for a few days, at least until Lucille is out of danger."

Tracey paled. "Lucille? Was someone else with you in the car?"

Poor girl probably imagined an overlooked body lying in the ravine.

"Lucille's my car."

Color returned to Tracey's face. Shirley Temple did an about face and left the room.

"Is there a hotel or rooming house in town?" Sam asked.

"My father runs a rooming house, Aaron Golden?"

"The town justice? Let me guess, he's probably the mayor, too."

"My father's a lot of things in Haven, Miss Knowles, except the mayor. My parents have a couple of rooms over the Lighthouse Lounge, a bar, but he doesn't serve any alcohol. The lounge is a restaurant, sort of."

"Sort of?"

"More of a hobby than a business. My parents don't have a license, so they don't charge. They figure they have a lot of company for supper every night."

An interesting concept—one that probably broke a hundred and one zoning laws. A town justice worth his salt should know that.

"Anyway, one of the two rooms is vacant. Leon rents the other one."

"Who's Leon?"

Tracey tucked the blankets around Sam's feet. "Leon's this old guy my parents have taken care of for years. He and Grandma Mazie moved up here when my folks did."

"He's not a weirdo, is he?"

"A little eccentric, but he's harmless." Tracey handed Sam a cup of ice-chips. "So what do you think?"

Did she really want to stay in a boarding house full of loons, a justice of the peace who skated on legalities, a questionably sane grandmother, and an elderly psycho? She couldn't get much rest if she had to sleep with one eye open. Then again, she'd been in more dangerous places, and this might prove to be an interesting diversion. Ironically, a haven from public enemy number one in Sam Knowles's Book of Thugs, Thieves, and Murderers. Vermont could wait; she couldn't ski in this condition, and Zack Bordeaux held more promise as a tour guide than Alonzo the Gorgeous.

"And does your father run his boarding house the

same way he does the restaurant?"

"Oh, no. That's all licensed and everything, along with the store."

"In that case, Nurse Golden, would you ask your father on my behalf? Guess I'll take your advice and stay a few days near the scene of the crime."

"Crime, Miss Knowles?"

"I did kill a moose."

Tracey giggled and left.

Shirley Temple returned, pulling a gurney with the help of a blue-scrubbed attendant. Sam strained to read the nurse's name tag—Tyra Bannings. She patted Sam's hand, a condescending, distancing gesture—six degrees of separation between the live patient and the name on the medical chart. "Miss Knowles? We're taking you up to the floor, now."

As the attendants whisked Sam down the hall, Zack sneaked into view and kept stride with the gurney all the way to Room 107, waiting in the corridor while the nurses got her into bed. He came in wearing a grin and holding a small, crystal vase filled with hyacinths. "I rescued these while you were treated in the ER. Do you want me to put them on your nightstand?"

Sam nodded.

"If it's all right, I'll come back tomorrow and see how you're doing."

"I expect I'll be cut loose by morning."

"Can I give you a lift anywhere?"

"Tracey's arranging for me to stay at your uncle's place."

Sam examined Zack's face, a place where kindness dwelled, a kindness she had never seen before, except in Johnny Miller's eyes, but Johnny Miller broke up with her after high school. Kindness didn't last forever.

"Uncle Aaron's place is a hoot. I'm sure he'll be proud to give you the tour, too. Don't fret over that ticket. Trooper Mitchell likes to go by the book, but Aaron's reasonable. He'll probably reduce it to a bald tire, what he normally does. Well, I'll let the nurses get to their paperwork." He winked at Tyra who winked back then left.

Sam's cheeks heated over the fantasies flitting in her mind. For all she knew, Zack and Tyra might be a couple and Zack's attentiveness no more than a courtesy.

Zack leaned in and whispered, "Tyra's my cousin on my father's side."

"Am I some kind of family project?"

Zack smiled. "Could be." He stood a head taller than Tyra. Then again, flat on one's back, anyone would look like Paul Bunyan's twin next to a female Tom Thumb. Zack squeezed Sam's hand. "I'll see you tomorrow, right after church. I'll go to the early service and be here by ten."

A male nurse came in and slapped a stack of papers on Sam's nightstand. "Let's get your particulars, and let you get some sleep." He harpooned a series of medical questions, hardly taking a breath as he scribbled her answers in tiny boxes on the forms. A waste of time. What did Sam's broken arm from twenty-five years ago have to do with hitting a moose today? She signed the paperwork, not legibly, but she could hold a pen. "Be grateful for small blessings," Justine would say.

When seventeen-year-old Samantha entered Columbia University, she vowed to deliberate her decisions, her mentors Reason and Practicality. Every pragmatic bone in her body pressured her to call Abe to come bring her home. For years, she'd envied those people who could decide at five o'clock what movie they would see at six. Or people who walked down a street with no particular destination.

What harm would there be in staying a few days in a friendly, quaint town with a safe name like Haven? Besides, curiosity demanded she find out how a town justice got away with operating an unlicensed business, no matter what he called it.

She sniffed the hyacinths, switched the overhead light to dim then shifted to her left side, uncomfortable, but satisfied. For once in her life, Samantha Knowles would do the incalculable thing.

4

Zack put away his dishes from the dishwasher, stretched his back muscles, then made himself another cup of hot chocolate. Taking care of his apartment and working two jobs seemed a bit of a stretch for a man who lived with his parents until six months ago.

It'd been a long day, anything but boring, packed with challenges that set his mind awhirl. The moon had already begun its descent into a new day, but one item still remained on his to-do list. He booted his Word program and opened up his resume. The Bronx needed a few good men. Why not him?

He corralled his errant thoughts, heaving back and forth like a stuck car, reasons to leave Haven, and reasons to stay. He'd taught the same grade for ten years and still lived with his parents, more pathetic than a sitcom mama's boy. No wonder Ellie called off their engagement.

If he made principal, then he'd have something to boast about—a school administrator's license and a master's degree good for little else. Unfortunately, Frank Simmons wasn't about to retire any time soon, at least, not in the next five years according to the teacher's pool. He was a good man, a faithful husband, loving father, and community supporter, but a lousy principal—only not lousy enough to be fired. Still, he didn't make a difference where the kids were concerned; his energies expended more on keeping the status quo, a better politician than an educator.

Zack pondered his imponderables. If he didn't make a move soon, he'd be doomed to spend the next half a decade in Frank's shadow. Frank's refusal to address discipline problems and his habit of ignoring staff problems left Zack with two options. Either fight his boss at every turn or slip into mediocrity. The students deserved better.

"Every negative has its positive," Dad always said. Finding a positive in swampy disillusionment would take more than a serenity prayer. Lately, between Jonathan's spiraling moodiness and Frank's escalating arrogance, Zack's roster of heavenly petitions grew exponentially.

Lord, isn't it time to leave this mountain?

Life in a teeming city would be different than Haven, for sure. No matter. He'd show Ellie he wasn't Mr. Dull—that Zack Bordeaux was more than a small town boy with a vision to match. He could be a school teacher by day, EMT by night, or possibly a New York City cop.

Not that he minded teaching, but he'd followed in his father's footsteps without ever entertaining an alternate career. In fact, he enjoyed teaching when Frank allowed Zack to manage his classroom the way he preferred, with fewer lectures and more interactive experiences. Frank measured academic success by achievement scores, not the stretching of a youthful mind, fitting it for the future.

Zack grabbed a pen and started writing his pros and cons. On the other side of the paper, he listed alternative careers should he move to New York City. If he didn't become a cop or teach in the slums or work as an EMT, he could write his own trauma series or a medical suspense novel like *Coma.* His hero could be an EMT who becomes a cold-case detective and figures out the identity of Jack the Ripper.

Get ready, New York, here comes Zack Bordeaux.

Visions of a red-headed tour guide danced across his mind, him and Sam holding hands as they tread Manhattan sidewalks, or strolled through Central Park.

Sam. Funny how the name fit her, an aura of witty attractiveness that etched a sensual sensibility—not model-pretty like Ellie. Ellie ripped out his heart and devoured it, like an ancient Medea, who killed her brother and scattered his parts on an island. "Love bites," they say. Maybe he wouldn't get so chewed up if he dated girls who were a little less model-perfect on the surface and had more inside the head.

Not as if Haven didn't have its share of available women. Five had asked him out as their Sadie Hawkins date for the fireman's fundraiser last month, though he'd turned them all down with the excuse he'd be out of town to run a marathon. He did go to Albany that Saturday, but sat the entire day by himself at the movie theater.

Zack reread his resume.

Bland—stick-your-finger-down-your-throat boring.

Not much he could do to soup things up without telling a tall tale. He'd never lived beyond the sanctuary of Haven, not even for school, a commuter right through his advanced degrees. Dullsville—that's where he lived, and why Ellie left him.

"Face it, Zack, old boy. You're doomed to live out your days in a place no one outside of Washington County has ever heard of." He yawned with the realization that not even his EMT experiences were worth putting on paper. Calls that made the headlines came infrequently, mostly tourists who got lost in the woods, or an occasional accident, like Sam and her moose.

Stuff Haven might talk about for a few weeks and then abandon when the next storm front moved in. Most of the 911 calls factored a little old lady who hadn't had a bowel movement in six days. Not exactly fodder for motion pictures. Unless Zack took the proverbial bull by the horns, he was doomed to stagnate, his epitaph a pitiful one paragraph obituary in the local paper.

Ellie stood in the shadows of his memory—eyes steely cold. "You're a nothing, Zack Bordeaux. I want a man who will excite me. I don't want a brick house and picket fence. I want to live where every minute is different than the one before it. Not you. You're a small town boy with an imagination to match. You'll die in Haven and be buried in the Bordeaux plot next to your grandmother and parents." Then she took off her one-quarter-carat ring, all he could afford, and jammed it into his palm, flipped her blonde curls, and pranced out of his life forever. He'd show her how wrong she was about him. He had to, or he'd die the most boring man in the world.

Jonathan had accused Zack of being afraid to try again after Ellie. If that were true, why did Sam slice at Zack's reticence? If she recuperated in Haven more than a few days, decided to make the town her home, she'd be the one reason he'd need to stay. She called out to him like the mythical sirens, wooing him into something dangerous, a perilous precipice, an earthquake certain to tumble his fears of withering away in Haven. Her eyes drew him like an ebb tide out to high water.

Zack closed his document. He'd send out the resume later. A few more days wouldn't matter.

&

Jonathan Gladstone threw another log in the den fireplace, then put back the file containing his father's will. The document confirmed his lot—neither a tenant nor a landlord. He closed the steel cabinet with a shove, "There has to be a loophole, somewhere."

He sat on Father's leather chair, its oily coating dank, like the memories soaring through his mind, of Angelica and Father's walks along the lake while he painted in the cabin. He could see them together, though they were too far away to read their faces. He knew Father was quite fond of her, but he'd never suspected subterfuge—until now. Had she colluded with Father against her husband—taken Dawn's Hope from him with no hope of getting it back? He'd thought of all people, Angelica understood him—that she saw his love for Dawn's Hope in his landscapes. She'd taken everything from him, his son, her life, and his own inheritance. Yet, he still loved her beyond reason, beyond the grave. Once he joined her in eternity, he'd forgive her, whatever her motivation, if he only had the courage to walk into the lake like she did.

Nor did he blame Father for his part, doing what he thought best for Dawn's Hope, though Jonathan hated him for a hundred other reasons. How could Father have known Jonathan's passion when father and son never talked? Richard Gladstone was a cold fish, as slimy as a swamp in late August, a deeper enigma than a Rubik's Cube—that puzzle was at least solvable.

There had to be an answer somewhere in Father's old journals, some clue that would prove Angelica's noble intent, her soul too pure to have imagined any evil, any deceit against the man she loved. Her death, and Elliott's just a bizarre accident.

Jonathan left the den and stormed into his adjoining studio. He threw the empty fuchsia paint tube across the room. Without the right color oils, he couldn't finish the portrait before Angelica's birthday. He'd promised her he'd join her after he completed this last tribute to her, and no other color would do for her gown. Now he'd waste more precious days. Sadie's art store would be closed tomorrow. He'd either have to wait, or drive into Albany, an option he refused to entertain. Sadie carried the exact color he needed. He'd have to wait.

5

Sam stepped from Zack's truck into a world from yesteryear, cobblestone as far as she could see to the east and west, brick façade that covered old factories remodeled into shops, and bakeries, and boutiques window-dressed to lure the wealthy tourist.

Zack retrieved Sam's bag of borrowed clothes and her still-soaked purse.

What would she do for money? She'd only put a twenty in her purse, intending to stop at an ATM when she arrived at Stowe. Her credit card and bank card had stuck together, and she'd damaged the stripping when she'd tried to pull them apart at the hospital. They needed to be replaced, anyway. Both cards had become so worn, the cashier at the grocery store had a hard time swiping them, and the numbers were worn to unreadable. One of a hundred things Sam'd put off to put Styles behind bars.

Zack pointed toward towering buildings resembling abandoned factories. "Haven had a few textiles in its heyday, but mostly the town catered to merchants and sailors who transported the goods from New York City up the Hudson, through the canals that emptied into Lake Champlain, then on up the St. Lawrence River to Montreal."

Sam veered to the side, and Zack managed to catch her with his free hand. "Be careful, Sam. A sling will throw you off balance. Dennis warned you your head injury might make you dizzy for a few more days, yet."

"I know what Dennis told me. No need to repeat it."

She took Zack's arm, grateful he was there to lean on, and giggled uncontrollably, a laugh that gurgled from an unknown tap, perhaps a free spirit that came with the Capri pants Tracey lent her. "Please tell Tracey I'm grateful for the temporary wardrobe. Looks like she thought of everything—even a temporary purse until mine dries out." Sam never would have bought a sequined, over-the-shoulder bag, but dry flash was better than wet practicality.

"I'm thinking maybe Tracey's tastes don't run along the same line as yours?"

"Still, it was very thoughtful of her. If she hadn't come to the rescue, I'd have had to parade around in hospital pajamas until I could retrieve my pilot case. Even if my clothes somehow survived, I only brought a couple of changes with me. I'd hoped to do some shopping in Vermont."

"Haven has a few boutiques on Main Street, although they cater mostly to the latest and zaniest styles, so Tracey says."

If the clothes Tracey put in Sam's pity bag were any indicator, a boutique too zany for Tracey must sell futuristic fashion, glittering baubles and lethally pointed shoes, way beyond the comfort zone of a hardly-ever-wears-plaid prosecutor. "I'd settle for anything, other than sequined tops and short-shorts."

"You'd look good in short shorts, Sam. You've got nice legs."

She should be insulted—the practical Sam would have been, but this free spirit she put on with Tracey's clothes soaked up the male appreciation. "Thanks for the compliment."

"If you want, I can take you to Albany to do some shopping, only about an hour from here. There're a couple of big malls there. Glen Falls has a mall, and it's closer. And Lake George has a lot of outlet stores."

She didn't need a closet full, only a few changes until she got back to Manhattan. She gazed the length of Main Street, a picture out of an impressionist painting. She imagined women in bustled day gowns and mustached gents in tailored suits strolling over the bridge or rowing down the canal that ran under it.

Zack pointed to three buildings resembling row houses. "Aaron and Sadie own these. They should be home since they go to a Saturday night service, and Aaron does his fishing in the early morning."

The Lighthouse Lounge was located in the middle between *Sadie's Gift Shoppe and Arte Supply* and *Main Street Boarding House*. Zack pointed to the farthest. "Aaron and Sadie live on the first floor. The upstairs is connected through all three of the buildings. The rooms are actually above Sadie's store. She plans to open up more rooms in the near future. Go on in while I get your bag from the back of the truck. No need to knock. The doors are always open. Just walk in."

"Which door?"

"Take the middle, but every hall and stairwell eventually leads to the Lighthouse."

Someone had replaced the handle with an intricately carved silver soup ladle. She pulled it open and it rattled shut behind her as she entered a long hallway. When she came to the archway, the squeak of the door behind her as Zack came in startled her. She teetered and would have fallen if Zack hadn't caught her. "Guess you were right about the sling."

"Sorry, Sam, I didn't mean to startle you." He cupped his hands around his lips, forming the oldest of megaphones. "Hello! We're here."

A man wearing a khaki shirt and pants approached them. A light beam ricocheted off tackle hanging from his broad-brimmed hat. "Welcome. I assume this is our lovely Miss Knowles?"

Sam shook the offered right hand. "You presume correctly, at least, the Miss Knowles part."

Zack handed Sam the bag of clothes then motioned to follow Aaron's lead. "Now, Aaron, you'd better be nice to our Miss Knowles. Remember the moose."

"I'm a lot tougher." Aaron winked—his flirtations unlike any judge Sam had ever known. "Sorry about your car, Miss Knowles."

"Sam."

"Sam it is. The troopers said your car's at Josiah's Towing and Salvage."

"Yes, that's what they told me, as well."

"Josiah McIntosh is the best mechanic in these parts. Well, the only mechanic within ten miles, but I wouldn't trust my vehicle to anyone else. That's for sure. Anyway, I called Josiah to let him know you'd be staying here. I'm afraid he says there's no help for your Lucille—"

Her heart sank. Poor Lucille. "How did—"

"My daughter told me. She thought Lucille was a great name for a car."

Haven's grapevine was faster than Facebook.

"He put a loaner aside for you until you figure out what to do about a vehicle."

"I'm not sure how long I'll be staying."

"You still might need wheels. Don't have cabs, trains, or buses in Haven, and it's a long walk back to New York City. Josiah knows every car in Haven, who drives what, when and where. If he says a car is dependable, you can go to the bank on it, literally."

Aaron droned on about the last car he bought from Josiah and how well it ran and never needed any work done, and that if a mechanic sold a car that good then he had to be pretty trustworthy as far as pre-owned cars were concerned.

Sam strained to pay attention. After all, Aaron would be hearing her case, assuming she had a plea to stand on. A fat yawn escaped in spite of her best efforts to stay focused. She clutched Tracey's clothes to her chest.

Zack came to the rescue again. "Don't talk the girl's ear off. She needs her rest." He turned to face her, want in his eyes. "If you'd like, I'll stop by tomorrow and give you a lift to Josiah's so you can get the rest of your things out of the car."

Sam exercised her jaw to keep from yawning again. "Tracey said you were a teacher. Don't you have school tomorrow?"

"Extended weekend—unused snow days."

Aaron took off his cap and threw it on the counter. "We shouldn't keep you standing here all day. I'll give you the quick tour, then show you to your room so Zack can go home."

"That's OK. I'll leave now. I'm supposed to meet Jonathan this afternoon. I'll pick you up about nine?"

"Sounds good."

When the door thudded behind Zack, familiar loneliness encased her.

Haven might be the bait, or maybe she was the

lure. Something beyond her control landed her in Small Town, USA. In fact, Haven was the smallest town she'd ever been in. Curiosity compelled her to ask. "What's the population here?"

Aaron lifted his hat and scratched his nearly bald head. "Last census said 1,500, half the size of Whitehall. Haven is an eclectic community—retirees, farmers, campers, mostly. Some independently wealthy folks live on the outskirts..."

Great, her temporary landlord liked to talk. At least, she didn't have to worry about carrying on a conversation. Ask any open-ended question, and he'd likely spew for the next five or ten minutes, or longer. Maybe if she kept him talking long enough, she could size him up to prepare for her defense.

When Aaron paused for breath, she popped a question. "What time is court?"

"I hold court on Thursday afternoon, when I get back from fishing. Doc and I fish most mornings on Mirror Lake at Dawn's Hope."

"Sorry?"

"Dawn's Hope—that's Jonathan Gladstone's place—where we found you."

"I don't remember you coming to my car. I'm glad you happened by, though. Who knows how long I might have been stuck in the ravine, otherwise. You probably saved my life."

Aaron clicked. "Funny how it all worked out. Doc left at noon, but I stayed on a little longer. I took the access road to shave off a few minutes so I could get back to help Sadie with supper. You were passed out, and I couldn't get the door open. I checked for any leaking gas. Quicker for me to hike up to the main house than drive the long way around.

"I appreciate your efforts."

"I like to think the Good Lord watches out for us, helping us even though we don't see His hand in things."

Another involuntary yawn erupted. This was not the time for a theological debate on whether God watched out for fools and fishermen. "I suppose that's true. You fish on private property?" She hadn't meant to sound so accusatory, but what else did this justice do to stretch the law like a rubber band until it snapped?

"Jonathan has a cabin he lets us use, and he keeps the lake stocked with bass."

"And he lets anybody on his property?"

"Not anybody. The property's posted…absolutely no strangers. Let me introduce you around." Aaron pointed toward two men bent over a shuffleboard table. Aaron's voice echoed from beam to beam. "Everyone, this is Samantha Knowles."

"Sam." She hurled her name to a detached audience.

"My apologies," Aaron said. "Sam Knowles. She'll be renting a room upstairs for a few days."

A rail thin man, late seventies, dressed in khakis and a camouflaged vest decorated with an assortment of hooks and bobbers, waved a greeting. If he and Aaron stood side by side, she'd have a photo op for *Field and Stream.*

"That's Doc Hensen. He takes his shuffleboard as seriously as he does his medicine, retired now though…from medicine…not shuffleboard. That's Murray standing next to Doc—Shuffleboard Champion four years running.

Murray hitched his backpacked oxygen tank to

one side as he studied the board.

Doc rubbed white powder on his hands, picked up a blue disc, poised himself, then shot it across the board, pinching his lips together as it glided toward his target and hit the red disc with sufficient force to knock it into the dusty gutter. "Got ya, Murray!" Doc kept his eyes trained on the shuffleboard. "So this is the moose killer you told us about?"

Sam offered a smile, then retracted it when she saw Doc's stoic face, an unreadable, not-even-Abe-could-decipher pose.

Aaron nodded in his fashion-twin's direction. "When Doc isn't fishing, he's up here playing shuffleboard. Most days, he doesn't go home until about six at night…says his wife doesn't like him hanging around the house."

Doc turned to face them. "Heard that Aaron. See, Miss Knowles—"

"Sam."

"See, Sam, my wife wasn't used to me being around all that much. So when I retired, I found a way to keep things normal. In the summer, I occupy my days by fishing. In the winter, I volunteer medical services at the city homeless shelters. The wife shops and sits on every charity board in Haven. Staying out of each other's hair keeps the marriage happy, and we both have something to bring to the supper table."

Perhaps Doc should moonlight as a couples' therapist. She studied the Lighthouse's décor.

Windows spread across two sides of the Lighthouse, each affording a view of the canal, while a fireplace took up most of the street-side wall. A series of doors aligned along the fourth wall, one she assumed led to a kitchen. Sam counted twenty lantern-adorned tables in seeming haphazard locations.

Aaron pointed toward white scripting on the crossbeams. "Those are Bible verses and prayers for the seafaring. Sadie did most of the painting and artwork …she likes to theme things. We found some of the first photographs taken of the place, so we're trying to restore it according to the original layout when it was built in 1849."

He led her to a card table where four very elderly ladies, old enough to be Methuselah's sisters, played bridge. Their gazes met hers, then returned to their cards, dismissing her like a minor disruption.

"Don't pay any attention to the gals, Sam. They're pretty serious about their Bridge Club. Mazie, that's Sadie's mother, entertains her friends every forenoon come rain or shine."

Sam turned back to the shuffleboard table as a red disc bumped Doc's blue one off the playing surface, followed by an enthusiastic, "*Touché!*"

Murray re-adjusted his oxygen tank then picked up another disc.

Sam glanced toward the bar where two hefty men drank coffee and sprawled over four bar stools. Maybe Aaron knew her brain couldn't handle a lot of names, and thankfully, he offered their first names only. Rusty, was Haven's only plumber while Myron was helping Aaron install the new drywall in Sadie's expanding gift shop.

Aaron walked behind the bar and filled a glass with tap water. "Dennis told me to make sure you drink lots of water. So here."

Like an obedient child, Sam took the offering and gulped it down.

Aaron put his hat back on. "Ready? Follow me.

Something I want to show you." He led her behind the bar through patio doors that opened on to a wooden deck. He leaned over the rail as he pointed down river. "This end of the canal connects to the Hudson River and Lake Champlain." He rattled off a series of fort names, a litany of landmarks he said were important during colonial times.

Some vague recollections of Mr. Gillette's seventh grade social studies class skittered through Sam's mind. Regrettably, the year was mostly a blur.

Aaron filled in the knowledge gap. "Ft. Ticonderoga's up the road a piece. Folks around here are proud of their heritage. Whitehall, our neighboring town, is the birthplace of the American Navy. I'm not a New York native. Born and raised in Middlebury, Vermont. I retired a few years back, and then the wife and I moved here. I'll tell you, Sam, I love this town as if I lived here my whole life."

If she hadn't yawned and nearly dropped her hobo collection crammed into a thirty-gallon garbage bag, Aaron might have rambled geography and history lessons the rest of the day. "Poor girl. You're probably exhausted. I'll bring you to your room, now. Have you had any lunch yet?"

"I had a few crackers at the hospital."

"That's not a lunch. Sadie will send up some pea soup and grilled cheese."

"She needn't bother. I don't eat much."

"My wife will consider that a challenge. She'll put some meat on those bones, or die trying."

Aaron led Sam up a series of steps, each stair set off by hand-painted grapevines and labeled with two cities separated by a number. "What do these numbers stand for?"

Pride etched on Aaron's brow. "These are the nautical miles from here to distant locations. Town legend says this bar was an inn for sailors making their way to the St. Lawrence River. Did you know that you can get most any place in the world by water?"

She figured she could have lived a lifetime without that piece of information, but didn't want to alienate the judge. "No. I didn't know that."

Aaron led the way up another set of steps, but these spiraled and narrowed at the top. At the landing, he pointed to a closed door. "This first room is Leon's. He was a high school English teacher in Albany. A philosopher, too, of sorts, I'm told. He wrote a lot of essays—never widely published, though, mostly a few literary journals. Leon's ninety-four years old. You'd never guess it by the looks of him—takes the steps like a twenty-year-old and still walks a couple of miles every day, too. Out walking now, matter of fact."

Aaron opened the door at the end of the hall, and Sam gasped at the Arthurian theme. Faux stone adorned the walls, and a circular, five-foot chandelier berthed the ceiling. In the midst of Camelot, four framed landscapes of a glassy lake surrounded by hyacinths caught her attention, anachronisms in a three-dimensional storybook.

Aaron answered before she asked. "That's Mirror Lake in the middle of Dawn's Hope, where Doc and I fish."

A pungent, floral scent filled the room, and her eyes watered.

"You OK?"

"Fine." She reached for a tissue from a canoe-like holder. "I get these olfactory hallucinations from time to time, where I think I smell hyacinths—probably a reaction to the landscapes."

Aaron laughed. "No. You're not hallucinating. Look over there on the side table. Zack brought these over this morning before he went to church."

This kind of male attention she could get used to. "Zack mentioned Dawn's Hope had hyacinths growing in the wild. Highly unusual."

"Lord Gladstone, Haven's founding father, planted gardens all around his estate and brought over a variety of plants from England, including the hyacinths. Unfortunately, Dawn's Hope has had a century of troubles, and the gardens have fallen into disrepair, but the hyacinths, a hearty plant I'm told, survived. The groundskeepers manage beds throughout the estate at Jonathan's insistence. However, most of Dawn's Hope has reverted to the wild, except where the house stands."

Sam's eyes locked on the landscapes. "Did Jonathan Gladstone paint these?"

"I believe so. Gifted artist don't you think? At least that's what Sadie tells everyone. She's his biggest fan."

Serenity pulled her into their scenes. "I'd like to buy a landscape like these. Where can I find one?"

"These aren't for sale, but Sadie has a few in her store."

"Soups on!" The high-pitched voice wailed like a noon-day whistle. Soon, a pudgy, slightly-past-middle-age woman carrying a loaded tray appeared in the doorway. "I figured you might be a mite hungry…that hospital food ain't fit for human consumption. I threw a couple of chocolate chip cookies on your tray, too. Leon's favorite."

An elderly man with a wispy voice bounded up the steps. "Now, Sadie, don't go blaming me for making those cookies. I'm not the only one who's partial to them."

The woman turned. "Hello, Leon. Didn't hear you come in." Sam remembered the squeaky front door. How could anyone *not* hear someone come in?

Aaron kissed the woman on the cheek. "Sam, this is my wife, Sadie. And this crotchety fellow rents the room next to yours."

Sadie turned toward Sam again. "I'll put the tray in your room, dear. Now go on in and eat, while it's warm. Then you can settle in. We'll talk business later. This door doesn't have an exterior lock but you can bolt the door from the inside for privacy."

Leon stood in the hall, a gangly assortment of misshapen features—a nose too long for the face and protruding ears. "I usually take my meals downstairs. I came up to get my wallet. The boys challenged me to a game of shuffleboard soon as I came in the door." He cupped his hands over his mouth and lowered his voice to a near whisper. "Beat 'em every time, I'll have you know." He opened his door, but from where she stood, she couldn't see inside, and she wondered if Leon's room had a theme, too. "Nice to meet you, Sam. I hope you'll join us for shuffleboard when you're feeling better." He offered a flirtatious wink, hardly offensive; at ninety-four, probably all for show.

Sam winked back. "Hope so, too."

"Get your stuff, get back downstairs, and leave the girl alone," Aaron said, giving Leon a nudge. "She just got here."

Leon laughed, went into his room and came out stuffing something in his pocket, presumably his wallet.

Sadie lingered in the room. "Need anything,

dear?"

"No. Tracey thought of everything."

"There's a phone on the bedside table. Bert's Tackle and Bait carries cellular phones, but the reception's almost nil around here."

"I'm not one for gadgets, except my computer. I only carried a cell for emergencies, and it didn't do me any good when I finally had one."

Sadie laughed. "The library has an Internet connection for the public and one of the cafés has that service, oh what do you call it?"

"Wi-Fi?"

"That's it. Don't use a computer myself. I do my bookkeeping the old fashioned way with pen and ledger."

Sam shook her head with disbelief. Had she landed in a 1950's sitcom?

"Holler down if you need anything. We practically live in the lounge."

Sam's spaghetti legs wobbled from exhaustion. She sat in a velvet-covered bedside chair, a queen's throne, while Sadie lit the cast iron candelabra centered on the bureau. "I'll bring up a snack around three, and supper about six o'clock. Maybe tomorrow you'll be able to join us in the lounge for your meals." She opened the armoire doors. "There's the television. Make yourself to home. You can put your tray outside the door so we won't have to disturb you." With that, she left.

Sam managed to down half the soup, a few bites of the sandwich and one cookie. She put the tray into the hall as instructed, returned to the room and bolted the door, smiling as she traced the delicate carvings of the antique knife, forged and reshaped to function as a door handle, similar to the one she noticed on the street entrance.

She dumped out the bag containing borrowed clothes and a plastic tote with hospital-issue toiletries. She stored Tracey's kind assortment in the top drawer, kicked off the sandals, then closed her eyes as she stretched out on the bed.

The late morning sun warmed the room, and visions of dancing hyacinths by a quiet lakefront filled Sam's senses. What a wonderful place she'd happened into. Or, maybe she hadn't been rescued as she thought. Maybe she died in that accident, and this was the heaven she didn't deserve.

6

Zack cast his fishing line into the deeper water to his left while Jonathan kept his line in the shallows to their right. "Glad you finally changed your mind about fishing with me. Seems like old times, doesn't it, you and me out here by the lake. Where did those teenagers disappear to, do you suppose?"

"You're still that kid. As for me? Don't know. Don't know where I am half the time."

"Hold that thought…I got a bite." Zack reeled in the bass and measured it. "Twenty inches…a keeper."

"Depends on whose chart you're following. How much does it weigh?"

Zack placed the fish on his homespun scale. "Eight pounds, give or take a few ounces."

"No game wardens here. Keep it. I'll never tell."

"This baby will make my mother happy. Mom loves freshwater fish." Zack reached in for a worm, baited his hook, and recast to the same location. "Looks like I found a good spot. How's your line coming?"

"Not a thing. That's OK. Never got the thrill from fishing that you get. I thought I should try it one last time, though. But, whenever I'm near this spot, I wonder if I wouldn't be better off if I joined Angelica."

Did Jonathan intend to walk into the lake like Angelica, and a few of his ancestors? Suicide ran too rampant in the Gladstone legacy to ignore a statement like that, although Aunt Sadie would call Zack an alarmist. Let her. He refused to be one of those friends who skirted around the symptoms.

"Is that a threat, Jonathan?"

"No threat. I'm leaving for Paris soon. Maybe I won't bother to come back."

"You had me concerned there for a moment. I really wish you'd see a doctor about your depressed moods. Given your family history…"

"I'm not depressed, Zack. Just some days, I'm tired of living."

Zack grabbed a can of coke, snapped open the tab, and guzzled it down. "Paris, huh? A bit of a jump, isn't it? You hardly ever leave Dawn's Hope. Why Paris?"

"To study."

"Study what? Your landscapes have made you famous. What would Paris teach you?"

"Something other than landscapes."

"Is that why you called me yesterday? You don't need my permission, you know. Go if that's what you're itching to do."

"Not that simple, Zack. Father's will…it's complicated. That's why I'm looking for some legal help. Whoa…got a bite."

Jonathan's face tore into a smile. He'd rarely smiled in his youth, but his marriage to Angelica made him the smilingest man in Haven. After she died, a smile became as rare as when they were boys. If a little thing like catching a fish could make him smile, maybe all Jonathan needed was a little pleasure instead of psychoanalysis.

Jonathan reeled in the bass and measured it.

"Well?"

"Twelve inches…but they're my bass, aren't they?

Here…throw this in your basket with the other one." Jonathan re-baited and re-cast, staying in the shallows. "Maybe that guy's big brother's in there."

"Seems kind of cruel when you put it that way, fishing…I mean."

"We humans are cruel to the core. Don't you know that?"

Change the subject…Don't go to the deep end with Jonathan. "So about that question…I teach history…that doesn't make me a legal expert by any shake of the imagination."

"Yeah. I know. I realized that after I called. What about your new girlfriend?"

"Sam?"

"Whatever her name is."

Zack bit his lower lip. "She's not my girlfriend. She's a stranger in Haven, is all. Besides, she banged herself up pretty bad, and needs to rest. I don't think it's fair to put her to work." His bobber dipped twice. "Got another one!" Zack yanked to his left. "Gotcha!" He reeled it in and measured, more out of curiosity than necessity—eighteen inches. He took out a dollar from his wallet and placed it on the rock between them. "Let's see who hauls in the most, like we did when we were kids."

"No contest. You're the hunter and fisherman. Me? I'm a wanna-be naturalist. I spend my days either painting, or taking long walks around Dawn's Hope. I like to watch the deer, not shoot them."

"There are some folks who envy that kind of life."

"Let them. Most days, I think I'm going to start painting something other than landscapes…but lately, I've been remembering too much."

Zack didn't want to remember, either. "So why do

you want to hire Sam?"

"Sam who?"

"Sam Knowles. The attorney they found on your property. Why hire her? Why not Aaron?"

"Aaron was Father's attorney."

"So?"

"So you know how well Father and I got along."

"About as good as a gazelle and a lion." Zack recalled his boyhood visits to Dawn's Hope. The tension between father and son was so thick, the air bent with hostility, and even more so after Jonathan's mother died. But when Angelica came, fresh breezes blew at Dawn's Hope. Zack re-baited his hook and cast again at the deep end. "Might as well stick with a good thing. Want a soda?"

"No, but I'll have more pizza. I feel hungry all of sudden." Jonathan reeled in, hooked his line on the rod, put his pole on the ground by his empty basket and grabbed a slice of pizza from the box between them.

Zack reeled in his line to recast. "The fish must have moved to another spot, or maybe all our talking scared them away."

"Sorry."

"It's OK. We haven't talked about much of anything since..." Why open Jonathan's wounds again? Zack wanted to avoid talking about Angelica's death as much as Jonathan. They'd known each other, considered each other a friend, since grade school, though more through church than school. Zack had avoided Jonathan at school functions, fearful his association with "Glum Boy," as the others called Jonathan, would cost Zack his popularity. Outside of school, though, Zack enjoyed being with Jonathan, fishing and hiking their common ground. That, and being the only two boys in youth group with fifteen girls, cemented their friendship.

Jonathan stared over the lake, not to the other side, more like under the water. "I guess I'll talk to Aaron about the will. I have to go to the art supply store tomorrow, anyway."

"Good thing you're too fussy to have them delivered. You'd never come off this mountain otherwise."

"I'm not a hermit. I don't like social situations. Is that a crime?"

"No, of course not. Sadie worries about you."

"Sadie worries about everybody, including you. She says you're still not over Ellie. Are you?"

Zack bristled. "Don't go there, Jonathan. She's ancient history in my book." He'd come here to help his friend, not be analyzed by a textbook neurotic. Zack reeled in his line, hooked it to his pole, stood, and picked up the basket. "I'd better go home. I still have a pile of papers to correct and lesson plans to get ready for next week. Enjoyed the fishing, Jonathan." He had enjoyed most of it, anyway. "Up to taking the ATVs out for spin next weekend?"

"Maybe. Depends on the day."

"How's that?"

"You know, Zack. Sometimes I wish I was at the bottom of the lake so I could see Angelica, again."

Not now, not when Zack's patience had been tested to the limit. He replayed the smile when Jonathan got a bite. No. Jonathan would get through it, maybe like an ice-age, but his pain would melt in time. However deep the sorrow, Jonathan's will to live and a faith he once treasured would pull him from the depths of despair. “And is today one of those days?”

“No.”

7

A rap on the door brought Sam from the depths of slumber to the warmth of her sun-drenched room. "Is everything alright, dear? It's Sadie."

She looked at the clock. Nine. She'd slept through the night for the first time in three years.

"Of course. Come in, please."

"Door's bolted."

Still groggy, Sam teetered to the door and pulled the knife handle to disengage the latch, but it stuck. When she jiggled the handle, a screw from the bolt assembly fell to the floor; the knife dangled along the door jam. "Oh, dear. I think I broke your beautiful handle, as well as the bolt. I'm so sorry."

Sadie pushed the door and brought in a breakfast tray. "No need for apologies. That door sticks all the time. I'll see if Aaron will put up a temporary hook 'til I can conjure up another decoration. A young girl should have some privacy."

One hook?

Her apartment door contained a dead bolt and five locks as well as an alarm. Most of her friends settled for three, but a girl couldn't be too cautious. Sam shooed away the worry. Nothing much a thief could take from her now—Tracey's clothes, dime store toiletries, stuck-together credit cars, and the twenty dollar bill so wet, it might crumble in the thief's hand. Maybe she could wrap it in tissues to soak up the excess moisture.

"Don't worry about it, Sadie. I don't think I'll be here more than a few days. I'll manage."

Sadie shrugged her shoulders. "Might as well stay until court, Thursday. Makes no sense to hurry off someplace then have to scoot back here so soon. All that driving will wear a body out, and the Good Lord knows, you need your rest. Besides, I hoped you'd like us enough to stay a bit longer than a few days. I brought your supper up last night, but you didn't answer my rap, so I left the tray outside. When I found it untouched this morning, I got worried. Hope I didn't startle you."

Sadie's concern soothed like a mother's sweet lullaby. "You know, I feel really good this morning." Sam took off the sling and rotated her shoulder—only a slight twinge. "Thank you for breakfast. But I don't think it's necessary to be carting my tray up anymore. I'll join the group for lunch. What time?"

"Noonish. Folks kinda wander in and out. Breakfast starts at six, lunch noon, and supper at six. Doc Henson is particular about the times he eats, though. Sugar, don't you know."

"He's diabetic?"

"Don't tell him I told you. He don't like it broadcast."

Sam moved her fingers across her lips. "Sealed, like a juvie's record."

Sadie set the tray on the bedside table. "Do you know what you're going to do today?"

"I don't want to stay in bed, that's for sure. Zack's picking me up around ten to get my things from Josiah's. He managed to get Lucille's trunk opened and salvaged my pilot case. Not that it matters. The clothes are probably mildewed by now, and the laptop is probably ruined."

"You could take it down to Bert's Tackle shop. Their son is a genius about computers. I heard tell he got one up and running that'd been in a fire."

"I'll keep that in mind." Sam's gaze scooted toward the landscapes. "Since I have an hour to kill before Zack gets here, I'd like to wander around your store. Aaron said you had more Gladstone landscapes there. Then maybe I'll take a walk down Main Street. Familiarize myself with Haven."

Sadie shot an indefinable glare—concern, like the way Justine stared when Sam went days without sleep. Mothers, so some say, have a way of disciplining their children with certain glances. Not Mama. Mama kept her gaze cast towards the floor. Once, after Daddy ran out of the house in a drunken fit, she glanced up, and Sam saw Mama's swollen eyes, a slit underneath her right one.

Sadie's eyes twinkled, as if her mood belied her admonition. "Don't get your life reorganized all in one day, dear. Plenty of time for that. Mind your doctor, now. Goodness gracious. A body that's had to sleep for twenty hours probably needs a tad more rest, yet." She turned and left, closing the door behind her.

Sam gobbled all her eggs and toast, surprised at her ravenous appetite, then headed for the shower, lingering fifteen minutes, rather than the environmentally recommended ten—one day of self-indulgence would not bring the world to an end.

Putting on Tracey's tan Capri pants and a pink sequined, floral tee, Sam checked her outfit in the closet wall mirror and winced, imagining Justine's laughter if she could see Sam now. At least these clothes were clean and comfortable, not to mention a near fit. Sam slipped on the sandals, wondering if glitter clashed with sequins. She imagined Judge Normandy's scowl if she showed up in his court with this getup.

Sam eased down the steps, remembering Dennis's warning that she'd be prone to dizziness for a few more days yet. Seeing no one in the lounge, Sam pushed open the hinged shutters separating the lounge from Sadie's store and took a hesitant step inside a foreign world. Wind chimes rang over her head, and an assortment of paints and easels littered the storefront, while Sadie's cluttered counter took up most of the back. Barrels of paint lined either side. A lanky man, probably in his mid thirties, hovered over the farthest barrel, a rustic sort, with faded jeans and an open flannel shirt over a wrinkled thermal undershirt.

As she scanned Sadie's inventory, Sam found the landscapes on the wall near the street entrance. She gazed intently at the larger one, about five by three feet, panoramic, but a similar vista as the smaller landscapes in her room.

With Justine getting married, chick flick nights would come at a premium. Time to pursue a hobby of some kind—why not art? If she bought this landscape, hung it over her fireplace, then she could officially call herself an art collector.

She supposed she should squint, cock her head and offer an, "Ah" and "Ooh." But she couldn't see past the cartoonish, heavy-set lady with the garden hat standing in front of her. Sam tapped the woman on the shoulder. "Excuse me. I'd like a closer look at that landscape if you don't mind."

The woman smiled and moved aside. "I'm sorry, dear. Didn't know anyone was behind me."

"Is that a Gladstone?"

"Sadie only displays Gladstones. He's the most popular artist in these parts. I'm partial to the large one myself. But then, I've seen that lake a dozen times for real. My husband fishes up there most mornings with Aaron Golden. If Aaron can't go, I sometimes go with my husband so he won't pout."

"I thought Aaron fished with Doc Henson."

"That would be my husband. I'm Cynthia Henson. You must be Sam Knowles, Aaron's new guest. The moose lady."

"Yes."

Unobstructed, Sam studied the landscapes, wondering why they all featured the same lake, different seasons yet the same scene, painted from the same viewpoint. As if bonded to the land in some inexplicable way, Sam knew she had to see it for its stark beauty. "I'm sorry to bother you again, Cynthia."

"No bother."

"I understand the lake is posted. Is there any way someone who doesn't fish can see it?"

Cynthia leaned in and changed her tone to a whisper, casting a glance toward the long-haired man near the paint supplies. "You have to get Jonathan's permission."

"How do I do that if he's as reclusive as everyone says he is?"

Cynthia winked and pointed towards the paint supplies. "He's right over there. I think Sadie's probably the only one he talks to besides Zack Bordeaux. But you can try." She giggled like a fan-crazed teenager. "That's why I come in here so often…on the outside chance Jonathan's come down from the mountain."

Did she dare talk to this hill-dweller? Reclusive people could not be trusted. Well, that might be a bit judgmental since Justine criticized Sam for being a borderline hermit. "If you didn't have a job to go to every day, you'd probably never leave this apartment," she'd said at least a dozen times, gushing condemnation, designed to guilt Sam into going to a movie.

Sam forced her right foot forward and bristled over to where Jonathan stood enamored by a barrel of oil paints, or maybe water colors, not that she could tell them apart. Some art collector she'd be.

She picked up a tube of green something or other, and pretended to examine it while she studied Jonathan's height. Sam was taller than most women, maybe not WBA-tall or can't-wear-regular-size-pants tall, but certainly not petite. She dwarfed next to this Gladstone guy, the top of her head an inch above his shoulder. "Excuse me. Are you Jonathan Gladstone?"

"Ah. There it is. Fuchsia." He plopped the tube onto the counter. "Yes. I am. Who's asking?"

"Attorney Sam Knowles."

Most people hauled to attention in the presence of a lawyer, and even Jonathan abandoned his paints and stared down at her. She remembered a cruise she took with Mama to the South Pacific. Sam saw her first coconut on that cruise. That's what Jonathan's eyes reminded her of…coconuts, large, round, marble-like coconuts.

Mama's eyes were blue, but Jonathan's looked like hers, eyes that demanded pity.

"What would a lawyer need from me?" His smile

was unnerving, not in a sensual way like Zack's—more like she'd pierced him, penetrated his shell of indifference.

"I want to see your lake. I'll pay any price you ask."

"You are direct, I'll give you that. I don't charge admission to my lake." His lips parted into something that resembled a grin, convoluted by his caved cheeks, not unattractive, and sufficient to highlight wind-blown lips. For a recluse, Jonathan appeared to spend a great deal of time outdoors.

"I'm buying your painting. Would that help?"

A chuckle. "Look, Miss Knowles. The only people who see my lake besides me are fishermen. They like the bass I supply. Sometimes I sketch them while they fish—a symbiotic relationship. How would your seeing my lake help me?"

Until now, everyone in Haven seemed cast from the same civil mold, mysterious, but with a go-out-of-their-way friendliness. Jonathan was a dime out of time…a hippie in a Norman Rockwell painting, or maybe Haven was the anachronism.

"I'll give you free legal service. Need a will drawn up, or anything?"

"Actually, I do need some legal advice. Drop by tomorrow morning. Nine." He scribbled a note for Sadie then disappeared with two tubes of Fuchsia paint and a hundred unanswered questions.

8

Sam wrote a note to Sadie asking her to set aside the large landscape until she could figure out whether to ship it, or take it with her when she returned to Manhattan. Sam started out the street entrance as Sadie came in from the lounge.

"Good to see you up and about, Sam. I saw Jonathan leave in an awful hurry. He said you'd be going to his place tomorrow."

"I think so."

"That's nice. Jonathan doesn't have much company, especially over the last few years."

Sam joined Sadie at the counter. "I'd like to buy that landscape on the wall. I left you a note. Can you hold it for me? It'll take me a couple of days to scrounge up the cash. Not that I'm broke, I need to switch some assets around. My credit cards are no good…damaged that is. Can't get the numbers off them, either."

"Um….sure…no problem…it's that well, I don't know how much Jonathan wants for it. I'll have to ask."

"Doesn't matter. I can afford it."

Sadie skewered a look.

Sam realized that most young ADAs couldn't afford luxuries of this magnitude, and Sadie might be wondering where Sam's money came from. "I have independent resources."

Sam shuddered at the sound of that. How long would it be before the gossip trail suspected her wealth came from corruption?

Better to let Haven's town folk be suspicious, than explain her inheritance or why she rarely spent it.

"I'll put this out back in a safe place until you've come to some decisions," Sadie said. "Anything else I can help you with today?"

"I won't know what I need until I see what's going on with my car. I'd like to hang around Haven until the weekend, maybe longer. If I need anything, I'll let you know."

"I'm sure Josiah can fix you up with some kind of transportation."

"Everyone has been kind." *Except for that Jonathan.* "I wish there was some way I could show my appreciation."

Sadie wrapped the picture in bubble wrap as she spoke. "We're used to strangers here. Tourism is our bread and butter. Maybe you could put in a good word about our town to your city friends. Drum up some business for us."

She'd do just that—tell all her four friends. Word of mouth advertising from Sam Knowles would hardly cause a blaze of interest. Not even a spark. "I'll be certain to spread the word as best I can. Thanks for keeping the picture. I still have half an hour before Zack gets here. Think I'll take that stroll, now. Looks like a good day for exploring."

"It's nice and bright out for sure…but the sky was red earlier this morning."

"Is that a problem?"

"Don't tell me you never heard tell of the sailor's saying: 'red sky at night, sailor's delight, red sky at morning, sailors take warning?'"

Sam hardly grew up with rural wit. Mama and Daddy's conversations usually involved shouting and foul language. "No, I never heard that one before."

Sadie glanced toward the window. "Never seen it fail." She reached under the counter and handed Sam an umbrella. "I'd feel better if you had this on you."

"Thanks." If only Mama had been a little like Sadie.

Sam headed north, passing store fronts of every description, and a very old church, apparently still in use, since the sign read: *This Sunday's Message: Holiness is not a way of life, but a state of mind.* If she were still here, this might be an interesting church to attend Sunday. Maybe it was time to get back into the church habit.

She counted four boutiques among the novelty shops, bakeries, and used bookstores.

A few people meandered up and down the cobblestone road, and once every few minutes, a car sailed through. A van slowed when it neared Sam, crept alongside for a few minutes, then sped up and disappeared at the intersection. Odd. Probably a town person curious what a tourist was gawking at so early in the morning.

When Sam reached the end of downtown Haven, she caught the shadow of a gothic mansion, featuring gables on all visible sides, wings jutting from a main section. With her knowledge of architecture as scant as her knowledge of art, she could only describe it as a conglomeration of styles ranging from castle, fortress, to towers, as if sections were added on over the years, a mishmash of construction. And yet, in all its uneven presence, it stood proud, tall, and beautiful, a sentinel, its abutments like angel's wings, hovering over the town.

This must be the famed Dawn's Hope, the Gladstone residence. If she had an appointment with Haven's royalty, she should go prepared, do a little preemptive research. She crossed the street and checked the library's hours of operation, then headed back towards the Lighthouse.

Cinnamon aromas grabbed her senses. She shouldn't be hungry after Sadie's enormous breakfast, but she'd never been able to resist cinnamon, cinnamon anything, muffin, donut, bread, or tea. So what if she gained a few pounds while on vacation. Everyone said she was too thin, and her size two dresses had been hanging on her frame. She ducked into Well's Bakery, pulled out her soggy twenty-dollar bill, glad it hadn't disintegrated, and bought a cinnamon muffin, devouring it in four bites.

She walked the cobblestone sidewalk past the Lighthouse, past the bridge, to the south end of Main Street, where a sign pointed toward a small parking area to the right, room for ten cars. A narrow road, marked Emmanuel Lane, veered from the main drag up the mountain. At the north and south ends of Main Street, civilization stopped—not a single shop or house, an endless tarmac to nothingness except that eerie mansion.

Droplets pinged at her head. She opened the umbrella Sadie had given her and retreated to the Lighthouse where Zack waited on the stoop. "Ready? I saw you walking, but you looked pretty intense so I thought I'd stay here until you came back."

She hopped onto the runner and climbed into the cab. With any luck, she'd have some sort of independent transportation within the hour. More than likely, this would be her last ride in Zack's red truck. She liked Zack, she didn't like trucks. Daddy had driven a truck, a big black one.

As she clicked her seatbelt, her gaze caught Zack's unsettling smile, one that spiked a desire to flirt, a smile that splintered her resistance towards romance. She shook off the want, a risk she could not afford right now, not while Harlan Styles still had a chance at freedom. Yet, she couldn't shake off the wonder…what if she permitted the interest in Zack, let whatever feelings birthed between them take root? What was the harm in a little fling, if such a thing existed? Whatever it was wouldn't survive her return to Manhattan, where courtrooms and law books suffocated any burgeoning relationship. A little fling might prove to be fun, like a shipboard love affair, Zack a safe bet.

She chided herself for her premature thoughts. Zack might very well have a girlfriend, and besides, it had been so long, she couldn't remember how to flirt. Instead, she offered an unsure smile.

He hit back with a wider, eye-popping grin, and something like an electric bolt shot through her. Not even Johnny Miller made her feel heat the whole four years they went out. They'd agreed to be boyfriend and girlfriend through high school, to avoid the whole clumsy mess of dating. Until this tingle, she'd thought love was a convenience, not a discovery.

Why did Zack have to be so irresistible, like cinnamon? With his movie-star smile coupled with sincerity, Zack had to be the most sought-after bachelor in town. Sam pictured a line of airheads waiting for a Zack smile. Mama's warning rang in Sam's ears. "Handsome men are dangerous, Sam."

Daddy was handsome; handsome and kind didn't often go together, though they seemed to in Zack.

He didn't push for conversation, a trait Sam admired. Justine would get paranoid if Sam didn't fill up the room with chit-chat when they were together. Chit-chat didn't mean people liked each other. In Samantha Knowles's Book of Friendship, mutual quiet meant respect, a comfort in each other's company.

Maybe she should say something, in case Zack didn't like quiet, but was too polite to drill her with a lot of nosy questions. "Thanks for the lift."

"My pleasure. Find anything interesting on your walk?"

"I saw a house—more like a mansion—beautifully grotesque—up there on that mountain."

"Dawn's Hope. The Gladstone estate."

Should she tell Zack she had agreed to meet the nefarious Gladstone tomorrow morning? No. She'd keep that to herself for the moment—unless she needed a ride. "I hope I didn't intrude into your day off too much."

"Not really. I was supposed to go to baseball practice later. But I expect it'll be cancelled due to rain."

"You play baseball?"

"Not on a regular basis. A few of the teachers and firemen formed a team to compete in the charity tournament during Haven's Spring Fling next month."

"Spring Fling?"

Zack's face glowed like Abe when he took a bite of Bob's prime rib—prideful, as if he himself had cooked it. "It's the name we give our Founder's Day, the biggest day in Haven. Wish you could be here for it. There's a parade, carnival, and fireworks courtesy of the Gladstone estate. Say, maybe you'd come back for it? I'll make sure you have a good time, if you do."

The burn in Zack's boyish blush warmed her, prodded her to move a little closer to him.

"Sam, I hope I'm not out of line asking this."

"Ask me anything you want, but I reserve the right to refuse to answer."

"Fair enough. Now, I know you're not married because the police checked out next of kin at the accident, but I wondered if…well…if there was a special person—"

"No, Zack. I'm totally unattached."

He grinned.

"And I plan on keeping it that way."

Zack's face reddened—she'd either embarrassed him, or hurt his feelings. He might've been getting up the nerve to ask her on a date, and she'd trounced on his opportunity with as much consideration as squashing a cockroach. She regretted her action, even if it was for the best. Forget the idea she could manage a small town romance, then brush it off when she returned to the city. It had taken her two years to get over Johnny Miller, even though she agreed breaking up was the sensible thing. "It's too hard to keep a relationship going if we're attending different colleges," Johnny said. "We should be free to see other people, don't you think?" Johnny Miller had wasted no time in seeing other people, and he married during his junior year.

Zack moved his jaw back and forth. "I understand. You're not looking for a boyfriend. We can still be friends, can't we? Maybe I could come to the city once in awhile, and you could show me around?"

"I'd like that, but my job keeps me so busy, I don't

have time to develop relationships outside of work."

He stared straight ahead. "I see."

Could she rescue this moment without hurting Zack any more? "How about you? I take it from your question you're not exclusively involved with anyone."

"I dated a girl I met in college…off and on. A few years ago, I convinced her to move to Haven to take a teaching job. We were engaged. She up and left, and broke off our engagement in the process. Seems Haven wasn't exciting enough for her. Can't say I blame her. Not a lot happens here, and it's probably the reason why everyone can't stop talking about your moose incident."

"Incident?"

He smiled. "The feature article for the next edition of *The Haven Gazette*."

Justine believed there was a man for every woman, and did her best to help Sam find hers, fixing her up on dates, crazy dates—the stuff of comedies, and the reason Sam believed she should die a spinster, as Great Aunt Susie predicted: "It's a good thing you've got your own money, Sam. You're pretty, but not pretty enough to land a man worth any substance. You'd be better off never to get married, die an old maid, like me." Between those crazy dates and now, being the lead article in a newspaper, Sam was sure Aunt Sadie was right.

The rain abated, but black roving clouds promised another downpour soon. Zack pulled onto a side street, made a few more lefts and rights and then parked in the dirt driveway of an old barn on the other side of Haven's mountain. "We're here."

The sign said *Josiah's Towing and Salvage. You break 'em. We fix 'em.* If reports were right, though, Lucille was a lost cause.

A short, dark-complexioned man with flaming red hair, four shades brighter than Sam's, approached and shook hands with Zack. She tried hard not to stare at the comical contradictions in his appearance.

"Morning, Zack. Nice of you to give Miss Knowles a lift." He offered Sam a handshake. "I'm Josiah McIntosh."

She accepted the handshake, but still couldn't drag her eyes away from Josiah's crop of curly, clownish hair. "I'm sorry. I'm being rude. I apologize."

"No apology necessary. Most people react the same way when they first see me." He grunted a minute laugh. "I managed to pry open the trunk. Your pilot case, as well as your laptop, is in my office for safekeeping."

"Can I see her…Lucille? I know it's silly, but I'd like to say goodbye."

Josiah smiled compassionately, as if he understood the special attachment some people developed to their cars. "Of course. Follow me." He led the way past his barn through an orchard of mangled cars, Lucille's final resting place, a graveyard in exchange for her spare parts or as scrap metal.

Zack held Sam's arm, guiding her as if fording a river. Josiah had a big enough lead, and Sam's curiosity got ahead of her manners. "What gives with his red hair?"

"Josiah's a descendent of Patrick McIntosh, an early settler of Washington County, a former plantation owner who freed his slaves, married his housekeeper against the scorn of his family and friends, and made a new life in the Adirondacks—a close friend of Lord Gladstone, actually. Josiah is president of the Haven Historical Society."

Josiah stopped. "Don't think I can't hear you. Zack got it mostly right. He worked as a tour guide at the town museum during the summers. His father and I taught him everything he knows about Haven's history."

Sam buzzed with discovery, so much she could learn from a place, until two days ago, she'd never heard of.

"My story isn't so unusual, lots of interesting folks in these mountains, Miss Knowles. As for my freakish hair, I like to think I'm a symbol of the American Melting Pot. Like the best Columbian brews, I'm an exotic cultural blend."

Sam laughed. She liked the odd-looking man, about the same age as Haven's justice of the peace, yet still putting in a day's labor, and probably had no time to fish like Aaron. As town historian, Josiah might be able to give Sam a bit of a history lesson on the Gladstones. "Zack mentioned your ancestor was a friend of Lord Gladstone. Would that be Jonathan Gladstone's ancestor?"

Josiah stopped and turned. "Yes, it would be. Now that Jonathan's a story. Sad, really."

"Why's that?"

"Jonathan's the last of Lord Gladstone's heirs. Rumor is he has a hankering to go to Paris if he can figure out a way to shed responsibility for Dawn's Hope."

"Really?"

Josiah pointed toward the hinder portions of the Gladstone mansion. "See that house up yonder? That's the second house on Dawn's Hope, built by Henry Gladstone about 1825. The first house burnt down soon after The War of 1812."

Finally, some history Sam remembered. "The British?"

"More likely it was an act of revenge. Folks in Haven didn't cotton much to Henry, though the mills he built brought prosperity to the town and also made him wealthier and more powerful than his father or grandfather. Legend has it tragedy's followed the Gladstone clan ever since." He shook his head with sympathetic resignation.

Josiah stopped in front of an unrecognizable heap of metal. "As you can see, Miss Knowles, your Lucille has passed on to the Great Parking Lot in the Sky."

Sam sobbed…the first real cry since…since she could remember. The heavens opened, sharing Sam's grief.

Zack covered Sam's head with his jacket. "Here. This might help a little. We should find shelter."

She shoved the jacket back toward him. "I won't melt, Zack. I might be a little emotional over Lucille, but I'm hardly a delicate flower that'll bend with a little rain. Lucille has been like a friend. I bought her my senior year of high school…oh…my keys. Do you have them, Josiah?"

"Right here in my pocket. I brought them in case you wanted to look inside." He unlocked the doors then threw her the keys. "Makes no sense keeping a dead car locked, anyway, so you might as well keep 'em."

"My life in keys," Sam said, as she plunked them into her purse, her words cracked with sorrow. She peered inside as one would view a dead loved one at a wake. "Bye, old girl. I'll never forget you."

More tears.

Zack squeezed her hand, and this time Sam let him hold it. "I'm sorry for your loss, Sam."

She wiped the tears from her eyes. "I'm being silly. She *is* just a car, a hunk of metal, and I should learn to accept that." She heaved a sigh that seemed to come from her toes. "There. I'm done with grief. You're getting soaked with rain."

Josiah pointed towards his garage. "Follow me. We'll talk turkey where it's dry."

Once inside he listed Sam's options...encouraging her toward buying a car from him. "I've got a used Focus, loaded."

"Loaded? Now Josiah McIntosh, I'm sure you figured out that I know blip about cars. What do you think, Zack?"

Finally, he felt useful, and his cheeks warmed that Sam actually looked to him for help. He felt an inch taller, bursting with pride. "I've seen the car, Sam. It's a good deal."

"Well, then, if Zack recommends it, that's good enough for me." She looked right at him with those little-girl eyes, but spoke to Josiah. "I trust Zack. Aaron trusts you. I think we can do business."

Zack leaned in towards Josiah. "What will you give Sam for Lucille's salvage?"

He scratched his head. "A hundred is the best I can do on a car that old. Now Sam can—"

"Hey, you two. Quit skirting around me like I'm an old lady. Talk to me, Josiah. I appreciate Zack's expertise, but I'm the one who's paying."

Josiah scratched his head and shrugged his

shoulders. "As I started to say, I can give you a daily rental rate or we can deduct the salvage and you can purchase the Focus outright. Did you have collision insurance?"

"No. Standard liability is all. Look, I need a vehicle. I can pay cash for it, but I'm afraid my bank cards are useless. The numbers are unreadable, and I left my checkbook in Manhattan. I could write you a cashier's check, I suppose. What do you think, Zack?"

Now she wanted his opinion again. He looked at the whole of her, her neediness and refusal to admit it, her shape—thin, but meat on all the right places, smart, too. Absolutely, a few slips and slides would be worth having her on his arm. He'd have to learn to keep better balance.

Josiah was the trusting sort, would probably let her drive it away and wire him the money from Manhattan. But, if she found that out, Sam might leave tomorrow, not bother to wait for her court date. Zack needed a little more time to get her on his good side; and if that smile was a clue, there was a start of something between them, even if he'd stepped knee deep into her moat of resistance.

"It's a good car, Sam. That's all the advice I'll give you. If you want it, go for it."

"Thanks Zack. I appreciate your help and advice. I can take it from here. I don't want to keep you from your baseball practice, or if it's cancelled, I'm sure you've got better things to do than hang around while Josiah and I conduct business."

Sam's tone was undeniable—dismissed like a valet. He'd thought there'd been a spark of something between them, as much as a city gal would loosen up to a backwoods local like Zack Bordeaux. He'd hoped to follow her into town and spend a few hours showing her around Haven, the real Haven—the Haven he'd grown up in and loved, not the tourist block on Main Street. Instead, she pushed him aside like his jacket. Samantha Knowles could take care of herself. He should take the hint and forget about her. He should, but he couldn't. Might as well jump in with both feet, right up to his neck. "Will I see you later, Sam? At Sadie's? I usually have dinner there."

She cast her glance downward. "I suppose I'll see you, then."

He returned alone to his truck, scuffed his heels on the ground as he walked, got in, yanked the ignition and revved the engine a little too loudly. Pebbles flew every direction as he spun out of the parking lot.

9

Sam slung her pilot case into the backseat, allowing herself a sense of pride both in her nearly new car and in her spur-of-the-moment decision. According to Josiah, the former owner had hit a deer, not a moose, and opted for a replacement vehicle, selling the damaged one to Josiah, who fixed it up like new. Not a Cavalier, but red. Lucille II was a fitting name.

The transaction had taken more time than she'd expected, eating up most of the morning. She could barely believe that a total stranger would trust her, be willing to forego a security deposit, and let her drive away, leaving only a copy of her water-damaged driver's license.

She should probably go back to the Lighthouse for lunch, possibly even a nap. Buying a car was more exhausting than she remembered from fifteen years ago. Besides, she should make a few phone calls before she went to the library—call Justine, and cancel the rest of her vacation at Stowe. Why not stay here in Haven? Good people…eccentric…but kind.

Zack had left in a huff. She should have told him about Jonathan and needing to rest, and she should have let him take over more on the car. Sam spun out of Josiah's parking lot and headed for Aaron and Sadie's enterprises, trying out the radio as she drove. Nothing but static, but along with other handy features, the car did have a CD player. She could purchase a few jazz albums at one of the bookstores, or see what Sadie had in her store.

She parked in the lot on the south end of Main Street, looking forward to a quiet afternoon. When she went to the library later, she'd check out a few books. Haven probably folded up at dusk, the hottest spot in town, the Lighthouse, the television her only other after-supper diversion. It might be worthwhile to drop her damaged laptop off at Bert's Tackle, though she doubted it could be salvaged.

Sam stepped inside the lounge to see who might be playing cards or shuffleboard. If Leon was there, she might take him up on his offer to teach her how to play the game. Perhaps exercise would shake off this exhausted feeling. She scoured the Lighthouse, but no sight of Leon, only a half dozen elderly men who seemed glued to the shuffleboard table.

Sadie bustled to and fro with lunch preparations, and Sam glanced at the sign as she breezed by: *Today's Special: Barbeque pork on a bun and vegetable soup*. By the time Sam reached the steps, a few customers—no, Sadie would call them company—wandered in.

The aromas punched at her stomach with more demand than the cry for rest. She sat on a stool near the Shuffleboard Gang, Murray the only one she recognized. He waved and grunted a quick greeting, "Howdy, Sam."

"Howdy yourself, Murray. Where're Leon and Doc?"

"Leon went upstairs to get his wallet and Doc had to take Cynthia into Albany for a doctor's appointment," he said, without taking his eyes off the shuffleboard.

Sadie served the gamers first, setting down six plates on the rectangular table to the right of the shuffleboard and another four plates on a table left of Mazie's bridge group. Not one gamer stopped to acknowledge delivery.

"I win!" Mazie hauled in her jackpot, all of twenty cents.

The losers got up and moved to their lunches, and Sam overheard someone whisper, "I'm getting tired of letting Mazie win all the time…she can't even remember what trump is from one play to the other."

Mazie stood up and hollered at the women. "Well, ladies, let's get started on our card game, shall we?"

The whisperer helped Mazie to the table. "It's lunchtime, Mazie. We'll play again after lunch."

"We always have a game *before* lunch."

"We already played a game, Mazie, now sit down and eat your lunch."

Sadie brought in a fresh carafe of coffee. "You're such a sweet gal," Mazie said. "I think I know you. What's your name?"

"Sadie. Yes, you do know me. We're great friends." She poured the coffee, her eyes moist.

Sam wondered how it had been with Sadie and her mother before dementia robbed them of their special relationship.

"I'll be right with you, Sam." Sadie scooted into the kitchen and came out with a tray filled with choices for a king. "We're not really open for business, but if people wander in here, I certainly can't send them away without a full belly."

"How do you manage to make ends meet if you give away all this food? You shouldn't let strangers take advantage of you like that." Sam's cheeks heated with the realization of how much she sounded like Justine. Preaching must be contagious.

"Oh, no one takes advantage of me, dear. Folks generally plop down some money on the table afore they leave…most times it's a generous amount. The Lighthouse Lounge is a hobby, and we always have enough to cover our costs." Sadie leaned in. "And sometimes a little extry."

She zipped back into the kitchen, returning with more coffee urns for the visitors. One could only speculate how long before Sadie and Aaron would officially open for business, or if they truly wanted to. How did a town justice get away with scamming the IRS like this, even if they billed the lounge as a hobby?

Sam dug into her soup as Aaron sat at her table. "How is it?"

"Delicious."

He eyed Sam like a defense lawyer studies the jury. "Sadie said your friend Justine called about an hour ago and wants you to call her back."

"Thanks."

Sam rushed to her room. Lunch and a nap could wait. She found her door slightly ajar, but her bed had been made and the bathroom smelled like pine. She picked up the phone and punched in Justine's number. Something must be wrong if Justine called her first, when she expected Sam to call this afternoon. Acid erupted with each ring, relief when Justine answered in her usual cherry tone.

"Thank goodness. You scared me half to death."

"Whoa, girl. Stop and catch your breath. Abe wants me to run a few errands for him this afternoon, and I didn't want to miss your call. I've been worried about you. That was no picnic you had with that moose, you know. Since you were out, I take it you're feeling better. When are you leaving for Stowe?"

"I made a slight change of plans. I decided to stay here for my entire vacation. Tell Abe I'm sorry. I hope it didn't put him out too much."

Justine giggled. "Not what I expected at all. I'm proud of you. Abe will be, too."

Might as well tell Justine the whole of Sam's newfound spontaneity. "I bought a car today."

Justine squealed, and Sam moved the receiver away from her ear. "You are so full of surprises, girl." She stuttered a few errs and ahs, then finally, "There's another reason I called."

"Thought so. It's not about Robert, is it?"

"Robert's fine. It's the wedding that's not so fine. We can't get the reception hall we planned for, and the next available date isn't until after Robert goes back to the Middle East. We've been trying to find another decent place to hold the reception, but so far no luck. Life is so unfair, sometimes." Justine the Serene spewed a few choice phrases, cagily sounding like expletives without actually swearing. She'd do that when she got mad, then lift her eyes towards heaven and say, "Lord, forgive me."

"What happened?"

"Apparently, someone else booked the hotel for the same time as our reception, but they supposedly made their plans before we called. The other party's guest list is a lot larger than they anticipated and they need the extra space. My cousin who works there told me the other party was a city council member."

Sam could hear the sobs in Justine's voice.

"The wedding's only six weeks away. What should I do, Sam? Should I sue a city council member?"

"Probably not the best thing to do if you want to keep your job."

"We weren't having a big to-do, about fifty people, but I'd like to have a place a little more festive than our church basement, more than a covered dish reception, at least."

Sam blurted the thought before she'd even let her brain digest it. "Why not ask Sadie to do your reception? You could have it here at the Lighthouse." Sam gave Justine an in-depth description of the lounge and Haven. "I saw an old church on my walk this morning. I'll ask around. It's possible you could have your wedding there, too. Make the whole affair a getaway weekend. Sadie loves to theme things, and you like themes. The two of you could whip up a humdinger of a party."

"I like it…love it, actually. I'll see if I can get Abe to drive me up and take a look—that is, if you don't mind some company. Abe and I have been out straight with the Styles case. We both could use a break."

It wasn't what she said that caused alarm, it was the way she didn't say it. Something was wrong, or Justine would have blasted Abe for making her work so much overtime when she had a wedding to plan.

"What's going on with Styles?"

"The usual drama that doesn't amount to anything. Darnell Washington keeps throwing motions for a mistrial and Judge Normandy keeps throwing them out. And Abe and Darnell have held a ton of meetings behind closed doors. Nothing you didn't expect, Sam. Darnell's not letting so much as a pebble go unturned…what he's noted for. You predicted Styles wouldn't give up without a fight."

Yes, she had, the reason Sam hadn't wanted to take a vacation in the first place. "Maybe I should come back to Manhattan sooner?" A sense of loss crept over her with the thought of leaving Haven so soon.

"Don't you dare! Abe would have my head if he knew I told you."

"I'm glad you did. Promise you'll let me know if the case gets any more complicated than Darnell Washington's posturing."

"Sam—"

"Promise me, or I'm leaving tomorrow." How she hoped she wouldn't have to, as if something held her in Haven, compelled her to stay.

"Fine…don't get all righteous on me. I promise. Now, let's get back to my reception. You really think Sadie could manage it on short notice?"

"I'm sure of it. Not only manage, but enjoy the challenge. The whole thing would have to be done like a gigantic house party. They don't have a license."

Justine laughed. "A New York City prosecutor is recommending work under the table?"

"Not like that at all. You'll see when you get here. They might push the envelope so far to the edge it hangs off, dangles a bit precariously, but I don't see the harm. Besides, Aaron's an attorney, too, and the town justice. Who's going to complain?"

"Sounds great. I can't wait to see it. So, what kind of car did you get today?"

"Focus. Zack said it was a good deal."

"Zack, the EMT guy? What gives?"

"Nothing. He's merely being nice."

"Nice is a good start."

Sam was on a roll, might as well keep the surprises coming. "I bought a painting today."

Justine roared with excitement. "Shut up. Really? You? The girl with the lowest grade in her Art Appreciation class?"

"A Gladstone landscape." Sam let it fall off her tongue as if she'd visited every gallery exhibit in New York City.

"A Gladstone? Really? How did you manage that? He's one of the most well-known landscape artists in post-modern circles. I can't afford his pieces. How did you get one?"

That famous? And Sam had insulted him. "I'm going to his estate tomorrow to see the lake while the hyacinths are still in bloom."

Justine gulped in disbelief. "Get out. You met him? Jonathan Gladstone lives in Haven? I knew his estate was somewhere in the Adirondacks. That's way cool. Color me jealous."

"He's not as nice as his paintings."

"Then why are you meeting him?"

"The lake, for one thing, intrigues me…so clear, like glass. I want to see if it's as surreal as he paints it. And I'm curious. The town mechanic said the Gladstones are cursed."

"That's ridiculous."

Probably. She wondered if the legend self-perpetuated, if by believing they were cursed, the Gladstones brought tragedy upon themselves. "I thought you'd be happy that I've finally taken an interest in history, as well as art."

"More like you've taken an interest in the artist, not the scenery."

"Not so. I've also become interested in history. Haven's is fascinating. Did you know that the southern Adirondacks played an important role in both the

French and Indian Wars and The Revolutionary War?"

"Everyone knows that."

Everyone except me. "I always crammed for the test, then forgot everything I studied as soon as the exam was done." Storing facts and figures in a crowded brain was not among Sam's preferred activities. Why strain with the weight of useless knowledge when libraries and the Internet were easily accessible?

"No wonder you stink at Trivial Pursuit. So, Jonathan Gladstone…I've seen pictures of him, a hunk—although there hasn't been much publicity on him lately, almost like he dropped out of existence."

Haven had now officiously moved from the quaint to the mysterious, another compelling reason to stay—the whole intrigue surrounding Dawn's Hope a enigma Sam could dig her teeth into. "I suppose he's good looking in a rugged sort of way. I hadn't noticed."

"I heard he was married once, that his wife died. Drowned, I think. Well, anyway, I expect a full report when we come up. Haven sounds wonderful. I can't wait for the tour."

The rattle from the closet sounded like ten mice on a rampage. Sam jumped and the phone dropped to the floor, the loud buzz evidence she'd lost her connection with Justine. She needed a weapon of some kind…Sam picked up the handset from the floor and tiptoed toward the closet door.

Ajar.

She took aim and pulled the door open.

Leon cowered and covered his face "Don't hit me!"

"Don't worry, Leon." Sam set the handset onto the cradle. "See? I'm not going to hurt you. Now tell me what you're doing in there."

He slunk out, a scolded puppy. Sam pointed for Leon to sit on her bed while she imitated Judge Normandy's you-have-one-minute-at-my-bench glare.

"I'm sorry, Sam. When you came in, I got scared and hid in the closet. I thought you were a burglar."

"That does not explain why you were in my room."

"This is your room?"

"Yes. Your room is down the hall."

"Oh. That explains what all this furniture was doing here, though, Sadie's always changing things around, putting new stuff here and there. I thought the room looked a little girly. But I'd never complain to Sadie. She's the salt of the earth, that one."

Sam studied the defendant's mannerisms. His pupils never dilated as he spoke, although his hands jerked, and he scratched his head almost continuously. Obviously, Leon had some kind of dementia, like Mazie.

"Come with me. I'll take you to your room."

He opened the door and went in. "That looks more like I remember."

Maps and charts covered the walls, and one legend read: *Asia and Africa in 1945.*

"Do you collect maps?"

He moved four tacks from England to France, as if evading the question.

"So, are you a collector, Leon?"

"Of what?"

Sam pointed to the wall. "Of maps?"

"Might be. I don't remember why Sadie put them there. I think I might've been in the war."

"Which one?"

"Which one, what?"

"Which war do you think you were in?"

"Sadie tells me I was in that big war with Japan."

"You mean World War II?"

"That sounds right."

If she needed a reason to head back to Manhattan, she now had a justifiable one—she'd managed to become a loon's neighbor. She worried about Leon taking walks by himself when he needed closer supervision.

Sam glanced around the room. The yellowing maps encased in glass set off the rest of the 1940's memorabilia: a bayonet, a grenade, a poster of Betty Grable, even an old-style cabinet phonograph.

She pointed to a stack of 78s. "May I look at these?"

"Be my guest."

Most of the artists had unfamiliar names, but she did recognize Frank Sinatra and Glen Miller. "I love swing…the big bands." She held up a record and squealed. "Look at this one… Doris Day…Sentimental Journey."

"1945…her first hit."

Sam had researched Alzheimer's for a case she worked on during her internship, a woman with dementia who'd speared her caretaker with a knife. The patient pleaded self-defense since she forgot she had a caretaker and thought the woman was an intruder. The patient knew every movie made in 1935, the year she was married, but forgot her husband died three years ago. Apparently, recent memory went first, and long-term memory often stayed intact with confusing accuracy.

"What were you doing before you came into my

room?"

"Don't remember." He acted out his recollection. "Let's see, I went out for a walk. Saw you drive by with that new car of yours. Focus, isn't it? Nice little car. I'd get me one if I remembered how to drive."

Something didn't add up. Leon couldn't remember how to drive, but he knew Sam had bought a Focus? "Murray said you came upstairs to get your wallet. Is that it? Did you come to get your wallet and went into my room by accident?"

"Sounds right."

This was getting her nowhere. "Leon, did you have lunch?"

"You know, Sadie comes to get me and bring me down. So I probably didn't."

"Why don't you and I go downstairs and see what's happening? And if you haven't had lunch, Sadie will give you some of her good soup."

"That's so nice of you, young lady. What's your name?"

"Sam."

"Now that's an interesting name. A nickname?"

"It's short for Samantha, but not really a nickname. I use it professionally, too."

"Professionally?"

"I'm an attorney."

"Oh. You're the girl who killed that moose."

"That would be me." Sam took his arm and helped him down the stairs.

Sadie rushed up to meet them as they entered the lounge. "There you are, Leon. You had me worried. I went up to get you, and you weren't in your room. I was about to organize a search party."

Sam switched to Leon's defense. "He mistook my

room for his."

Sadie chuckled and cocked her head. "That so, Leon?"

"That so, Sam?" Leon winked.

Sam had been the mouse and Leon the cat, his dementia a game an almost believable defense when caught snooping in her room. Why was he there in the first place? Nothing was missing and no harm done that she knew of. He probably ducked into her closet when he heard her coming to avoid a cross-examination, the ruse another attempt to keep her from questioning him.

Justine accused Sam of having no sense of humor. No time like the present to prove her wrong. "Cute joke, Leon. But watch out for payback."

10

Frank Simmons had to be the craziest principal Haven's school district ever had...probably a close second to its craziest citizen, Pete Nugent, a burly fireman as loony as he was big. The rain had eased to a slow drizzle, but the baseball diamond was still slick with mud. Zack wanted to win as much as any other man on the team, but not at the expense of a broken leg.

Teams of two and three scattered around the field warming up with stretches, while some picked up a few bats and practiced their swings. Frank signaled a time out and walked past home plate. He leaned against the fence, his face a grayish white.

Pete slapped Frank on the shoulder. "What's the matter, old man, no more wind in the sails?"

Frank straightened. "Positions, everyone. I'll hit a few balls to the infield then we can take turns at the plate." Frank grabbed a bat and did a couple of practice swings. "Pete and Zack, change positions. I'd rather hit off of Zack's ball than one that might start a grass fire."

Pete kicked up mud as he stormed to the catcher's spot. "Zack throws like a girl. You just don't want to look bad. You know you can't hit mine."

Frank threw a second mask over to Pete. "Quit whining and put on your gear. Zack, don't hold back."

Zack threw Frank a helmet. "Better put this on."

"Batting helmets are for women and boys." Frank threw it to the side.

"Remember, you asked for it," Zack jibed. When Pete was ready, Zack fired one across the plate. Frank let it fly by.

Pete laughed as he scooped up the ball and sent it back to the pitcher. "What's the matter, Alice? Afraid to swing?"

Frank scowled as Zack wound up and threw a fastball. Frank swung too hard, and missed, the bat coming around with a smack to the collar bone. There was brave and then there was downright foolish. Frank edged both fronts. "You OK, Frank? Thought I heard a crack."

"My bones are made of rubber…not to worry. Show me what you got, Zack."

Frank always swung like he had something to prove…like he was twenty-five and not fifty–six. He swung the bat like he swung his golf club…with way too much aggression.

"Just meet the ball, Frank," Zack said. "You don't have to kill it. Try bunting and see if you can get to first."

"Hey. I'll do the coaching, if you don't mind. I started running bases before you learned how to walk." Frank took a couple of practice swings, so hard his 250 pounds teetered backward a few yards. He regained his balance, and repositioned himself in a batter's stance.

Zack zipped another fastball, and Frank swung late. "Hey, hot shot. That was outside."

Zack tugged at his cap. "Ready for a real pitch now, Frank?"

"Give me all you got."

Zack wound up again, throwing every inch of pent up frustration into his pitch, and Frank swung, a wannabe Joe DeMaggio. Too hard, he stumbled forward and caught the ball at the tip of the bat; the ball hissed backward, bounced off his head, and he dropped to the ground.

Rushing to Frank's side, Zack checked for a pulse and looked for signs of breathing. Nothing. He started CPR, and yelled to the field, "Someone call 911! Come on, Frank. Breathe. Don't make me a killer."

Zack whistled with relief when he felt a faint pulse. Slow, but he was alive—and pallor returned. Zack examined Frank's forehead where the ball hit and felt a small contusion on the scalp. It was better to swell outside than in; however, the slight bang on the head didn't explain Frank's symptoms. Nobody goes into cardiac arrest from being clobbered by their own foul ball. Unless…Frank did swing awfully hard…

Of course.

The signs had been there all the time—Frank's frequent indigestion, rubbing his arm, shortness of breath whenever he crossed the room.

Distant wails. "Help's on the way, Frank."

Within seconds after arriving, the paramedics had Frank on a gurney and loaded into the bus. As the ambulance sped off, Zack ushered a prayer for Frank's recovery. If Zack's suspicions were right, Frank would not be returning to work any time soon. As the only teacher at Haven Central with an administrative license, Zack would probably be moved up to acting principal before the week was out. He wanted Frank's job, but not like this.

11

Harlan Styles sauntered into the visitation room where Darnell Washington waited. "Tell me you've got some good news, Darnell."

Washington tugged at his suit. "We've got her…Knowles. I checked the PI's info and I've had a bunch of confabs with Hilderman. I threatened to sue the city for negligent handling of evidence and prosecutorial misconduct."

Harlan smiled. A crumb…not enough to satisfy…not even a career ender. "Miss Perfect? Thought you said she was the most thorough prosecutor you ever dealt with. Besides, what's a civil suit gonna do to get me out of here?"

"The law bends to the highest bidder, Harlan."

"I know some folks can buy their way out of a jam. Done it myself a few times to beat a couple of drug raps. But I don't see how it applies here. Knowles won't budge no matter how much money you throw her way. Hilderman's no crook, either."

Washington leaned back in his chair and snickered, the way he did when he knew he had someone cornered. "Even brick walls fall down, Harlan. Hilderman has a lot to lose if this case goes sour, if we keep the case tied up in courts for years to come. I told him we'd take it to the Supreme Court, if necessary."

Washington might find Hilderman's plight

amusing, but what good would a case in Supreme Court do Harlan now? He needed out. He squeezed his head. "I can't wait years, Darnell. You've got to get me out of here. I don't care what you have to do to make that happen."

"Glad you said that, Harlan. I do have a plan." Washington tapped his file against the table. "Hilderman doesn't think the case is worth the expense, so he's willing to cut your sentence if we drop the suit."

Life couldn't be that simple—nothing came to Harlan Styles on any kind of platter…least of all, a silver one. "Doesn't sound like Hilderman. He's almost as hardnosed as Knowles."

"I upped the ante. I told him Knowles was a whack job and we had the proof. She should never have been allowed to try your case, but the city let her."

Harlan smiled—the first since he'd been put in prison. "You seem pretty sure of yourself, Darnell. Must be Saint Samantha's sins are pretty severe."

"You should have seen Hilderman's face when I told him she had an abusive childhood. The psychiatrist's report indicated that Sam suffered from a suppressed desire to take revenge against her perpetrator—her father."

"How does that help me, Darnell?"

"Feeds right into the theory of prosecutorial prejudice. She's trying to get back at her father by putting you away."

"Might work, at that."

"But…"

Another contingency? Washington's deals always sank his clients deeper into the pit. "But…what?"

"It'll cost you pretty to cover my tracks…how I got this information."

Every time Washington took a deep breath, Harlan paid pretty…so pretty he'd have to rob a bank to pay Washington off. "Money's no problem. You know that. I'll get it from somewhere." Maybe his brother Reg could find some action. "How are you going to get a judge to release Knowles's juvie record?"

Washington stiffened with Harlan's challenge.

Pride goeth before a fall. That's what his foster mother said when she pushed Harlan into a closet for hours on end to think about what he'd done wrong. He'd spent so much time thinking about his sins, he learned how to pick locks.

Washington leaned forward. "When it's pertinent, there are ways."

"Sounds impressive, Darnell."

"Sam Knowles never should have tried your case, Harlan. We'll make sure the public knows she used your case to get revenge…not justice. The stink would be noticed from here to San Francisco, and that's something Hilderman wants to avoid. Seems he's up for a promotion, and it wouldn't look good if one of his subordinates was disciplined for prosecutorial misconduct, especially for a case he helped win."

"I thought Hilderman and Knowles were tight."

"If the price is right, there's not a soul wouldn't turn on their own mother. If Knowles backs down, Hilderman takes over. Simple as that."

Street thugs knew Knowles's reputation for taking the hard-line approach to all her cases. It'd take more than a few threats to get her to back down, even if Hilderman tried to make her.

"I don't care what you have to do to get me out of

here. Just do it. I've got a score to settle." Careless words that had tripped off his tongue faster than his brain could process his thoughts. Prison did that to a man, mushed his mind.

"Be careful, Harlan," Washington warned. "Talk like that could ruin everything. In fact, Hilderman told me he had to register a threat you made to Knowles at the sentencing hearing."

"The PI told me she sleeps with all her lights on. I made a joke, is all."

"From now on, you've got to be a model prisoner, if you want out of here. Go to those Bible meetings—get some religion. We've a good chance to make this happen, Harlan…"

Washington paused, and Harlan braced for the catch. With Washington, there was always a catch.

"That is, if you're willing to sing."

"I don't know, Darnell. Sounds risky."

Washington whistled. "Hilderman's after Ingram. If he shakes off this lengthy civil suit, busts up the Ingram family, he's a shoe-in for his promotion. You got more goods on Ingram than Jay does."

Thanks to Brenda.

It was her idea to use the pharmacy to front both crime-lords. He shouldn't have listened, but the money kept Brenda supplied with drugs and expensive perfume. Made sense now, why Jay had been so generous to hire Darnell. Harlan had been set up—Jay's retribution for the double cross. If Harlan turned on Ingram…Jay got rid of two headaches at once.

No one crossed Ingram and lived.

"What did you do, Darnell? Why didn't you come in here with a dagger and get it over with?"

Washington laughed. Harlan glared. If he lived

long enough to get Knowles, Washington would be next. "I fail to see the humor in this."

"I know we're doing a tango with the devil, but don't shut your coffin lid, yet. I think we can pull this one off. Hilderman's offered protection."

Lies…more like Ingram would slice Harlan in more ways than a Sicilian pizza. "None of this was supposed to happen. How did the charges go from criminal negligence to murder? You told me not to deal when they first arrested me. You said they'd never be able to make the charges stick. You know as well as I do, Ingram's going to get me. Well, let him. I got no reason to go on living without Brenda. She left me."

"I heard. You're over-reacting, Harlan. I told you, you'll get protection and there're a lot of Brendas out there for you to pick from once you're out of here."

"Nothing else you can do? No way to get Ingram out of the equation?"

"Here's the problem. I can't shed enough reasonable doubt where Kiley's death is concerned. You've got to pay up somewhere."

Harlan stiffened. "I didn't kill Kiley. She was a brat, but I didn't kill her."

"So you say, but Knowles's evidence, except for the TOD typo, is solid."

"I'm telling you, I don't care what the evidence looks like, I didn't kill Kiley. I'm a sinner going straight to hell when I die, looks like that'll be soon, thanks to you and Hilderman, but I'm not a child killer, never killed anyone on purpose, for that matter." Visions of Knowles in a pool of blood tickled his fantasies. "At least, not yet."

Washington slapped the file on the table. "I told you to quit talking like that. Threats won't get us anywhere."

"Are you telling me I have to confess to something I didn't do?"

Washington sat back down, his eyes pleading. "You only have to give up Ingram. If we can get your sentence reduced…maybe even house arrest…will you do the time and sing?"

Not even Washington believed Harlan's innocence…only Brenda could clear him and she'd sooner swallow a pit of vipers than come forward.

Washington put the file back in his briefcase, closing it with an aggravated zip. "It's all I got. We either run the legal gamut with a civil suit—and, if we do, we're talking years before a settlement is reached—or, we take Hilderman's deal. As your attorney, I recommend you start practicing your scales."

Harlan squeezed his head until he thought he'd pass out, then let go. Yeah, he'd belt out an entire opera if he had to, his swan song. Once he was out, though, he'd hum a different tune. Knowles claimed she only wanted justice for Brenda's kid. What about justice for Harlan Styles? Once Ingram heard about the deal, whether Harlan rolled or not, the clock would start ticking on Harlan Styles's death parade. If it had to be, it had to be, but Justice demanded a life for his life, too. That was the verdict in Harlan Styles's court of law.

12

She glanced at the clock as she picked up the handset on the fourth ring. She'd slept for three hours. "This is Sam Knowles."

"Sam, it's Justine. I got worried when you disconnected. So I called Aaron. He told me about Leon giving you a hard time. The old man sounds like a hoot. Wonder why he yanked your chain like that?"

Something Sam wondered about, too. "Nothing was missing in my room, but there's a fresh batch of hyacinths on my table." Sam yawned and rubbed her eyes. "So what's up?"

"I promised to let you know if I heard anything. Styles's defense team requested a resentencing review for later this week."

"Not on the grounds of the ME's wrong TOD? Styles has no alibi for the corrected time."

"Something else is going on. Abe's had all kinds of meetings with Darnell Washington, He won't tell me anything about them and said not to bother you with the case details, that he had everything under control."

Every prosecutor had at least one case go sour in spite of planning for every contingency imaginable. Asa Abbington had to go to retrial because Judge Normandy accidently left a microphone on during a private chat and was heard pronouncing the defendant guilty before the jury returned. The law most often worked satisfactorily—eventually in favor of justice.

But at times, the guilty did go free. Fear caught in Sam's throat to think Styles still might walk after three years of constant vigilance, and all because of a typo.

She'd been so thorough, read and re-read her briefs, pored over evidence with a microscope. Kiley Smith cried out from the grave, and Justice might be forced to turn a deaf ear. Sam screamed a silent prayer. *Oh, God. Justine calls you the Great Avenger. Please don't let Kiley's death go unpunished.*

Anger pushed aside fear, anger over Abe's intrusion. He had no right to be making any kind of deals with Darnell Washington without consulting Sam. Why hadn't he called her, asked for her input? This was her case, not Abe's. She should pack her bags right now and leave for Manhattan, give Abe a piece of her worried mind. Aaron would understand…he was a lawyer, too. She could always mail in her fine. As for Jonathan Gladstone—she didn't owe him anything if she never went to see the property. "I can be there tonight."

Justine screeched. "You'll do no such thing. Abe was afraid you'd say that. He said if you argued to remind you he was your teacher and you were the student. He can handle it."

Sam laughed. "One crazy professor, for sure. But, yeah, I did learn a lot from him, and I used every trick he taught me to earn that conviction."

Justine sighed. "I'm worried about you, Sam, worried you won't let this go. It's time you trusted someone else with this burden."

"Abe?"

"No, God."

"I suppose you're right."

"I know I'm right. When's the last time you asked

for God's guidance with this case?"

Of course, she'd prayed for intervention, but as Justine suspected, she'd never asked God for wisdom. "An eye for an eye, Justine…isn't that what the Bible says?"

Justine squealed like a mouse in a trap. "I give up trying to put sense into you. But don't you dare give up on your vacation. Abe will find a way to keep that jerk in jail."

"Urgh."

"I'll take that as a yes, you'll stay in Haven as planned?"

Justine would have taken a no for a yes, and Sam had no defense against that kind of determination. "Keep me posted. See you soon. Oh, and bring my spare laptop and some clothes when you come."

"I'll have to get your laptop back from Abe. He said he needed to check some files."

More intrusion. Sure, she'd let Abe keep an extra key in the event of an emergency…like a fire, or if she didn't show up to work for a couple of days. Not to help himself to her laptop whenever he felt like it. She had personal stuff on there, stuff Abe had no business seeing.

Justine skirted another sermon. "If you can't trust Abe, then who can you trust, right?"

"Right."

"Enjoy your vacation. I can't wait to see Haven. Love ya…bye."

"Bye." Sam disconnected.

She paced the room for a few minutes, willing her ire into submission. She'd have to stay calm if she were to find anything out on Jonathan Gladstone. The library would be closing soon. She had slept too late.

Now she'd have to wait until tomorrow to get to the bank.

She replaced the handset, grabbed her purse and checked the closet, the only place an intruder could hide. No Leon this time. She navigated the steps and headed out the lounge door.

Sam waved to Aaron. "I'm heading for the library."

"Say hello to Lillian for me."

"Lillian?"

"My sister, Lillian Bordeaux, Zack's mother…she's the librarian."

Everyone in Haven was probably related somehow or another to everyone else, if not by blood then by heritage, a stream of love enveloping one's every breath. Sam envied the connectedness, wishing she could belong, in spite of her past, in spite of the secrets. But then, Haven had its secrets, too. Another reason to stay…mysteries to unravel.

Jonathan turned the landscape toward the light. No, the colors were all wrong! He paced the length of the cabin. Why couldn't he get the shades the way Angelica would approve? He stopped pacing, and opened the tubes he'd bought at Sadie's. He filled in Angelica's gown then dabbed the hyacinths with different colors, stroking the petals one by one.

He stopped…his breathing rapid and exacerbated.

The rage again.

He threw the palette across the room, sank into a recliner, and buried his face with his palms. "I'm sorry, Angelica. I can't do it."

She seemed to call him from every corner of the cabin, her summons more intense each day. *Come to me, Jonathan. Come join us. We will be a family again.*

"I will. I promise. When I finish your portrait. "

He intended this canvas to be his masterpiece, a portrait of Angelica next to a vase of her beloved hyacinths, like the works she had inspired him towards before her death—where flowers danced in joy. Now he could only paint when in a rage, and his rages produced dead hyacinths, brutalized, bleeding. Jonathan longed to join her and Elliott, until he went to the canvas, and his genius became imprisoned. He couldn't join her in failure.

Jonathan peered out the picture window, the lake still hazy from the morning rain. "I can't come to you now, Angelica. There's another voice calling me. I don't know whose it is, and I don't know whose to listen to. Don't you see? That's why I have to go away from here…away from your memory. Please, don't be angry with me."

Jonathan slammed the door to the cabin and mounted his ATV. Mud splattered onto his pants and shirt, and he laughed at the sheer magnitude of the moment, the ping against his legs like a rhapsody of hope.

He must live. For what, he didn't know, any more than he knew the source of this certainty. Paris would have the answers.

13

Sam gazed at the brick and wooden structure, perhaps one of the oldest left in Haven, with the exception of the church. According to the outside placard, Arlington Memorial Library was donated by Muriel Gladstone Arlington, Emmanuel's daughter, in memory of her husband, Congressman Franklin Arlington. Had Muriel married Franklin out of love, or prestige? So much of the Gladstone hierarchy steeped in intrigue.

Inside, a white-haired woman in a striped, charcoal-gray pantsuit stamped books at the counter. A younger girl, possibly sixteen or seventeen, took books off the counter and placed them into a rolling cart. The older woman gazed up. "May I help you?

"I'm—"

She smiled. "I know who you are. You're the girl who's rooming at Aaron's place."

There was something to be said for anonymity, something not so difficult to achieve in Manhattan.

"You have me at a disadvantage. Seems everyone in Haven knows who I am, but I've only met a handful of people. I'm assuming, though, you're Lillian Bordeaux, Aaron's sister? I see the resemblance. You both have kind eyes."

"Nice of you to say."

"Everyone in Haven has been kind." *Except Jonathan Gladstone.*

Lillian pushed out a *humph*. "My dear girl, no town is without its dirt roads. But I'm glad your first impressions are favorable. What can we help you with?"

"I'm interested in any information you have about the Gladstones."

"Miss Knowles—"

"Sam."

"Sam…we have a whole wall dedicated to that subject. And then there's the microfiche from the newspaper, *The Haven Gazette*, a weekly paper, more of a hobby than anything else, barely supports itself. My husband, Tom, edits it." Lillian came out from behind the counter and walked into the lobby, reappearing arm in arm with a thin, tallish man wearing a medieval monk's garb, complete with a Friar Tuck hairdo.

He offered a handshake. "Tom Bordeaux. You must be Sam Knowles. Zack speaks highly of you."

"I think highly of Zack, too. He's been a great help to me."

Tom glued his gaze on Sam as if studying an anomaly. After a few awkward moments, he removed his wig, revealing a full head of cropped gray hair. "This costume's for a skit I'm doing in Zack's class next week, tried it on for size. Pardon me for staring, Miss Knowles."

"Sam." Maybe she should just wear a sign.

"Haven gets a lot of tourists, but we rarely have a moose murderer among us. You're famous."

Would it be wrong to ask God to send a blizzard so the people could forget her and the moose and find something else to talk about?

Lillian squared her shoulders. "Tom is an adjunct history professor and also a writer. He's an expert on the Gladstone Legacy. He'll tell you anything you need to know. Save you hours of going through books and newspapers, and Tom likes to show off his knowledge." She rubbed his arm. "My Tom has three PhD's from Columbia. It seems I've spent my whole life the wife of a college student."

"Now, Lillian—"

Justine said that the world was so small a toothpick connected the two hemispheres. Must be true. "Dr. Thomas Bordeaux? You're a guest lecturer at Columbia."

"From time to time, yes."

"I attended one of your lectures a few years back about the impact of waterway development in American History."

Tom smiled. "Well...well. Most of my lecture audiences are captive, required attendance if they want the grade. I'm not the most gifted speaker, I'm afraid, and the students use the time to sleep or write letters. I'm pleased someone actually paid attention, even more so that you remembered."

Sam's cheeks heated with embarrassment. "Not me. Actually, my friend was the one who attended and dragged me along. But something you said did stick with me."

"What was that?"

"History is what connects us as people and should not be taken for granted. Studying our common heritage unifies us as a nation and a world. Or something like that."

"Close enough, I'm sure. Sounds like something I might have said."

No need to spoil the man's moment by admitting the thought came back to her only now; though, at the time, his words pricked her conscience, ignited a latent desire to learn more about history. Unfortunately, the interest suffocated under a mountain of legal studies.

She could pursue it now, and she had a living, breathing encyclopedia ready to spit out his knowledge at will. "What can you tell me about Jonathan Gladstone?"

Tom tossed his wig on top of the counter. "Anything you want to know. I've written volumes on the Gladstone estate, and I'm considered the foremost biographer on Jonathan Gladstone."

"My friend Justine said he was famous."

"He was, in art circles, anyway, at least up until five years ago. Some say he could have been the Rembrandt of landscapes. I published a few essays on his work in *The New Yorker* and *Newsweek.* He stopped doing gallery exhibits after the accident."

"You mean when his wife drowned?"

"Come upstairs in the meeting room and I'll explain."

Sam mouthed a "thank you" to Lillian and followed Tom up two flights of steps into a spacious lounge, probably colonial, but then she knew as much about architecture as she did art. A marbled fireplace took up most of one wall, and a massive, intricately-carved wooden table centered the room. The walls were adorned with portraits and landscapes of every period in history.

"This lounge is used for various community events," Tom said. "And a good place to display art." He pointed across the room. "Over there is our colonial collection."

Sam squinted to read the names—under one she made out, *Paul Revere*.

"Colonial artists painted portraits, mainly, and usually in the winter, too busy in the summer and fall with crops and such. Many of the artists painted figures with blank faces. When they received a commission, the artist filled in the face of their patron." Tom pointed to the central portrait, and Sam peered into the same coconut-brown eyes she'd seen at Sadie's shop. "I assume that's Emmanuel Gladstone."

"Why, yes it is." Tom stopped in the middle of the room by a series of paintings, all of Mirror Lake, many of which featured hyacinths of various colors, some with buds poking through a thin layer of snow. "Jonathan donated these at the height of his popularity."

Sam scrutinized the landscapes, not sure what she should be noticing. Tom pointed to a second set. "These were donated last year. Notice anything different?"

Her untrained eye caught the obvious absence of light. No happy play like the others. An eerie moon cast protracted shadows along the violet red hyacinths masquerading in grotesque human form. "I'm no art connoisseur, but I see the differences. What happened?"

Tom's smile vanished. "Jonathan's life seemed to fall apart after his wife died. He painted these early masterpieces shortly after he married. Everyone thought he and Angelica were very much in love. Sometimes the couple could be seen fishing on Mirror Lake. At other times, Angelica would take the boat out while Jonathan sketched."

Tom pointed to a painting of a young woman seated in a row boat and holding an antique fishing pole. "All that changed after she had the baby. Not surprising. Tragedy seems to follow some families. Many town folk believe the Gladstones were cursed after the first mansion burned to the ground."

While Tom's side trip proved to be interesting, Sam prodded him toward more immediate information needed to prepare for her interview with Jonathan. "My friend thought Jonathan's wife drowned. Is that true?"

"They both did—Angelica and Elliott. Rumors quickly spread after Angelica's disappearance that she had taken Elliot and run away. After their bodies were found a year later, some speculated that Jonathan had killed them both. Other rumors circulated that Angelica suffocated the boy, then drowned herself."

"Why would she do a thing like that?"

"Elliott was born with a rare disorder called schizencephaly, Type II."

"I've heard of it. In law school, we studied a few adoption cases involving the disease. But these children were from overseas. I thought the disorder was rare in the United States."

"Rare, but not unheard of. That's what the kid had, all right. Seizures, paralysis, blindness, nothing more than a vegetable, really. At age four, Elliott still wasn't responsive. He'd make a few guttural sounds when he rolled his eyes, but that was about it. Angelica's journals state that the boy didn't even respond to her voice. Something like that is sure to break a mother's heart. It might have caused her to do something brash."

Sam felt a ping of sympathy toward her prospective client. No wonder he was standoffish, gossip must follow him everywhere. Sam remembered the tabloids after Daddy died. Curses were as medieval as Tom's costume; yet, something sinister seemed embedded in the Gladstone legacy.

"Did the autopsy reveal anything?"

"The bodies apparently had become lodged under the rocky ledge, and the spring thaw pushed them loose a year later. The autopsy proved both Angelica and Elliott drowned, and, after months of investigation, their deaths were finally ruled accidental." He clicked his last statement.

"And you don't agree with the findings?"

"Not my place to agree or disagree, but the circumstances were very mysterious and the investigation failed to explain everything. Jonathan testified that he had been in town getting art supplies. When he returned home, Angelica and Elliott were missing. He searched the entire estate and found the empty rowboat adrift in the water. He notified the authorities. Divers looked for them but couldn't find anything. Some speculated Jonathan had murdered his wife and child, buried their bodies, and staged the drowning."

How awful to be so uncertain for so long.

Tom contorted his lips to one side. "Thing is, no one can figure out why Angelica would have brought the boy out in the rowboat to begin with, especially without a life preserver. Jonathan took Angelica's disappearance pretty hard. He stopped painting entirely until the bodies were found. Then these dark landscapes followed. Although judged to be artistically brilliant, they sell sluggishly. Rumor is that Jonathan hasn't had a commission in over a year."

The landscape she'd bought in the morning must have been an early Gladstone. "So what you're saying is, he's broke?"

Tom smiled. "Hardly. Jonathan receives a substantial allowance from his father's estate, and monies were left in trust at the Haven Savings and Loan for the upkeep and maintenance of Dawn's Hope. Aaron serves as executor according to Richard Gladstone's will."

"But Aaron has only lived in Haven less than a decade."

"Aaron visited Haven frequently to see us, and he and Richard Gladstone became friends. Jonathan made millions on his earlier landscapes, but, his career has come to a tragic standstill. Some speculate he'll never get it back."

Sam glanced at the clock in the hall. "I'm keeping you past closing. Lillian would probably like to go home."

Tom reached into his shirt pocket and offered a business card. "If you need anything else, let me know."

"Do you have any idea why Jonathan Gladstone would want an attorney?" Sam ventured the question, though it might breach an expectation of confidentiality. Sadie's rule-bending must be wearing off.

"Not really, although Zack said something about Jonathan wanting to go to Paris." Tom led the way to the lobby. Sam shook hands with Tom and Lillian and headed towards the Lighthouse Lounge. The late afternoon sun, a cantaloupe against a darkening sky, matched her subdued mood. She'd come to find reasons to hate Jonathan Gladstone, but instead discovered a soul that had been wind-tossed and storm-driven, even more than she had.

She thought of all the Haven residents she'd met

so far: Aaron, Tracey, Leon, Josiah, Zack, Mazie's bridge club, and the shuffleboard players—people cast from an odd mold. Something surreal rode on the canal that ran through Haven, drawing her in, her belonging to Haven as anachronistic as a light bulb in a Renoir. Yet, she wondered if Haven would be the briny balm that could finally heal her wounds, wounds still deep and raw, like Jonathan's.

So far, Haven had proven to be a place of rest, and she couldn't remember when she'd slept so soundly. *Haven, a place of rest*. A tune burst from a crypt of buried memories, a melody Justine's church people used to sing—

I've anchored my soul in the "Haven of Rest,"
I'll sail the wide seas no more
The tempest may sweep over the wild, stormy deep
In Jesus I'm safe evermore.

14

She was late, and she'd agreed to meet Zack at the lounge. She stopped at the front to read the sign: *Yankee Pot Roast with all the trimmings.* When she entered, the place was filled to capacity. Apparently, Aaron and Sadie didn't pay any more attention to seating limits than they did zoning laws. She searched the lounge for Zack but couldn't find him. Maybe she should wait for him before taking a seat at a table…besides, there didn't seem to be an available spot, for the moment.

Sam sat at the bar and watched Sadie whiz to and fro, carrying large trays teeming with guests' suppers. An African-American man, dressed in an Armani suit, rose from a single table near the door and walked toward Sam. She recognized him almost immediately—Darnell Washington, the last man Sam thought to look for in Haven.

He nodded his greeting. "A pleasant evening, Miss Knowles, wouldn't you say? I trust you're finding Haven a nice place to rest after your horrible accident."

"Don't bother with the small talk, Darnell. It's not your strong suit. What do you want?"

"Let's just say I'd like to make an offer you can't refuse."

Like a jewelry assessor scans a fraud, Aaron raised an eyebrow and shot Sam a glance that silently rendered assistance if needed. "Everything all right,

Sam?"

"Yes. Mr. Washington and I need a private place to chat."

"You can use my office." Aaron pointed to a closed door at the far wall behind the bar.

Washington extended his right arm and bowed, an affectation that nauseated more than impressed. "After you, Miss Knowles."

Legal books lined the shelves, interspersed with nautical novels. Sam counted ten copies of *Moby Dick*. Washington pointed to a chair, perhaps wanting her to sit first. Chivalry went out the door with the joust, yet he oozed sickening politeness, and Abe had taught her to beware of overly polite defense attorneys.

"I'll stand if you don't mind." Sam glanced at her watch. "You've got two minutes before I ask Aaron to boot you out of here. You know this is breaking protocol, cornering me like this while I'm on vacation."

"And I apologize, Miss Knowles, but expediency demands I break protocol." Washington put his briefcase on top of Aaron's desk, owning the room—his cold, hard eyes splintered his too-collected demeanor, as if he thought he had the upper hand, Lucifer defending his demon."You know we have requested an expedited hearing on my client's unjust sentencing."

She didn't know, but she wouldn't let Washington in on how much she was left out of the loop. "You didn't drive all the way up here to tell me something I already know. Go on."

"My client is prepared to make a deal."

Sam's mouth went dry. "Not on your life. He's already been found guilty, and I intend to make the verdict stick. You know the ME's typo isn't enough to warrant a mistrial. You've got nothing, Darnell. You should back away from this case before you lose all credibility as a defense attorney. So why don't you pick up that leather briefcase and get your suited self out of my vacation."

Washington chuckled. "I love your spirit, Miss Knowles. For a wisp of a gal, you stand your ground…don't even flinch."

"One minute left."

"I'll cut to the chase. Mr. Styles wants you off the case, permanently."

Was this some kind of joke? Did Abe send Darnell up here to give her a good laugh? "Neither you, nor your client, has the right to decide who will prosecute. How dare—"

Washington pulled out paperwork from his briefcase and handed her a copy of an affidavit. "We've done detective work of our own, Miss Knowles. You are not without ghosts in *your* closet."

"What are you getting at? I've never been arrested. Not even so much as a traffic violation." At least her license was clean until she met with Aaron on Thursday. "I refuse to play your game."

"Very well. But you should do yourself the favor of reading that affidavit."

Sam shoved the paper into Washington's hand. "Get out. And if you dare approach me again in such an improper way, I'll report you to the Bar Association for ethical misconduct."

Washington's laugh reverberated off the walls, a rude, maniacal snort. "I don't think you want to do that, Miss Knowles."

Sam's cheeks burned and her spaghetti legs wobbled. She grasped a side chair for support. "What are you driving at, Darnell?"

"We are prepared to demonstrate prosecutorial prejudice against my client and mishandling of evidence on your part."

"Ridiculous. If you did your homework, you'd know race has never been an issue with me."

He bared his teeth, a grimace more like a snarl than a smile. "Race is *not* the issue, here, Miss Knowles."

"Out with it, or I'm calling Aaron in now."

"I'm talking about your hatred toward men, a fixation that stems from the abuse you received from your father."

"Get out."

Washington shrugged his shoulders, seemingly obtuse to her rant. "Have it your way, Miss Knowles. I hoped we could avoid unpleasantness." He tossed the unread affidavit into his suitcase. "By the way, do you still sleep with a light on here in Haven?"

Fear crept up her spine and anger surged. How did they know? But of course, neighbors would have commented that Sam's lights were on all night. Not really so hard a thing to discover. But judging from his sneer, he knew why, too. How? The records were sealed.

He picked up his briefcase and nodded. "You'll be hearing more from us, Miss Knowles—through appropriate channels, of course. But you can't say we didn't try to keep this civil. All we wanted was for you to step down from this particular case. And you will—"

"I doubt that—"

"One way, or another."

Washington left, and Sam felt the full emotional

blow. Her knees caved while the room spun; the weight of her body headed towards the floor, surprised when Aaron's arms caught her. She hadn't heard him come in.

He eased her into a chair. "Sam? What happened? You look like you're going to lose your supper and you haven't eaten yet."

Sam took a deep breath, but her legs still trembled. "Just got some bad news. I can't talk about it right now."

"Is it about Harlan Styles?"

"How did—"

"We get television up here, Sam. We've tried to respect your privacy, but we all know who you are."

"I'm not at liberty to discuss—"

"Of course, but lawyer to lawyer, if there's anything I can do—"

"I appreciate your concern, Aaron. Mr. Washington won't be returning anytime soon. If he does, I want to know about it immediately."

"Let me help you to a table, at least."

Sam stood to prove her phony courage. "I'm fine, really. I would like some of Sadie's pot roast, though, if it's not all gone. I'm sure it's delicious."

Aaron walked beside Sam like a guard dog, like the father she wished she'd had, a protector, not an accuser.

"Sam!" Holding a bouquet of hyacinths, Zack arched a wave. When their eyes met, he pointed to an empty seat next to him. She managed to cross the room before collapsing, grateful for something other than the floor to hold her up. Zack thrust out the flowers like a schoolboy's offering, and she buried her face within the blooms.

"Easy, Sam."

She raised her head, exhausted, but no longer afraid, Zack's presence the proverbial port in the storm, a safe hedge, one she should embrace. "Been a long day."

Sadie came to the table with a glass of water. "Might as well put those in here until you go upstairs. Can't have them wilting in the lounge. People might think the air's contaminated. So what'll you have?"

Sam felt Zack's searching eyes—she studied his jutted chin, like Abe's when he worried.

"Ladies first."

"I'd like the pot roast, small portions—"

"The question was for Zack. I've already fixed your plate, dear. I won't abide any argument, either. Goodness gracious, if that's how you eat in Manhattan, no wonder you could hide behind a flag pole."

Zack rubbed his stomach. "The works, of course." As Sadie turned toward the kitchen, he placed the blooms into the glass and pushed the arrangement toward Sam's side of the table. "I've seen lots of girls with flower preferences. My ex-girlfriend liked roses. Pink ones, actually, Carnations, too. But I don't ever recall meeting a girl with a passion for hyacinths."

"I can't be that odd. They're a beautiful flower."

"Wait a minute. Yes, I have. Jonathan's wife, Angelica, loved hyacinths. Jonathan hired a botanist to make sure they'd continue to thrive on the property in the wild."

Truth was, Sam didn't know how or why hyacinths comforted her, or how the scent came to her in stressful moments. If she confessed all that to Zack, he'd have her committed to the nearest psychiatric ward. He sat there all inquisitive, like a puppy surveys its master. She had to give him some kind of explanation, and their relationship had not yet progressed to the point she trusted Zack with intimate confessions. "My mother had a bed of hyacinths when we lived in Westchester."

"That explains it, I guess. Sam…I've been thinking about our date for the Spring Fling—"

"About that, Zack, I might not be able to come back for the festivities."

"Why not?"

"I received troubling news today on a case I've been working on—"

"Harlan Styles?"

Did the whole world know her business?

"I can't discuss any particulars, but the case doesn't want to go away. I think it might be best if I go back to Manhattan sooner than expected. I promised my friend Justine I'd finish my vacation here, but I'm going to have to break that promise, too."

Zack's eyes veered away. "When will you leave?"

"Probably right after Aaron's court. Besides, Justine wants to have her wedding and reception here so my boss is driving her up to talk to Sadie."

Zack brightened. "A wedding? When?"

"Six weeks."

"Then at least I'll see you again." He smiled. Why did he have to be so poster-boy perfect?

Sadie brought their dinners, Sam's plate heaped with enough to feed three truck drivers. Zack dug in, and she welcomed the respite from conversation, but found even Sadie's mashed potatoes hard to swallow.

Zack lifted his head and peered directly into her eyes, a gesture Sam used on hostile witnesses. "Do you want me to go with you to Jonathan's tomorrow?"

"How did—"

"I stopped by his place yesterday and he told me."

"No need for you to babysit me. Besides, you probably have school tomorrow. I don't want you missing work on my account. And there's the issue of confidentiality. Must be some reason he wants an attorney."

Zack's lips curled. "Or maybe he wants to see you again, too."

Sam glared. Not now, she didn't have the energy to deal with Zack's possessiveness. They hadn't even dated yet. "Zack—"

"I know. That was uncalled for. Jonathan said he wanted legal advice, but his reasons can be masqueraded sometimes. You're a beautiful woman, Sam."

"Thanks for the compliment, but I told you—"

"You're not interested in getting involved with anyone." Zack's eyes filled with warning. "Be careful around Jonathan."

"Why?"

"He's been through a lot. He doesn't use the best judgment, sometimes. Goes days without eating or sleeping—"

Something Sam could relate to.

Zack's eyes met hers. "Something tells me, though, you'll understand him in a way nobody here in Haven can."

Dueling aromas of roast beef and hyacinths attacked her senses. Her stomach heaved and acid rushed to her throat. "I'm sorry, Zack. I can't eat. I have to go up to my room."

Zack threw his napkin on the table. "Why are you always running away from me, Sam? If you want me to leave you alone…say so. Your smiles say you like me, but you push me away right when I think we're getting close to something."

"I do like you, Zack. I'm sorry I've been so rude. It's…I don't feel well."

Zack reached across the table and handed her the makeshift vase, a huff of disbelief in his voice. "Don't forget these."

"I'm sorry, Zack." She rushed to the steps. Her Manhattan apartment was on the fourth floor and most days she took the stairwell for the exercise. Never had three flights seemed so far up. She barely made it to her room before the urge to retch won over. She dropped the flowers on the bathroom floor, cognizant of breaking glass but too sick to care.

Relieved of the mounting abdominal pressure, she flushed the toilet, covered her face with a wet washcloth then fell onto her bed. She turned on the bedside lamp, and soon sleep overpowered her until the dream intruded.

Darnell Washington and Harlan Styles stood by her bed, Washington waving an affidavit, their shapes grotesque, but recognizable—their mingled demon laughs shook furniture and Jonathan's landscapes fell to the floor. Then, Washington and Styles disappeared, and Daddy's face hovered over her. "It's your fault I'm dead, your fault I'm in hell."

Awakened by her own screams, she opened her eyes and darted to a sitting position. The hyacinths were in a clean vase. She glanced into the bathroom—the glass shards had disappeared. Then she realized Leon sat on the bed next to her. He swooped her into an embrace and rocked in rhythm to a soft lullaby. "Sssh, Sam. No one's going to hurt you."

15

Sam took Leon's hankie and allowed a tender kiss to her cheek. A younger man might have received a swift slap for such forwardness, but his comfort seemed paternal. Daddy used to hold her like that after a nightmare, before his rages started. After that, his touches only brought pain, usually from a belt; sometimes a board, while alcohol-coated breaths slurred obscenities like, "Just…punishment."

Daddy's indictment—bloodied behinds.

Until that moment, she hadn't quite made up her mind to consider Leon a friend. Now wrapped in his sympathetic arms, the previous deception was so forgivable. He caressed her, not from anger or lust, but with love, and he hummed the melody she had recalled on her walk. As her sobs quieted, the words soothed.

O Come to the Savior,
He patiently waits
To save by His power divine;
Come, anchor your soul in "The Haven of Rest,"
And say, "My Beloved is Mine."

She joined Leon's soft notes on the chorus, the only portion she remembered—pleased Leon had no remarks about her off-key vocals. The new flow of tears brought peace. Stilled within the storm, she thanked Leon. He loosed his grip and handed her the filled vase.

Sam scrunched her face into their soothing fragrance.

"I see you like them as much as I do."

So that's why Leon was in her room, not to steal, but to sniff. "Was that what you were doing in here, before? Smelling the flowers?"

"Guilty. The scent lured me like honey to a bear. I'll confess. I love flowers. In my younger days, I visited almost every botanical garden in the country, even Canada. Hyacinths have a perfume about them I can't explain, but these Zack gave you are stronger than any I've smelled. I got curious. Do you suppose that when they're picked, the scent intensifies, like roses?"

Sam stared him down. Was Leon still dancing around the truth?

He lowered his head like a sentenced convict. "I did lead you on a bit too much, and I'm sorry. Men aren't supposed to be partial to flowers, so I don't let folks know how much I enjoy them. When I heard you coming, I hid. Truth is I *am* very forgetful. Getting worse. Sadie wants me to go so a specialist. What for? Forgetting half my life won't be so bad."

"But there must be good things to remember inside that half."

He shrugged his shoulders.

Not that Sam blamed him for wanting to forget. She should listen to her own advice; she'd erased far too much of her childhood trying to forget Daddy. Why couldn't she remember the good without remembering the bad? If only the mind siphoned the unhappy thoughts into a throw away container and left the pleasant ones.

Sam offered Leon a smile of forgiveness. "You did

convince me you belonged at a mental facility, or in a nursing home." She sat up straight and arched her shoulders. "I'm not easily fooled, by the way. You're that good."

Leon's cheeks reddened. "Aw...You make me blush. Anyway, I heard you thrashing about awhile ago. I knocked but you didn't answer. Since your door wasn't bolted, I peeked in to see if you were all right. I saw the broken glass and the flowers on the floor. You started to quiet some, so I swept up the mess and put the flowers into a clean glass. Then you started screaming. So I sat here to sing to you."

Sam sniffed the blooms. "Zack brought me these."

Leon winked. "I know. I saw him hand you the bouquet. I see the way he smiles at you when you're looking the other way. He's sweet on you."

What did an old, confirmed bachelor like Leon know of love?

"I felt the same way about Sadie's mother once upon a time."

"Sadie's mother? Mazie? You and Mazie?"

"That was years ago. We're friends, now. Mazie spends her days playing bridge while I play shuffle board, but once in a while, she goes with me on a walk. Not far, though. Her legs get tired, or she gets frightened when she can't remember where she is. Occasionally, we sit and have dinner by the water. Most of the time, she doesn't remember me, but I think I still remember enough for the both of us, and I thank the Lord, I can be with her now after so many years apart." The wells in Leon's eyes thickened with reminiscent dew. "Well, I'll let you get back to sleep. You'll need to be rested if you're going to handle that Jonathan Gladstone fellow. He's a walking

Shakespeare tragedy if ever I met one."

More, Leon. Give me more. Don't whet my curiosity then leave me hungry. Sam wanted to talk until the sun cracked over the horizon, anything to keep from going back to sleep.

Leon stepped toward the door. "I notice you have a light on all the time. Is the lamp by the bed enough? I'll flick this switch off, and you won't have to get up."

Sam nodded and Leon left. She sat in the subdued lighting for what seemed hours, checking the clock every few minutes. She spotted the pilot case she'd shoved into the corner. Now would be as good a time as any to unpack. See what might be salvageable.

Mildewed, every stitch, except for one pair of tan dress slacks, a crewel-lined, satin top, and a chocolate cashmere blazer, still damp, but otherwise undamaged. She sniffed the extra pair of pumps. *Yuck.* She tossed the pumps and the rank clothes back into the pilot case.

She filled the sink with water and hand-washed the slacks and top, then hung them up to dry on the shower rod, along with the blazer. She plugged in her hair dryer—no sparks—probably safe to use. Setting it on high, she spent the next half hour blow-drying her sparse wardrobe.

Now what?

Still only five o'clock in the morning—too early to stir around without waking someone. She turned on the television, muting the sound and clicking on the closed captions, the out of sync lettering as annoying as the instant replays on the sports channel. Pulling up a chair, Sam sat in front of the television, clicked off the closed caption, and turned up the volume a few notches.

Was she still dreaming? She pinched herself to be

certain. Yes. She was awake, not believing what she saw—a video replay of Darnell Washington being interviewed by a reporter. "If there is any justice in this world," he said, "my client will earn a swift release. Harlan Styles is innocent, imprisoned by the hand of an overzealous prosecutor with a personal grudge. I intend to prove prosecutorial misconduct and untoward judicial prejudice towards my client."

The clip flashed to her photograph. Where had they dug up that one? She squirmed at her sour face, and grabbed the phone to call Justine. "Why didn't you call me? I saw that horrible clip on CNN," Sam blurted as soon as the click indicated Justine had picked up. "Why am I on trial?" Sam relayed Washington's earlier visit. "He wasted no time making good on his threat. If he thinks he can—"

"I'm sorry, Sam. This news broke late yesterday. I knew you needed to rest. I planned on calling you this morning. Honest. In an hour. By the way, what are you doing up so early?"

"I woke you, didn't I?"

"Yep."

"I'm repacking my things, and I'll be there as soon as I can."

Justine's disgruntled groan snapped in Sam's ear. "No. You will do no such thing. Abe thinks you should stay put. If you come back to the city, the paparazzi will have a heyday. You've got to give Abe some room to square this thing away. Washington is merely trying to garner media sympathy. You had a tight case, Sam. Don't let them get to you."

"Against my better judgment, I'll stay put. You're right. Abe is more than capable of handling this." Sam spoke the words for her friend's benefit, but was unable to convince herself, logic screaming that Washington's antics were way out of the norm, even for him. "Something's not right about this, Justine."

Hesitation.

"I'll call you with an update, later. Don't worry. Stay on course, and keep a low profile. These country types probably don't even watch the news."

Sam wasn't the only one who'd underestimated rural people.

"Go back to sleep. Don't worry. Remember Romans 8:28."

"Well, I must confess, my Bible reading has been as sparse as my prayer life. But I remember the verse: "All things work together for good…"

"Remember the other part?"

"For those who are called according to his purpose?" Justine quoted it as well, her tone readying for a twenty-minute sermon, "soul-talks," as she called them. Preaching should be left to ministers, not best friends. "You have to ask yourself if your, and I use the term sarcastically, *dedication* to this case is really stemming from some personal need."

Maybe Justine should remember the verse in Matthew about not judging lest you be judged. "He's sleaze, Justine…and he needs to be taken off the street…for good."

"By whose judgment?"

"Duh…I *am* the prosecutor."

Justine snarled. "That's not what I meant. Oh…it's no use trying to talk sense into you."

"Still love me?"

"Of course. Now go back to bed. Bye."

Disconnected.

Sam regretted her argument with Justine, but how

could any good come from this mess?

16

Zack woke with a start, shaking off his dream. He'd been chasing Sam through Dawn's Hope. She called out to him, but she wouldn't stop running, and he couldn't catch up to her.

He got out of bed and paced his studio apartment, his thoughts flitting from one thing to another like a housefly looking for sugar.

Within a few days, he'd be asked to become acting principal…what if Frank couldn't come back to work? What if the school board wanted him to take the job permanently? There goes New York. Now, everything seemed as muddy as the baseball diamond. Why couldn't he get a grasp on what he wanted?

Have you asked Me?

No, he hadn't consulted the One he should have gone to in the first place. "So what do I do, Lord?"

Take My hand and put one foot in front of the other.

"To where?"

To the other side of darkness.

What did that mean? Why couldn't God write him a letter or something? Zack remembered how Pastor Rick said that the answer to every question could be found in God's Word, but first one has to be hungry enough to look for it.

His Bible reading of late had consisted of a few devotions he planned on using for the youth group and a Bible Study the young adult class was working on. He read like he would study for a test, cramming the info so he could lead without seeming ignorant, not with an expectation that God might actually bring clarity to the muddled existence of Zack Bordeaux's life. He read for an hour and his spirit calmed. No great vision, but peace that God had a plan, a different plan than Zack's, but most definitely a better one.

He closed his Bible, sat on the edge of his bed, his sofa during the day, and clicked on the television, flipping through the channels until he came to CNN. Was that Sam's picture? Where did they get that one? Made her look twenty years older—and so unattractive.

He listened to the news clip, and a Voice within his soul roared. *Sam doesn't need a lover, she needs a friend. Will you be one for her now?*

17

The sun glowed on the horizon, enough light for an early morning walk, and early enough to escape anyone who might demand an explanation of why she'd been on television.

She showered and dressed in record speed, thankful for her one good set of clothes. She pulled on her still slightly damp blazer then slipped on Tracey's sandals. If Zack were still willing, she'd ask him to go with her to a nearby mall…later. First, more than clothes, she needed to get to a bank. With no usable credit card, no ready access to the Internet and no checkbook, she felt like a charity case. She recalled seeing a bank on Main Street. After her interview with Jonathan, she'd see if she could transfer some assets from her Manhattan accounts.

Flinging her purse over her shoulder, she tip-toed past Leon's room where peaceful snores carried into the hall. She took the steps with all the stealth of an experienced burglar, and then grasped the soup-ladle door handle.

"That you, Sam? What are you doing up so early?" Sadie's shrill greeting smashed any hopes of an alternate career as a thief.

"I thought I'd take a little walk before breakfast."

Sadie tilted her head to one side. "You know, Sam, that picture on the television doesn't do you justice."

Had Sadie made an offer to talk? Sam released the

door handle. Not much she could say to Sadie without divulging a past Sam thought buried with Daddy. Refusing Sadie a chance to "sit a spell" as she would say, seemed out-and-out rude. The woman was a fountain of energy, bustling to and fro like a chipmunk storing nuts—if not minding the store, then cooking up a storm; if not cooking, she painted; if not painting, she wiped tables and scolded Aaron for being out fishing too long. If Sadie thought Sam's company worth breaking her routine, it was a gift of attention Sam could not refuse.

"Maybe a cup of coffee and some toast before my walk would be good. It was a long night."

"Figured it mighta been. Course with you having your light on all the time, I never know if you're asleep, or not. I'm up at four every morning anyhow. Gets powerful lonely in the mornings, sometimes. Aaron only rises early if he has a fishing date. Funny about men, hey? They'll get up before the sun to bait a hook, but never ask them to get up early to run a vacuum cleaner." Sadie laughed at her own joke and went into the lounge.

Sam followed, but Sadie had already disappeared into the kitchen. A conditioned sprinter couldn't keep up with her.

Sadie trailed in with two mugs, a filled coffee urn, and plates of scrambled eggs, toast, and ham. "Already made up breakfast and it's sitting in the warmers. So, no arguing. If you was up all night, then you've got to be starving. I know I could eat a team of horses. Mind if I join you?"

"Please do."

Sadie plunked down the tray, filled the mugs and set the plates on the table, then scooted back into the kitchen with the empty tray and returned before Sam could open her napkin.

"Hope you don't mind the mugs. I use the cups for our guests, but seems like coffee ain't coffee 'less it's in a mug. Funny how set we get in our ways over some things."

Sam sensed Sadie's rants had purpose. Like pumping the gas pedal, she revved conversation with banter before heading on the road to more important matters. Sam took a bite of toast and tested Sadie's counsel while brushing off the crumbs from the tablecloth. "So you saw the clip about Darnell Washington and my photo of shame?"

Sadie sipped her coffee, a picture of confidence. "I don't pay no mind to anything I hear on television. It's like all those news channels decide what's true and promote that. Then they decide they'd better have the other view show up. I did happen to catch that report. Yes, indeedy."

Frustration surged as Sam put down her toast. "Harlan Styles deserves to rot in hell. Life with no parole is too lenient."

Sadie took a quick sip and winked. "Ouch. That's harsh."

"But he's a murderer."

"Ain't a one of us that hasn't butchered something in our life…guess that makes us murderers, too, in a way."

"How many times do I have to apologize for killing that moose?"

Sadie laughed. "Not what I was getting at. I suppose you've had enough ribbing on that score. But here's what I think. Every one of us has a heap of guilt inside. Some we deserve. Some we put on ourselves.

Either way, at the end of the day, we're all guilty."

Not Sadie who was as kind as the day was long. "You're the most guiltless person I've ever met. Except maybe you work too hard." And that she bent zoning laws. "Other than that, there's not a fault I can find. And I do have a discerning eye."

Sadie laughed again, more like an ellipsis of snorts, three in a row. "You don't know us yet, dear. Being a tourist town, we put our best foot forward to strangers. You'll see us for our true selves if you stay here much longer. Ain't a one of us that don't have as many skeletons as a Gladstone. Some of us, though, have made peace with our ghosts."

Sadie dangled the statement like one of Aaron's minnows, and Sam dived in for the bait and waited for the yank. "What skeletons could you and Aaron possibly have?"

Sadie took another sip, a long one this time, before putting her cup down and leaning in. "For starters, Aaron and I both know we're bordering on the illegal with the Lighthouse. We think it's worth the risk."

Incredulous that two intelligent people would do that. "Why?"

"It's a long story. You see I ran a catering business in Vermont...very successful and owned three companies...one in Burlington, one in Brattleboro, and one in Montpelier. Thing is, it was so successful, I stopped going to church, stopped praying, and acted like I was the one who made it so good, instead of thanking God for his blessings."

Unlike Justine, Sadie preached through her life, a quiet faith that shouted her love of God from morning to night. "I think I understand. My friend Justine, the one who wants to have her wedding in Haven, likes to preach at me a lot. She says I've let my career become my idol." Sam smiled as she brought Sadie into the conspiracy. "She's right about most things, but I refuse to tell her so."

Sadie patted Sam's hand. "I suppose we can let a lot of different things get between us and God. I sold my businesses when we moved to Haven, but God didn't take the caterer out of me. When we bought this property, He put this idea into my head to turn it into a place of hospitality where we could share the gospel in a non-churchy way, for God's profit, not mine. If I license the place, then I'd be right back into what took me from God in the first place. Do you understand?"

"I think so." That is, Sam understood the motive, but Sadie still skirted the rim of a misdemeanor. "Ever thought of registering the Lighthouse as a non-profit?"

Sadie brightened. "Say now, that *is* a good idea."

"I'm surprised Aaron didn't think of it."

"If the thought crossed his mind, he said nary a word to me about it. Course, the enterprises are in my name, not Aaron's, he don't want nothin' to keep him from fishing, but he tolerates my hobbies and helps out now and again if it gets busier than I can handle. I'll give your suggestion some thought. Suppose you could help me with it?"

"You don't need me to do that. Aaron will know what to do. Besides, I won't be here more than a few more days. I should get back to Manhattan by the week's end." If only she hadn't promised Justine to stay a little longer. Some vacation, if all she could think about was the possibility Styles could go free.

"Aaron and me will have a little chat, then. Thanks for the idea." Sadie put down her coffee cup, took a deep breath, staring at Sam with deadened eyes, sorrowful—the sudden change unsettling. Sam wrapped her hands around her mug.

"How long do you suppose Aaron and I have been married?"

"Guessing Tracey's age, I'd say about thirty years."

"Tracey's my step-daughter. I don't have any children of my own."

Sam put her fork down and gulped as the eggs slid down her throat. She'd never been comfortable playing the priest, hearing other people's confessions. Before Sam could object, Sadie kept on rambling.

"Aaron and I got married a week before we moved here, but we've *known* each other a lot longer." Sadie paused. Momentary silence from a woman who could fill a day with chatter, probably was meant for dramatic effect…to give Sam time to digest that Sadie meant *known* in the Biblical sense.

"That's our sin, Sam. Aaron and I met soon after he finished law school. He helped me get my catering business off the ground. We fell in love. He left his wife for me and planned on getting a divorce until he found out his wife was pregnant. Seemed the right thing to do was to try to make his marriage work. Separately, we started going to church, got our hearts right with God."

To see them now, to see Tracey's love for Sadie…the whole story was unbelievable. Why share it now?

"I never would have guessed. So how did you and Aaron get together? Is Aaron divorced, then?"

Sadie's rosy cheeks deepened as she spoke. "You see, Sam. God is merciful, even when we act in ways that must disappoint Him. As I told you before, my business made me a powerful lot of money, and I was too busy to marry, although I had my share of suitors." She pulled on her size 20 dress and chuckled. "You might not believe it, but I had me a good figure in those days."

"I believe it."

"About ten years ago, Aaron happened into a café I wanted to buy. We struck up a conversation, and he told me his wife had been gone a couple of years."

"She left him?"

"Not by choice. She died of cancer."

"So you started dating again?"

"Not right away."

Sam glanced at the clock. Sadie kept stalling, like a reluctant witness during cross-examination. "So…?"

"Tracey got us together again. After her mother died, she found an old photograph of him and me. She got it out of him about the affair and that he'd seen me recently. When he told her I wasn't married, she insisted Aaron try to take up where we left off."

"And she wasn't upset over the affair?"

"Maybe, at first. She knew her parents weren't really happy together. Maybe she blames herself for that, though we told her over and over again it ain't her fault she came along during a tough time for her folks. She wanted her father to be happy, and she'd leave the right or wrong of what we'd done up to the Lord to judge."

Although Sadie's story might be fodder for a Lifetime television movie, what did her confession have to do with anything? "I'm glad you and Aaron finally got together. You seem happy."

"We are. My point is that when God forgives a person, the past is erased, and He doesn't hold it against them, so why backpack our guilt and carry it around like that woman in that there story…you know…where she wore this *A*…"

"You mean *The Scarlet Letter*?"

"That's the one. Our backpack of guilt is our scarlet letter, Sam. But, it's something we put on ourselves, instead of other people marking us. God doesn't make us wear an *A* …he erases our guilt, and we go and put it back on, sling that old backpack over our shoulders and parade around stooped over from the weight of our self-inflicted guilt." Sadie took a long sip of coffee then stared into Sam's eyes. "Tell me, Sam. Are you a Christian?"

"If you're asking me if I ever asked Jesus to be my personal Savior, yes."

"And now?"

Sam sighed as she relinquished a crumb of trust. "I feel like God's far away…maybe He's given up on me."

"If God didn't give up on me, He ain't giving up on you. More'n likely, God hasn't budged…it's you who's taken yourself away from Him." Sadie leaned back in her chair, her eyes moist with pleading. "Am I making any sense, dear? I'm not a preacher. And I'm not one to go spouting off my personal views or sharing my dirty laundry, either. But you seem like someone whose carrying a dozen backpacks."

Did Sadie expect Sam to take a turn at this confession game? How could she talk about Daddy's death, how Mama killed herself soon afterward, about the investigations, and being sent to live in Brooklyn with an elderly aunt, how her friendship with Justine led her to God, but that somewhere between law school and hitting that moose, her faith became less important than putting Styles away—permanently—Justice, Sam's idol…Daddy's death, her backpack?

She couldn't even whisper the deed to herself, let alone tell someone else. Not even Justine knew the truth—only that Daddy died when he got run over by a truck. Although, by the time Sam returned from the Gladstone estate, her sins might very well be broadcast across the nation.

Sam seethed with renewed resentment. Juvenile records were supposed to be sealed, yet somehow people like Washington managed to get hold of them. What was his game? She could countermove by a petition to have him disbarred—there was certainly enough dirt she could dig up on the man—one notch higher on the sleaze ladder than Styles. Washington was too far ahead of that race, the damage he'd inflict might be terminal. Not only to her career. How would the revelation affect her friendship with Justine, who treated people according to sin classification? The uglier the sin the more Justine distanced herself. Once the truth was broadcast, Justine would never speak to Sam again.

What about the kind people of Haven? Wouldn't they hate her, too?

Sam searched Sadie's eyes, patient, like Mama's, when Daddy went into rehab the first time.

Sadie's eyes begged for Sam to let go of her backpack. But she had too many to take off so quickly. "When I thought for sure I was going to die after I hit the moose, I prayed. Do you suppose God hears the prayers of the desperate even when the desperate have ignored him for years on end?"

Sadie's tears spilled. "I'm sure of it. God musta been pleased that you finally called to Him. He has so much to tell you, but you've gotta be willing to listen." She wiped her eyes on a table napkin. "This whole mess with that Styles person will work its way out. You wait and see. Sooner or later, you've got to start trusting God again. Time you took those backpacks off for good."

By now, the sun had claimed the morning sky. Bright red stripes ripped through the blue of promise. Sadie stared out the window. "Red sky at morning—"

18

Sadie's words echoed in Sam's ears as she careened her way along the mountainous path toward Dawn's Hope wishing she had the willpower to cancel this ridiculous agreement. She owed Jonathan Gladstone nothing as long as she didn't see the property, no contract, nothing binding, not so much as a handshake. Then why this compulsion? Something about Mirror Lake possessed her, wooed her like a lover's whisper through Jonathan's brushstrokes, bonded her to a land seen only through fantasy.

She pulled into the arched driveway at the foot of the mansion. She quickly scanned the area and noticed a van and a truck lined on a cement pad. Maybe that's where she should have parked. A wide trail led from the pad towards the back of the mansion. Should she take that walk way or ring the front door? Was she a servant or an honored guest? In the distance she saw a three-compartment barn, she assumed to be an eighteenth century manger, with slanted roofs and open feeding troughs, but no livestock…empty and deserted…like the huge house, a hint of a once thriving era. She felt like Charlotte Bronte's Jane Eyre. Would Jonathan Gladstone prove to be her Rochester?

She opted to leave Lucille II in the circular drive in the event she needed to make a fast exit. Hesitating near the wide, cemented steps, she surveyed the full height of the building—five stories, if the top counted as one, a narrow portion, like the top of a tiered cake. An exterior railing encircled the utmost heights, possibly a widow's walk.

Her head ached from arching back so far. She heaved her shoulders, took a deep breath, then rang the doorbell, resisting the urge to peer through the narrow glass panels that hugged the sides of the broad mahogany door.

She expected a typical valet from a classic novel, a Mr. Jeeves type perhaps—or television's rotund butler, Mr. Belvedere, or, more in keeping with the surroundings, *The Addams Familys's* Lurch. Instead, she peered into the somber, coconut eyes of Jonathan Gladstone, his hair roughly corralled into a mannish ponytail. "You're late," he said, "I thought attorneys were punctual."

Confrontation riled her, urged her to turn and leave. She thought she'd come to be of help, not be accused. "I try to be. The drive took a little longer than I anticipated."

Jonathan motioned for Sam to come in. "We can talk in my den. That's where the papers are. Then I'll take you to the lake if you still want to see it." He turned and led the way, and Sam followed. So much with the small talk, not even an inquiry to her welfare. Some aristocrat he turned out to be.

The décor intrigued her—a mingling of grotesque modernization and old world gauche. Modern electric lights illuminated Louis XVI settees while iron-clad jousting suits and tall padded chairs lined the halls, a garishness resembling a B-rated horror flick.

He breezed down the corridor past an open door, but she managed a quick survey of what must have been a parlor or sitting room, complete with a

Steinway grand piano, roped off like a museum exhibit. She gasped when Jonathan opened the door to the den, containing a turn-of-the-century library, heavy cherry shelves from the floor to the ceiling filled with every imaginable literary work. A pair of enormous leather chairs sat in front of a marble fireplace. Sam half expected to see the fictional detective Sherlock Holmes, standing by it, smoking a pipe, scolding her with his admonition: *elementary, my dear Miss Knowles.*

With the exception of metallic file cabinets, this den probably had seen little change since former Gladstones used it, four times the size of Aaron's office, larger than the book room of Arlington Library. If the spiral staircase was an indicator, the den birthed at least one other story, or perhaps led to the master bedroom.

Jonathan stepped into the back of the room, grabbed a manila folder and then sat on the chair nearest the fireplace, leaving Sam in limbo. Since no invitation to sit seemed forthcoming, Sam claimed the chair across from Jonathan, slid her purse from her shoulders and took out a notebook. "What can I do for you, Mr. Gladstone?"

"Please. My name is Jonathan. Mister seems artificial." He raised his head, meeting her gaze. If what seemed a petrified frown cracked, even a glimmer, he might actually be attractive—if he were the least bit civil…or shaven.

A half-open door in the back part of the den caught her attention. From her vantage point, she saw a cobbled path leading to what, at one time, might have been a greenhouse. But given the supply of canvases, paints and easels, she assumed this was the artist's lair, the studio of his genius.

Jonathan reached forward and handed her a manila folder. "This is a copy of my father's will." Then he straddled his long legs and stroked his scraggly beard as she perused the document.

She had taken a course or two in civil law, however, estates and wills were not her forte. "I'm sorry, Jonathan, but I'm a criminal lawyer, perhaps you'd do better hiring someone with more expertise in civil matters."

"My father might've been a hard man, but I suppose he did what he thought best for the estate. If Elliott had lived…" Jonathan's face paled, his jaw tightened; pain etched across his face like a taut canvas. "I know you did some research on me at the library. Zack told me when he stopped by before school this morning."

"I'm sorry if I'm prying—"

Jonathan raised his hand. "I expected as much. Let me see if I can put this will business in concise terms without rehashing my miserable existence."

"If it's too uncomfortable—"

Jonathan uncrossed his legs and put his hands over his knees, his eyes crusted with unimaginable heartache. Yet, honesty dwelled in them. "Hear me out. If you're going to help me, you need to understand my perspective. In a nutshell, Dawn's Hope was founded in 1765 by my ancestor, Emmanuel Gladstone. He obtained a vast tract of land from King George as a reward for his service in The French and Indian War. When he turned patriot during The Revolutionary War he parceled the land, establishing Haven in 1794, a year before his death. According to his journals, Emmanuel hoped his direct descendents would inhabit what was left of the estate in the English tradition, awarded to the oldest surviving male child. In accord with Emmanuel's wishes, Dawn's Hope has been inherited by a direct male descendent since that time."

"But the Rule Against Perpetuities—"

"Lord Gladstone was well aware of the British law, predicting the new world would adopt it. He understood he could not force his will upon a generation not yet born. Emmanuel, however, was an imposing figure in his day, heralded as a hero in the eyes of Haven. Every direct descendent complied with Emmanuel's wishes—"

"Except you?"

"Yes."

So this Rochester was a rebel. Sam fanned the brief—all ten pages of stipulations. "I figured more than wanderlust stood between you and your father."

"Every Gladstone heir before me has served the public in some capacity: senators, ambassadors—all men of influence. Henry Gladstone was a Supreme Court Justice. The women were activists, too, like Muriel Arlington. She labored for equal rights for women and blacks, an early abolitionist."

"Impressive lineage."

Jonathan moved forward, his gaze towards the floor. "Not one Gladstone heir ever pursued the arts. Although, my great-great grandfather married an actress against family practice, and some of Father's wives were less than socialites."

A smile erupted, proof he did not suffer from a muscular disorder, a smile broad enough to expose his teeth, nice teeth—even, white.

"My father knew from the time I was twelve I could not be cast into the Gladstone mold. I will give him credit. He didn't try to force me down a path I'd fight to avoid. Instead he lured me…enticed me with Angelica."

"Your wife?"

"She was a distant relative on my mother's side who visited Dawn's Hope every summer. As I look back, I see how my father fostered our fondness, for she loved Dawn's Hope more than even he did."

Jonathan stood and paced. "Since Elliott was a direct descendant, Father registered the will the day Elliott was born. Father died three weeks later, unaware of Elliott's rare condition."

"What provision was made in the event Elliott predeceased you?"

Jonathan sneered. "If Elliott had lived, Father arranged for Angelica and I both to receive a generous stipend from the estate, providing we continued to reside here, Angelica's to continue if I died before her. If Elliott died before either one of us, the stipends would continue as long as we resided at Dawn's Hope. In a nutshell, I can live here, but I can never own it. When I die, the property is to be donated to the town of Haven as a museum and nature center."

Jonathan's father must have had pulp where his heart should have been. "If you don't want to contest the will, what do you think I can do for you?"

Jonathan's face turned scarlet as he grasped the chair handles. "I want off this place. Let the town have it for all I care, the allowance be hanged. I don't need the money. The revenues from my landscapes are more than sufficient."

Abe always said that a person's vehemence often indicated hidden desires. Could Jonathan's sarcasm indicate he didn't want to lose Dawn's Hope? He wanted her advice, and she'd provide it. "You don't have to go to that extreme. You could hire a caretaker and meet the residency requirement with periodic visits as long as you lived here for one day more than half a year."

Jonathan glared—his stare accusatory. "I'm not an idiot, Sam. That's where you come in. I need a lease agreement drawn up so I don't violate the terms of the will."

His raspy comments irritated like a dripping faucet. To shut it off meant to dig deeper, find the cause of his ambiguity, energy Sam had neither the inclination nor the time to expend. She hitched her weight and re-crossed her ankles. "I suppose I could manage that for you. Where would you go?"

"Paris."

"Why Paris?"

"Personal reasons—reasons you don't need to know to handle a simple lease agreement."

Did his well of rudeness have no bottom? She'd have to suffer it if she wanted to see the lake. She held up the manila folder. "May I keep this for a few days?"

Jonathan nodded. "The bank has the official record. Aaron has a copy, too."

She tucked the brief into her purse.

"You came as you promised, and I promised a tour. Are you ready?"

"Yes."

"Forecast is calling for rain. We might get wet."

"I won't melt."

"Can you drive an ATV?"

"ATV?"

"All-terrain vehicle. Don't they have those in Manhattan?"

She talked to his back as he raced out of the den,

down the hall, and to the main foyer. "I know what an ATV is…no, I've never driven one…can't be too difficult to manage…can they?"

"I'll show you out, then bring the Max II around front. It has a passenger compartment and is good on water, in case you want to go on the lake."

She'd imagined an idyllic stroll down a flower–strewn path into the woods, not a ride on an ATV that could swim. Maybe she should rethink her curiosity, let Aaron handle Jonathan's business. A lease agreement wouldn't be that much of a conflict of interest.

Jonathan led her through another maze of corridors, grabbing a jacket off a rack in a room. A hint of hyacinths filled the room. Another hallucination? Zack said the property was loaded with beds. Maybe Jonathan flung his coat into one while he sketched.

Jonathan continued his parade, ending at the door leading to the circular drive. She wondered if she'd ever be able to find her way around, or if she were left alone in a place like this, would she die trapped in a maze of rooms and corridors?

"Wait here by the steps." Jonathan disappeared along the cobbled path from the parking lot behind the house. Sam walked to her car. Opening the trunk, she threw in her purse. Should she wear her expensive blazer in the woods? She hadn't dressed for hiking, and the morning chill had given way to slightly warmer temperatures. She took it off and placed it by her purse, then shut the trunk with authority as Jonathan pulled up in a green jeep that resembled a row-boat.

"It's cold by the lake, you know," Jonathan said, his tone like a scolding parent. "You might wish you had that blazer on." He sat tall on the monstrosity, regal in a woodsy sort of way.

"I'll be fine." She climbed into the Max II's passenger seat, scanning the mansion one more time.

Jonathan had described Lord Gladstone as an imposing man, but Sam wondered—did Emmanuel crave opulence or was the grandeur the pursuit of his descendants? If matters in Manhattan weren't so pressing, she would enjoy deeper study of this legendary family, to learn why a nobleman spurned his bequeathed aristocracy to side with rebels, and how a man who had been dead for over two-hundred years still controlled an empire.

Jonathan spun the ATV around, handed her a helmet, then revved the engine while she put it on. Not quite the mountain man Justine wanted for Sam, yet, seated on his toy, he oozed a spirit of playfulness, a likeable rogue ready for adventure.

19

Warm raindrops turned into freezing pellets. Jonathan stopped the ATV where the paths that encircled the lake converged. Sam sat perched, a pitifully drenched, yet defiant, Raggedy Ann. He should offer to bring her back to the house, let her try again another day. Something told him she'd insist on enduring the downpour, forcing him to honor their agreement.

"There's a cabin at the cliff where we can wait the rain out. It has a picture window on the lakeside. We're almost there."

She pulled at her water-logged slacks. "I suppose that would be the smart thing to do if you don't mind. If the rain stops soon, could we try again?"

He grunted and bobbed a half-hearted agreement. He'd hoped to show her the lake, dump her off at her car, and resume his work on Angelica's portrait. Now he'd have to spend the next hour or more in conversation. What could he possibly find in common with a citified red-head?

Jonathan pulled up as close to the cabin as he dared. "The Max II is too big to get to the cabin from this direction. We'll have to walk from here. Give me your helmet."

"Catch." She tossed it.

He put the helmets into the hatch, then offered to help Sam down. Ignoring his hand, she jumped, teetering perilously toward the edge. He should have parked a little further away from the cliff but he wasn't used to passengers and forgot they had to get out on the other side. He instinctively pulled her to safety.

"I'm quite capable of self-navigation, thank you very much."

"Suit yourself, but be careful. There're a lot of ruts around here. The terrain isn't very level, and those sandals weren't made for trail-blazing. Don't you city folk own hiking boots?"

"For your information, these are the only shoes I can use at the moment. If I had another pair to wear, I would have. I wanted to see this lake. I'd have come barefoot if I had to." She glared at him with marble eyes, a mixture of blue and green. No wonder Zack was smitten—wild eyes buried beneath mostly sensible attire, a caged feline begging to cut loose, a latent nature lover in glittered sandals.

"My apologies. Follow me."

They strode side by side as he led her to the cabin. The treetops swayed to the wind's symphony while Jonathan ducked underneath low-lying branches. When they reached the door, she stood to one side, backed away, ready to scurry like a distrustful rabbit.

"What? Are you afraid? Do you think I have less-than-honorable intentions? "

She surrendered a faint smile. Good. Humor wasn't one of his strong points. He'd hate to think he wasted his one joke a month on a surly sightseer. He opened the cottage door. "Not very roomy, but I have food, a stove, a bedroom, a sleep sofa, and a television. There's a fireplace, too"

Sam stepped into the living room. "You don't lock your door? Doesn't anyone in Haven lock their doors?

Isn't it reckless to leave a cabin in the woods unattended like that? Might as well have a sign on your front lawn inviting intruders."

Jonathan slammed the door; this would be one long day. "I leave the cabin unlocked for the fishermen. They always let me know if they're using it overnight. Most of them bring their own food, but I keep staples on hand for when I paint here, and I do often enough. And I have a team of groundskeepers so it gets looked after, not that this is any of your concern."

Sam searched him, first his eyes, then his lips, down to his hiking boots. "Guess I didn't expect you to be so—"

"Civilized?"

"I meant open. You're different than I expected."

"Different than what? What did you expect?"

"Jeremiah Johnson."

"Who?"

"Jeremiah Johnson. You know, the movie starring Robert Redford about a man who lived a secluded life in the mountains during the early 1800s. Hardly a word said in the whole movie."

"Oh...*that* Jeremiah Johnson. Sorry to disappoint you, but as much as I love nature, I draw the line at wrestling grizzlies."

She snickered. Another bulls-eye—two in one day. He was on a roll.

"The cabin looks comfortable, for fishermen, I guess."

He pointed toward the main room. "I'd give you a tour, but what you see from there is pretty much it. Like I said, that picture window gives you a good view of the lake."

Sam fairly waltzed to the other side of the cabin.

He'd expected a few "oohs" or at least an "ah." She said nothing…stared…lost…her mind elsewhere. The rain pounded a harsh melody against the pane while a drizzly mist rose off the lake and hovered like a quilt.

"There's a recliner next to the fireplace if you need to rest."

She turned and sank into the leather as if the weight of the world pushed her down. "It's beautiful here, but I'd still like to see the lake when the rain clears." Sam stared out the window. "On a clear day, can one really see their reflection on the lake, like Zack said?"

"Family legend says Emmanuel Gladstone saw an angel's reflection, and like Jacob of old, he wrestled all night. In his journals, he said he built an altar to honor his changed life. From that day on, Emmanuel walked with an inexplicable limp."

"Is that when he fled the British army and joined the rebels?"

"Not right away, but something changed him. Change can come about overnight, or simmer in a heart for a while. I think that's how it was with Emmanuel. We Gladstones don't make decisions on a dime."

Sam turned, a tear slipped down her cheek. What had he said? "I don't know why, but I have to see the lake, all of it, in the calm as well as the tempest." She shook like the earth had given way.

"Are you cold?"

"I'm fine."

She'd probably object, but he put his jacket around her shoulders. Instead of rebuke, she smiled, and sniffed its sleeve, nearly buried her head in it. Strange thing to do.

"I'll get the coffee started, then I'll put a log in the fire place. Hungry?"

"No. Sadie filled me up at breakfast."

"I didn't have breakfast. I might have some English muffins in the cupboard. Sure you don't want one?"

"Only if you're going to have one yourself."

Sam's gaze seemed glued to the window. Good. He wouldn't have to make small talk while he prepared the muffins. He dumped them into the toaster, then started the fire as promised. When the muffins popped, he brought them over to where Sam sat. He pulled up a wicker chair on the other side of the fireplace. "Sorry, they're so dry. The muffins, I mean. I don't have any butter or jam."

She looked up, eyes brimming with tears. Maybe she hated dry muffins, or maybe he offended her in some way. Should he say something? Offer her a tissue, an apology? "Something wrong, Sam?"

"Jonathan, do you believe in God?"

He anticipated she'd ask him a lot of questions like a typical sightseer, inquiries as to the history and personal lives of his ancestors. Not this question, not so intimate an inquisition. "Are all lawyers so nosy?"

"I'm sorry. I shouldn't pry."

"If it matters, yes I do. I have faith, though believing and accepting are two different things."

"The lake…so beautiful…how could anyone not feel close to God here? I think I felt a Presence when I saw your landscapes in my room and Sadie's shop, but the later ones in the library seem…violent… undercoated with rage."

He certainly hadn't anticipated her perceptiveness, or her directness, either. "I think sometimes people get angry at God, but they don't stop believing in Him. When I read some of the Psalms, I think David had issues with the Almighty, certainly Solomon did."

"Maybe it's not God you're angry with?"

Perhaps. Easier to blame an unseen deity than admit he hated the woman he most loved for taking the life of his only son. "You're smart, lawyer lady."

Sam didn't respond.

When Jonathan glanced over, her head rested against the wings, the muffin untouched, her heavy breaths almost a snore. Should he wake her? Anyone who fell asleep that fast probably needed it. He'd watch the rain a little longer and leave her be. A strange peace came at the thought. It had been over five years since he watched a woman sleep.

A slight shake of her shoulders pulled Sam from wherever she had slipped away to.

Jonathan handed her a warm mug filled with steaming brew. "Here's your coffee."

She yawned, stretched, pulled Jonathan's jacket tighter around her, and accepted the offering, wrapping her hands around the plain white chipped mug, soaking in its warmth, inhaling the steam as well as the charred aroma wafting from the fireplace.

Jonathan sat in his wicker chair. "Do you always fall asleep like that? I've seen babies do that, never a grownup."

No way would she tell Jonathan Gladstone that she'd spent the last three years in perpetual motion, sleep a luxury, and one she rarely afforded herself, even if she could. Yet, since she'd been in Haven, she fell into near coma states like a post-hypnotic suggestion. At least she had an excuse for today. "I woke up way before the sun even threatened the horizon."

"Worried about Styles? I do get television up here."

"Not worried, exactly." She lied.

"So what are you going to do? Zack hopes you'll stay in Haven, finish out your vacation, at least."

"Look, there's nothing between Zack and me. We're friends."

"He likes you, Sam. But I'm sensing you don't share his interest."

He might be Zack's best friend, but that gave him no right to pry into her relationships. "Not that it's any of your business, I think Zack's a great guy, but I'm not the right girl for him, and this isn't the time for me to get involved with anyone."

Jonathan glanced out the picture window. "Rain's lifting. Do you still want to brave the trails? It's cold and slippery."

"It'll take a little more than wet grass and plunging temperatures to scare me away. I want to see the scene in the landscape I bought."

"I'm surprised Sadie let you buy it. I brought a few canvases in after Angelica died and gave them to Sadie for her store. A gift. She said she didn't have the heart to sell them."

Sam felt another backpack slip onto her shoulders. She should have asked first, and not assumed the landscapes were for sale. "Sadie wasn't there…I sort of took it down myself…If I'd known—"

"She thinks the Lord must've wanted you to have it, or else she would have been in the store when you decided to buy it."

"I could give it back...donate it to the library, maybe."

Jonathan placed his coffee cup on the side table. "No. Please don't. I'm glad at least one of them is gone. I see them on the wall and relive that awful day—the day I found Angelica and Elliott floating in the lake. That's why I hate going into town, those landscapes are everywhere. I'll give you the rest of them, if you want, as long as I never have to see them again."

"Thanks for the offer…but I barely have enough wall space for the one I bought." An idea flashed. "Maybe, my friend, Justine—"

Jonathan squeezed his eyes shut. "Just a thought. Don't feel like you have to—"

"No. Really. She loves your work. I would take a few as a wedding present. She's getting married—here, in fact. Not here, but in Haven. First weekend in June."

Sam returned her gaze to the window. How sad that a talented artist would give away the best of his work. Should she tell him she knew without a doubt that removing one's self from the object didn't erase the memory? If she warned him, she'd have to tell him how she knew.

Sadie might be on to something with her theory that everyone wore their guilt in emotional backpacks, forgiven sins that people put on themselves, self-condemnation that God had already washed clean.

Jonathan had fallen silent, a brooding sort, typical of artists, she supposed, although she never knew one before, so she didn't have any comparisons to go on. She shouldn't fault him for his current moodiness. He'd tried to be sociable, probably a Herculean effort for him. She was the one who fell asleep.

The man annoyed her like an arid desert, sparsely entertaining, yet he also intrigued her…or was it Dawn's Hope that pulled at her? Might as well respect his space, whatever mental cave he'd crawled into. Any conversation with him could be perilous, a walk across an abyss filled with accusations and memories.

Hyacinths.

They could talk about hyacinths. Ignorant about most flowers, she did know a few things about hyacinths. She could ask him why they danced before Angelica died and why now he made them bleed.

"Jonathan—"

"I think it's safe to take that walk now if you still want to see the lake."

"Absolutely."

Answers would have to wait.

Jonathan supported Sam's arm as she took the steps from the rear lawn down the steep incline to the beach front. She went on ahead, and he stayed near the forest's edge, an observer to her spirited investigation. "Be careful, Sam. There are a lot of sharp rocks hidden by the sand. Those sandals don't offer much protection."

She didn't even turn around. Serve her right if she cut her foot. Maybe next time she'd borrow better walking shoes.

Next time? Wasn't this a one-time deal?

At least, for the moment, he didn't have to worry about carrying on a conversation. That woman rubbed his ire to full conflagration, her comebacks as meaty with sarcasm as his own. Maybe the best way to communicate with this volcano was to not say anything. Nobody could argue with a mute.

Angelica never minded his moods. "You don't have to say anything, Jonathan. Just being with you is enough." Sometimes she'd push a smile out of him by stroking his cheek while he painted.

Sam took a sudden lunge forward, probably tripping over a hidden rut, and landed on her posterior, water lapping at her feet. Great. Would he have to carry her back now? He walked over to offer assistance, half expecting her to shove him away. She didn't. He helped her to a stand. "Can you walk?"

She put her full weight on her ankle, wincing, but apparently too stubborn to admit to any pain. "Lead on, Daniel Boone."

To where? Back to the cabin, the house? How much more should he risk showing her?

"Can we go there?" Sam pointed toward the hyacinth bed on the north shore. "That scene resembles the landscape I bought. Well, not quite, more buds on the painted hyacinths. Must have been done earlier in the spring."

"Good observation. Follow me."

Jonathan had hoped to circumvent the rocky ledge, the place where they found Angelica and Elliot. But when he and Sam arrived to the north shore, Sam ran on ahead and sat on the overhanging boulder. "Do you sketch here often?"

"Not since…I usually stay in the cabin. I still sketch the fishermen from the beach. Zack and I fished here the other day, though. Mostly, I avoid this spot."

"Why? It's so beautiful."

"This is where I spotted Angelica and Elliott's bodies—about fifty feet out from where you're sitting."

"I'm sorry if it's bringing it all back to you." Sam fixed her view toward the opposite side of the lake. "What's that structure, over there by the barn?"

"Triune Point…where Emmanuel wrestled with his angel."

"Looks like a shrine, almost."

"It is, sort of. There's a jut into the lake near the barn, rocky and covered with moss like this ledge. Emmanuel built an altar there, and his diaries indicate he went there to meditate."

Sam stood and brushed the moss from her slacks, her stance unsteady.

"Be careful, the terrain can be extremely slippery, especially after a heavy rain." He offered a hand to help her back onto solid ground. Once more, she accepted his help. "I'd hate to see you fall in."

"So would I. I can't swim."

Jonathan gazed at the thickening clouds. "We should probably leave. Looks like another downpour heading our way."

Sam squealed. He'd heard the sound before. Once in Sadie's store, a little girl ran over to a barrel of Old-Fashioned Licorice, delight in her shouts, absolute and unhindered joy in a discovery. Sam rushed to the bed of hyacinths, like that little girl rushed to the barrel, knelt down and buried her face amid the drenched petals.

He watched her, half amused, half amazed at the simplicity of her pleasure. He hated to end the scene, but big, cold drops, laced with snow, fell like warning bells from the sky. "Okay, Alice. Time to leave Wonderland."

They dashed back to the Max II and Sam climbed in, a calmer portrait then when they came, her wild eyes subdued, peaceful.

When he pulled in front of her car, she scrambled out. "Thanks for the tour."

She would leave, and he'd likely never see her again…unless…"Do you fish?"

"Never have."

"If you'd like, I'll make a trespassing exemption for you, and you can pick some of the hyacinths."

"That's why the property's posted?"

"Haven has a lot of nice folks. But, Angelica's hyacinths would be history if I allowed just anyone to tromp through these woods."

She cast her eyes downward. "Thanks for the offer, but I'll probably be leaving Haven in a few days. I need to cut my vacation short."

"What about the lease agreement?"

"I can always handle that from Manhattan. I'll mail it to you when I get it drawn up. All you need is a notary."

Sadness came over him, not one of foreboding or misery, but a loss of something he couldn't define. He'd actually enjoyed his time with Sam, if a blister could be categorized as pleasure, like a gardener's souvenir after a day of planting bulbs. Through her eyes, he'd seen the lake once more for its beauty, as it was when he and Angelica walked the beach front or sat on the ledge. He'd like to take more walks with Sam.

Was this attraction, then? How would he know, since Sam was the first woman he'd found interesting since Angelica died? He'd been in an emotional coma for five years, only now waking up, and like a gosling, imprinting to the first perfume.

20

Sam reached for her car keys and then remembered. "Oops."

"Now there's a precise legal term if I ever heard one."

Grrr. A perfect way to ruin what had been, until this moment, a perfect day.

"I locked my keys in the trunk of my car. They were in my blazer pocket."

"Clever move. I hope you're not as careless with your legal briefs."

She seethed. Criticism she could handle; it came with the job, especially the accusation-layered inquisition of the media. Jonathan's sarcasm unnerved her, made her quiver with anger. She liked it better when he forced a half-grin and droned his pathetic attempts at humor. She gave him a second to digest what he'd said.

His face muscles twitched with sudden realization. "I'm sorry. That was rude." He probably meant it to be, but his guilty plea softened its blow.

"This gentle rain is about to become another downpour. Why don't you come in, and I'll call Josiah. He'll have you going again in no time."

"That's stretching our deal a bit. Are you sure you don't mind?"

Jonathan leaned against the doorjamb. "You can wait in the den, where it's comfortable…" He hesitated. "Or, if you'd like, I can show you around the house."

Now that truly was an offer she couldn't refuse. She followed Jonathan back into the house, through yet another maze of corridors into a small alcove dressed with a small desk, laptop and landline. He picked up the handset and punched in the number.

"Got the answering machine…Josiah…Jonathan Gladstone. Sam Knowles's at my place. She's locked her keys in her trunk. Could you swing by and do your magic, ASAP?"

Hesitation.

Jonathan replaced the receiver and turned toward Sam. "Josiah checks his messages fairly frequently, so he should be here soon."

"You've probably got other things to do. I'll wait by the car."

"No bother. You seem interested in the house."

Interested? An understatement. "Since I first saw it from Main Street."

"If you're leaving Haven, this might be your only chance."

"Solid argument. Lead on."

He took off with a quickened gait, her shorter legs doing double time for each of his single strides. "You've seen the den and the foyer. This room over here is the sitting room."

"I caught a glimpse of it earlier. Steinway, right?"

"Yes…Angelica's."

"Why is it roped off?"

"I don't want anyone in there."

Why leave it open if the room brought him pain, or perhaps Jonathan veiled a need for self-punishment under this constant exposure to Angelica's memory.

Jonathan's backpack of guilt? For what?

"Why do you invite the pain if you're so bent on leaving here? Finding a caretaker isn't that difficult. You don't need a lawyer for that. So, what's the truth, Jonathan?"

"I'll never own Dawn's Hope. So why stay?"

Jonathan's face wore a different portrait, not of pain that came from loss, but one of betrayal. Was his desire to leave because of a lost love, or for some other reason—the curse of the disinherited? "Why don't you contest the will, then?"

"What's the point? My son's dead. I have no heir."

"No one knows what the future holds."

Jonathan raked his hair with his fingers, his gaze distant, as if fighting memories. "My father believed the only bond I had with Dawn's Hope was Angelica and Elliott. But he was wrong. I can't explain it. Something holds me here, something stronger than the insatiable will to run."

"Like a tug of war with your soul?"

His eyes changed in that instant, no longer dull, but liquid motion, a twitter, like the resonance of a severed chord. "Exactly."

"You're not the only one caught in a can't-fight, can't-flight paradox, afraid to move forward and unable to retreat. You're stuck, Jonathan—stuck in the mire of indecision. No one can help you until you know what you truly want. If you decide to stay here, we can contest the will. If you want to break free, I'll do what I can to help you find a permanent release. We can write up a transfer of property to the historical society, so that the land permanently belongs to Haven. I can't make that choice for you, but I can tell you that if we contested your father's will, you'd probably win. Isn't that what you hoped I'd suggest?"

"On some level—maybe."

He resumed his pace, then stopped by the main stairwell lined with portraits she assumed were his ancestors. Judging from the clothing and hair styles, they appeared to be ordered by ascension, the first a wigged man, fortyish, dressed in a blue, ornately buttoned coat, reminiscent of the late eighteenth century, with coconut eyes like Jonathan's. "That's Emmanuel. I recognize the face from the portrait at the library."

"Yes."

"I'm curious. Why did King George give him so much property? He wasn't even a general, a low-ranking lieutenant."

"A long story. In a nutshell, Emmanuel saved the life of the king's distant relative, and so George rewarded him with a title and land. The land tract is verifiable, but as for the heroic deed, that's oral history, not a shred of documentation anywhere. After the war, Emmanuel resigned his commission, married Lady Victoria Woolsey, and sired nine sons and five daughters. Only three daughters and one son lived to adulthood. That son's son started a mercantile business, a venture that brought prosperity to Haven."

"Henry?"

"Yes."

She studied Emmanuel's portrait, the eyes, somber and deep, like Jonathan's, eyes soaked with some other pain. What?

Jonathan motioned to follow into a small room to the right of the stairwell. "The family archives are stored here. If you're interested, you can browse through them."

Like footprints to a treasure, these tombs were the answer to the mysteries shrouding Dawn's Hope. Was it worth staying a few more days and let Abe deal with Styles? They climbed the stairwell, and Jonathan pointed to the last portrait in the group. "Father," he thudded.

Sam compared the eyes—Jonathan's mournful. The other Gladstone's were hard, fierce.

"I don't see any of the women's portraits."

"This way—at the top of the stairs." The landing opened into a spacious area twice the size of the Arlington Library meeting room. "The ballroom, my lady." He gazed into her eyes as if looking for permission. For what? Without warning and seemingly out of character, he spun her in an impulsive twirl, and waltzed her across the room, light on his feet compared to Sam's missteps.

Jonathan's playfulness took the wind from her, the twirling made her dizzy. Maybe she hadn't recovered to full strength as quickly as she thought she would.

He stopped his dance. "You look a little white, Sam. I apologize. Something came over me, a sudden urge."

"No harm, but these sandals aren't any better for dancing than hiking."

He pointed to the portraits on every side of the room. "The mistresses of Dawn's Hope." Sam recognized Muriel Arlington's portrait placed next to one that must have been the fashionable Lady Victoria Woolsey Gladstone. Sam followed the lineage of Gladstone women, by birth and by marriage, resting upon the ethereal Angelica, seated in front of a fireplace adorned with bouquets of hyacinths, a rosy-cheeked infant snuggled in her arms.

She'd seen artwork depicting Mary and the infant Jesus. Each one, although in varying degrees, featured a halo around Mary's head similar to the effects highlighting Angelica's portrait. "You painted this one."

"Yes. I did. But how did you know?"

"The brush strokes are similar, the way you hallow the hyacinths. That's your signature. At least the early paintings I've seen."

Sam stepped back to appreciate Angelica's perfect features, an oval face, her hair as black as midnight, eyes as blue as a cloudless day. "Beautiful is too weak a word to describe her."

He traced the outline of her form. "Sometimes, I think she holds me here."

"You mean like a ghost?"

"No. I'm not crazy, Sam. I don't see her. But I feel her and there are times I think I hear her calling me, as if she wants me to go to her and Elliott. Every spring she put up dozens of hyacinth bouquets. I haven't allowed a one in the house since she died, yet I swear I smell them in every room." Jonathan glanced in Sam's direction, concern in his eyes. "You're shaking."

"Am I?"

"Your face turned white when I mentioned the hyacinths."

"Smell is probably one of the most powerful memory triggers, especially those we'd sooner forget. In my case, the scent brings comfort."

"Invisible hyacinths? You, too?"

"Yeah, me too."

"I knew there was some reason I liked you."

She intended to offer a gaze of reassurance, to verify his sanity with her insanity. Instead, her eyes held at his chapped lips. Her legs trembled and blackness fell on her. She roused at Jonathan's gentle stroke across her cheek. "Sam, what happened?"

He must have caught her as she started to faint, brought her against his chest to keep her upright. His eyes matched the confusion in her heart, as she permitted a kiss.

No…this was wrong. She pushed lightly against his hold. She'd been impetuous to come here, to let him hold her like this, to let him kiss her. She couldn't afford any sort of romance, not even a fling. Not now. Not with Zack, and certainly not this strange man who filled her with as much ire as he did passion.

"You…looked like you were fainting—"

"Thanks for catching me."

Their eyes locked. "Sam—"

A distant chime. Jonathan's gaze held fast. "That's the doorbell. Probably Josiah."

"Probably."

"Should I let him in?"

"Probably."

"Yes. I should do that."

He sighed, turned, and headed back down the steps.

She'd done it again, guillotined a chance at something wonderful. She'd add that to her list of regrettable decisions.

21

Harlan Styles shook hands with a devil, the deal done and sealed according to Washington.

"It's all arranged, Harlan. I met with the DA this morning to finalize everything. This deal's been three months in the making, but it's finally come to light." Washington's face glowed, as shiny as if he'd had a snort…probably did, too. Harlan heard the words, but fear gripped him. No matter what kind of sweet deal Washington cooked up, Harlan Styles was a dead man walking, in or out of prison.

"The DA's not happy with our Miss Knowles. Not one bit. She'll be sacked, and Abe Hilderman will be assigned to take Knowles's place as lead prosecutor. DA doesn't want it leaked that the city put a child abuse victim at the helm of a child murder case, so they were ready to deal to avoid a civil suit. And your testimony put the icing on the cake."

Washington rubbed his tongue over his lips—the high that man got from turning the law in on itself. "Your hearing is tomorrow."

Harlan shook his head. "Judge Normandy isn't going to cooperate. You saw the way he stared me down when he read his findings. If beheadings were still done, he would've sent me to the chopping block right then and there."

"Hilderman thinks he can have Normandy removed, too. Seems he made some offhand remark in front of a juror that could be misinterpreted as prejudicial. He thinks the case would then go to a judge who owes Hilderman a boatload of favors. Gotta love it when politics works on our behalf for a change."

"Us, or for you? I don't see my situation improving much. I'm dead."

"I keep telling you, Harlan, Hilderman promised protection." Washington's lips turned upward in a hasty grin, suspiciously forced. "You should be happy, Harlan. You're going home, like I promised." He cleared his throat. "House arrest for a year. Better than being in here the rest of your life. Best I can do, Harlan."

"House arrest? I don't have a house anymore, Darnell. I got nothing left. I'll have to depend on welfare."

Washington clucked, a nervous chicken under a woodsman's axe. "You could go live with your brother."

"Reg isn't exactly much protection, now is he? It rots, Darnell. Why won't anyone believe I'm innocent?"

Washington's pleasant mask turned sour; he might as well have pointed a finger. "Because you've lied about too many things."

22

Sam looked out the window. The rain had stopped and the afternoon sun peeked out behind still grayish skies. Justine's call had been troubling, her tone muted, distant, foreboding, her enthusiasm coated with dread. Well, the truth would come out soon enough.

A faint rap and a weak, "Can I come in?"

"Yes, Leon."

She should give him Abe's how-dare-you-intrude look, but how could she stay angry with a man who rocked her to sleep? She melted in seconds.

"You look upset. I might not remember what I had for breakfast, but I can still tell a worried face when I see one."

Sam smiled. "That was my friend Justine on the phone."

"From Manhattan?"

"Yes."

"Something wrong?"

Everything's wrong, Leon. "No, not really. She and my boss are coming here tomorrow."

Leon brought his hands together and lifted his shoulders, "Ooh, I'll be so pleased to meet them."

"What did you want to talk to me about?"

"I'll confess. I'm nosy. I was curious about your visit with that Gladstone boy."

Now there was a memory she'd like to throw into

the forgettable half of her life. "Fine."

"He sounds like a sad bloke. I hear things. People think I'm crazy so they aren't very careful with what they say around me."

"What do you hear about Jonathan?"

"Can I sit a spell?"

"Of course." She took the Queen's chair and pointed Leon to the bed. "So?"

Leon sat and winked. "I also hear he's a handsome fellow."

"I suppose. I didn't go up there to rate his physical attributes."

Leon chortled. "Are you going to see him again?"

"Maybe...I'm not…probably not." There. She settled the matter in her mind. She would tell Jonathan their client/attorney relationship was over. He wanted her advice, and she had given it. Any competent attorney could represent him once he decided what he truly wanted. "Besides, I'm leaving Thursday afternoon. I need to get back to Manhattan."

Leon's face drooped. "I'll miss you."

"I'll miss you, too. I'll be back for Justine's wedding."

He turned to go. "Won't be the same. Nobody else's room smells so nice."

An unaccustomed sensation swept across her stomach. Hunger? Must be the mountain air combined with the savory aromas drifting through the planks in her room that stoked an appetite, but it was too early for supper. She glanced at her watch…with any luck she could make it to the bank before it closed. "Are you up for a walk, Leon?"

"I'd like that. Where to?"

"We could meander and see where we end

up."After the bank, the next stop would be someplace where she could buy sensible shoes. "I have a business matter I need to tend to before we leave. Justine wants to get married at the church down the road. Do you know who I should talk to about that?"

"That's Reverend Gottlieb's church, where Sadie and Aaron attend. Mazie and I go with them sometimes, but mostly they go to Saturday night service so Aaron can fish Sunday mornings. I was raised that Sunday's for church not for fishing, but I don't say a word of that to Sadie and Aaron. They've been mighty kind to me."

"Do you think Sadie could make a call for me?"

Leon beamed with purpose, his laugh heartier than a man of twenty.

Sam took his jutted elbow.

"Let's ask."

He left Sam at the bottom step, walked over and pecked Mazie on the cheek, then rejoined Sam as they walked to Sadie's gift shop. "I always say goodbye to my girl. Even if she doesn't know who I am."

Sadie finished helping a customer, then Leon motioned to get her attention. She hustled towards them. "What can I do for you two, this afternoon?"

"My friend, the one who wants to get married here, is coming tomorrow—"

"Oh, yes. We had a nice long chat this morning about what she wanted for her theme, menus, everything. I'm looking forward to meeting her." Sadie rambled on about pot roast versus roast beef and how chicken cordon bleu was preferable over orange-glazed chicken. If Sam was going to get to the bank, she had to leave soon.

"All very interesting."

"That's not what you wanted to know, is it, dear? I can tell by that yawn you're trying to hide."

"I am a little tired. Seems the least bit of exertion wears me out, and I must have walked for miles today at Dawn's Hope. Justine wants to be married in the old church on Main Street. She looked it up on the Internet, and apparently, it's a popular wedding chapel. Leon says that's where you and Aaron attend."

"Yes, lovely place for a wedding—"

"Would you be willing to call and set up an appointment for us, tomorrow, if possible?"

Sadie galloped to her counter, picked up the desk phone, and punched in a number. "No time like now. Want a thing done—do it right off, I always say. Hello, Pastor Gus—"

Sam wandered through the gift shop, sniffing the assortment of candles, settling on a pair labeled spring flowers, a hint of hyacinths and lilacs, perfect for her apartment. When Sadie disconnected, Sam brought the candles to the register.

Sadie's face glowed with excitement. "All set, dear. Pastor Gus will meet you and Justine around 9:30 tomorrow morning. The parsonage is attached to the church, so he'll pop in when you get there. The church is generally unlocked during the day. Is that too early for your friends?"

"They'll be here even if they have to leave before dawn."

Sadie wrapped the candles in tissue paper and slipped them into a green checkered gift bag labeled Sadie's Gift Shoppe. "Nice scent," she said. "Fills up the whole room. If you and Leon are going for a walk, do you want me to put these in your room for you?"

If the whole Earth were filled with people like Sadie,

there'd be no need for a Heaven. She nodded. "And could you put them on my tab? I'll make the bank my first stop so I can settle my bills. I plan to go back to Manhattan right after court."

Sadie smacked her lips in contemplation. "Well now, that's a whole 'nother day away. Lots can happen in a day, don't you know."

Sam made a quick stop at the bank, transferred some money to set up a temporary checking account, and withdrew a couple hundred for operating expenses. Feeling less like a vagabond as she put her receipts into her purse, she gazed up at the teller. "Are there any other clothing stores on Main Street besides boutiques for the frivolous?"

The teller shook her head. "Nothing much for the ladies, I'm afraid. Main Street caters to the tourists, the hunters, the fishermen, and the hungry."

Either brave the boutiques or go traveling after supper. She turned toward Leon. "Right now, I could go for a cinnamon muffin. Let's stop at the bakery. My treat."

"If you're buying, I'll have coffee, too. They've got a humdinger of a house blend there."

When she and Leon came to Wells Bakery, Sam took out a twenty and set her purse on an outside table. "Wait here and I'll get our orders. How do you want your coffee?"

"Two sugars. No cream."

Sam went inside, ordered, and came back out with a tray. No Leon. No purse.

"Over here, Sam."

She turned toward the tinny voice. Leon stood by the window holding her purse. "Where would you like to sit?"

She sighed. Was Leon playing another game or did he have a genuine memory lapse? "We can sit over there by the sidewalk."

"That'll be nice. Here's your purse. I found it on that table over there. You shouldn't go wandering off and leave your things out in the open like that. Somebody might've walked off with it."

"No harm done."

Leon took a knife and sliced off a nibble; Sam devoured her muffin in four bites. "Leon, tell me something, if you don't mind my asking."

"Don't mind. There shouldn't be any secrets between friends."

Pearls of wisdom from a man who probably would forget what he said by the time he finished his muffin—maybe before, at this rate. No, there shouldn't be secrets between friends. She should have trusted Justine with her past, if no one else.

"What do you want to know, Sam?"

"There's more to you and Mazie than the fact you once dated, isn't there?"

Leon took a sip of coffee. "Like I said, I don't keep secrets from a friend, so I guess I can tell you, but you have to promise not to go blabbering this to anyone else."

"If it doesn't involve a crime, I promise."

Leon sliced off another piece of muffin then took another sip of coffee. At this pace, they'd be here all afternoon. Sam chewed on the facts as she knew them, and pieced the evidence together. "Sadie's your daughter, isn't she?"

Leon took his napkin and dabbed his eyes. "For Mazie's sake, we don't talk about it. You see, I never knew about Sadie until she came to see me right after she and Aaron got married." He hesitated.

"Go on, Leon."

"Ours is the same as a hundred other stories, I suspect. We were young and in love, Mazie and me. When the war broke out, I wanted to get married before I went overseas, but Mazie had her heart set on a fancy church wedding. We put the ceremony on hold, but not our love."

"Mazie got pregnant?"

Leon nodded. "Back in those days, that sort of thing created a scandal. She never told me she was in the family way. Instead, I got Mazie's goodbye letter while sitting in a foxhole in the South Pacific. She told me she married someone else, a man she knew from work."

"She should have told you, Leon—trusted your love for her."

Sam had done it again, jumped to closing remarks before the jury heard every side. She reminded herself that the world was different for Mazie and Leon, than the jump-in-the-sack, let's-have-a-hook-up lifestyle her generation followed.

"I tell you, I was one shocked man when Sadie found me. Said she'd been cleaning out Mazie's apartment. Her memory was getting bad and she couldn't live alone anymore. Sadie said she was packing up Mazie's things and found her journal. In it, Mazie mentioned me, how sad she was to break off our engagement, but didn't see any other way out of her trouble. Mazie's Alzheimer's was too advanced, so after some digging, Sadie found me. Turns out she was my daughter, all right. So we arranged for me to move in with Sadie and Aaron, along with Mazie, so I could help them take care of her."

"And you weren't angry because she kept her pregnancy from you?"

Leon blew his nose. "Now Sam, don't be too hard on Mazie. She didn't see any other way. The supposedly premature birth didn't fool anybody, but Mazie's husband claimed Sadie as his, and that kept folks' tongues from wagging after awhile."

Leon talked, sometimes through tears, sometimes with smiles.

Sam sensed no remorse, but rather an account of wrongs long ago forgiven. "You still love her, even after she hurt you like that?"

"I was angry when I first got the letter—the hurt went powerful deep. I even thought about walking right into the line of fire and ending the misery. Instead, I prayed for the will to go on."

Sam saw peace in Leon's eyes, a peace with a life that had worked out far differently than he imagined. Would her life be different now? Her five-year goal had been to move up to a supervising attorney in the Special Victims Unit. Those hopes were falling flat with the Styles case in shambles. People continued to refer to the peculiarities of her accident, made jokes, but what if God had sent that moose not simply to get her attention, but as a road block, making her turn a different direction? Her head spun. How she hated analyzing situations. Life had lots of twists and turns, but that didn't mean God was behind every one of them.

"So what did you do, after the war, I mean."

"I went to college on the GI bill, became a teacher,

and helped shape young lives. I'll admit I wrestled with resentment off and on over the years. When Sadie explained everything, I could see God's hand in it all. Sometimes it takes a lifetime to heal from a hurt."

"How could you forgive her so easily? You were denied your own child?"

Leon took Sam's hand into his. "The way I figure, God worked it all out the way it was meant to be, and I had to learn to trust it. Mazie's husband raised Sadie like his own. He did a good job of it, too. Besides, why let anger over a past I can't change get in the way of the good time I have with Mazie, now?"

Would it take her a lifetime of hurt before she found peace with her past? Her thoughts veered toward Jonathan, how his brows drooped with pain. Leon might be right. Some hurts take years to heal, but eventually healing did take place—faith and time the best medicine for gaping wounds. But why was God so slow about it? *How long for me, Lord? How long for Jonathan?*

Sam picked up the mound of wet napkins, muffin plates, and empty coffee cups. "Ready to keep walking? Think I'd like to go to the library next."

Leon followed her to the trash bin. "For what?"

"Your story got me thinking."

He nudged Sam with his elbow. "About that Gladstone boy?"

"More like the Gladstone boy's father."

"Why?"

"A hunch. Besides, dinner won't be for another couple of hours. Want to join me?"

"To the library, then. I like reading the newspapers and talking to Tom. He's got more stories to tell than a king's cook."

"Let's hope so."

Zack held his breath, clutched the get-well card he'd bought at the gift shop, then entered Frank Simmons's hospital room.

Frank looked up, his face still pasty gray, but a little rosier than when Zack saw him on the gurney. "Hey, Zack. Good of you to stop by."

"Well, you sound pretty chipper for a sick man."

"I'm alive. Thanks to you. Hey, if the ticker had to give out, I'm glad it fizzled when you were handy."

In all the years Zack had known Frank, this was the most civil he'd ever been. Could be near death experiences tenderized the human spirit in some way. Zack tossed Frank the card. "I hope your heart can take a good laugh. I wouldn't want you to have another infarction."

Frank smiled. "No. Next one might do me in for sure. This isn't my first, you know."

"I didn't know."

"Last one happened before I came to Haven. About ten years ago. I'm afraid this time I wasn't so lucky, there's a lot of muscle damage."

"Anything you need? Something I can do?" Maybe he shouldn't be so quick to offer.

"No. Not really." He sat forward an inch or two. "I take that back. Might be one thing you could do for me."

Zack readied for mission impossible. "Anything. You name it."

"Doc doesn't want me back to work until the fall. I expect you'll be getting a call from the school board since you're the only faculty qualified to take over. I know we don't see eye-to-eye on a lot of things, but I know you'd do what's right by all concerned. That's what I told the board."

No surprise on that bit of news. "What'll they do with my classes?"

"I thought maybe your father could sub."

"Dad would like that."

"I'll put in a word for him, then." Frank pushed the control to elevate the head of his bed. "There's a chair against the wall. Have a seat."

Zack hesitated. Frank only offered a chair when dishing out bad news, or asking for a hefty favor.

"I want you to be our team captain in my place. Pete wants to do it, but…well…you know Pete." Frank winced.

Worried about Pete, or a twinge of pain? "You OK?"

"A little indigestion…they gave me Mexican food for supper…go figure. My chart says liquid diet."

Zack smiled. "And you didn't bother to correct them?"

"Where's the fun in that?"

"Are they shipping you over to the cardiac unit in Albany?"

"As soon as a bed becomes available. Might need a valve or two bypassed. Doc says there's a lot of blockage."

Another bit of news Zack expected to hear.

"You know, you've got one heck of a fastball, Zack."

They harmonized their laughter. "You accused me of using unwarranted deadly force with a lethal weapon. Maybe I should be a cop."

"Don't go beating yourself up over this heart attack. I was a ticking bomb, and you had the uncanny luck of pulling the pin with that pitch of yours. I knew I shouldn't try for it. Doc warned me to stop playing strenuous sports, stick to golf, riding a bike, and walking. I didn't listen and, well, here I am."

"I'm sorry, Frank. I didn't know you had a heart condition, or—"

"First one was at age forty-two."

Zack pulled up a bedside chair. "That *is* young."

"Bad tickers run in the Simmons family. My pop died of heart disease when I was only thirteen, and my brother died last year from heart trouble. On the golf course, though. Right after he made a hole in one. What a way to go."

"Absolutely."

Whatever faults Frank had, his sense of humor almost made up for them.

"I haven't been taking care of myself the way I should. If I don't straighten up, I won't live to see my oldest daughter get married next year. She's engaged, you know."

"No. I didn't know."

"Why should you? Not like we hang out that much. But I like you Zack, and I hope you accept the offer if the board calls. You'd be a good principal. Maybe you'll stick around Haven a little longer, too."

Zack felt his cheeks heat. "You knew I've been sending resumes out?"

"It's a small town, Zack."

"It's not that I don't like teaching…I do."

"Although, for your sake, it might be a good idea if you didn't take my job. Stick to teaching, you'll live longer."

Frank got high scores for directness if not for administration.

"Frank, I appreciate the advice, but…well…you know I'm a Christian."

"Yeah. So what?"

"So, it's not about what's convenient. It's about what God wants me to do with my life."

"Well…now…that's an interesting way of looking at things. But, maybe God's will is all about what He's gifted us with. Ever think of that?"

Zack laughed. Far as anyone knew, Frank never stepped foot in a church except for family baptisms, weddings, and funerals, not the sort of man associated with theological expertise. Yet, what he said made sense.

"Here's the thing. I was a better teacher than administrator. I miss teaching, Zack. I ended up doing a job I hated because the money was better. Nothing like coming close to death, though, to help a man think about his priorities." Frank pointed toward the ceiling. "Me and the Big Guy have been doing some talking." Frank belched. "Sorry. Gas is building up to almost intolerable."

"Want me to buzz Tracey for you?"

"I'll be fine. Mind getting some water in that pitcher for me?"

Zack got up and filled the pitcher with water from the sink in the patient bathroom. As Frank jabbered on about his goals when he got out of the hospital, how he wouldn't take life for granted anymore, Zack filled the glass on Frank's tray. Zack had worked for Frank for years, and this was probably the most they'd talked outside the school in all that time.

"So you really think I'm a good teacher? That's

high praise coming from you, Frank."

Frank gulped the water, then leaned back against his pillow. "What I'm saying is that I know you'll be a good principal. I have to wonder, though. Would you be as good a principal as you are a teacher?"

"Won't know unless I try."

Frank belched again, and tucked his chin against his chest. "Probably better take something for this, I guess. Anyway, what I'm trying to tell you, is that it occurs to me, you still haven't figured out whether you should get out of Dodge or stay put. Don't rush things. Maybe God wants you to stay here until you figure out what it is you really want."

"Right now, I think I'd like my supper. Hopefully, there's a pretty girl waiting for me at Sadie's, too."

Frank smiled. "The moose lady?"

Poor Sam. Would she ever lose the moniker? "We're friends—nothing more."

Frank broke out in a hearty laugh. "Yet?"

Zack grinned. "Yet."

23

Lillian Bordeaux greeted them with a wide smile. "Hello, Sam, Leon. Anything I can help you with?"

"Tom around?" Leon asked.

Lillian perked like the lead gossip at a quilting party. "No, he's a guest lecturer tonight at Albany University. He'll be home later tonight. Zack might need him to substitute for his history class—Zack's been offered a promotion as acting principal while Frank is recovering from his heart attack. Zack hasn't made up his mind, yet, though we're fairly sure he'll take it." Lillian leaned in as if sharing classified information. "Tracey said she wouldn't be surprised if Frank had to have a quadruple bypass."

Leon whispered into Sam's ear. "Woman's going to die of asphyxiation if she doesn't take a breath pretty quick." Then he looked to Lillian. "Sam wants to look something up. I'll go in the other room and read the *New York Times*."

Sam had spent the last ten years daily devouring not only New York papers, but the Washington Post. Since she left Manhattan, she hadn't so much as glanced at the headlines. The only television she'd watched was that horrible one-minute clip, the harbinger that three years of hard work had gone down the tubes. She squeezed Leon's hand. "I've been a bit out of touch lately. You can catch me up on all the news when we leave. I don't want to stay long. I think

I'd like a nap before supper."

He cackled all the way to the newspaper racks. Sam turned to Lillian. "Actually, I wanted to read older papers. I'd like to know what you have on Jonathan's father."

"Henry the Eighth?"

"Are you serious?"

"His real name was Richard Henry Gladstone. Henry the Eighth is our nickname for him—Tom's and mine—because he had six wives. Jonathan was Richard's only child, born to Richard's first wife."

Sam gulped. No wonder Jonathan seemed so distant—a cold father and revolving stepmothers, a dearth of stability for sure. "What happened to his wives?"

Lillian straightened and spewed every which way like a fully-opened faucet. "Wife one died of ovarian cancer when Jonathan was twelve. Wife two fell off a cliff during a hiking trip with her lover. Wives three and four were gold diggers—young, pretty things, Vegas showgirls—neither marriage lasted more than a year and both of them received hefty divorce settlements. Wife five seemed to promise a little happiness, and life seeped back into Dawn's Hope with extravagant parties and renovations."

Since there was a wife six, wife number five's day in the sun must have been short lived. Josiah had mentioned a family curse. Richard's string of bad marriages did little to quell the myth—maybe why Jonathan believed himself to be the victim of some malignant, cosmic rain.

"What happened to wife number five?"

Lillian leaned in, gazed around, as if to whisper, but spoke one decibel above normal. "Day after

Jonathan's college graduation wife five took off with Richard's accountant and a few million dollars that the bean counter managed to embezzle. Instead of pressing charges, Richard hired a different accountant. At least, he finally showed Jonathan some attention, especially after Angelica spent the summers at Dawn's Hope."

"And wife six?"

"She's still living. Richard married her right after Jonathan and Angelica's wedding. They traveled all over the world together. Some say there was no pre-nup agreement since she could buy out the Gladstones twice and still have money left over. Estelle was a refined woman, an art connoisseur, and probably the biggest reason behind Jonathan's success."

Sam did a mental recall of the Ladies of Dawn's Hope wall-of-fame. She couldn't remember seeing a portrait of any of Richard's wives. Jonathan's dourly grandmother's portrait stood out as the last of the matrons before Angelica's, and hers had been set slightly apart from the others.

"Does Jonathan keep in touch with his stepmother?"

Lillian grunted, scanned another book then tossed it into a bin. "Richard's widow moved to Greece after he died. She wrote to Jonathan, even after Angelica's death, although Zack doesn't think Jonathan ever answered her letters. His stepmother asked Sadie to keep her informed. You know Sadie. You can go to the bank on her promises, and she writes Estelle faithfully once a week."

Sam followed Lillian into a large room filled with video tapes, computers, a microfiche machine and a file cabinet marked *The Haven Gazette*. "The drawers are labeled by years, starting from 1798, the year the

Gazette was founded and ending in 1989, the last year of its daily publication before it became a weekly release." She pointed toward the computer. "I'm afraid you'll have to do most of your digging on the Internet for more recent info. Although we do have *The Times Union,* the Albany paper, on microfiche. Probably the best coverage would be *The Post-Star,* the Glens Falls newspaper. They cover most of the events for Lake George and southern Lake Champlain region."

"Thanks."

Lillian turned, and left Sam to her research without another word, but hovered nearby.

Not certain what to look for, Sam stood in the room alone. "Why do you even care," she asked herself aloud. She'd made up her mind to go back to Manhattan. Why waste her time drudging up dirt on a family, up until a few days ago, she never knew existed? As far as a computer search, she could do that in Manhattan, on her own computer, or with the full resource of a law library. She glanced at her watch, already four o'clock. Sam found Leon in the other room, reading the headlines. "Murder Case Takes On A New Twist."

Sam veered her gaze. She couldn't take any more bad news right now. Whatever the new twist, she'd find out soon enough. "Come on, Leon. Let's go back to the Lighthouse. If you don't mind, I'll stop at one of the boutiques. Trendy or not, I desperately need a change of clothes. This outfit bordered on musty when I rescued it from my pilot case. After today's deluge, it'll rank worse than a football locker room."

Leon smiled. "Are you staying for a few days more, then?"

"I still plan on leaving Thursday." Anger soured

her stomach. How could a sharpshooter like Abe let her case go so awry? She'd show Justine around tomorrow, have her say in Aaron's court on Thursday, then head to Manhattan to undo Abe's mess and forget Haven—forget the moose accident—and forget Jonathan Gladstone.

Jonathan stormed through the mansion, his prison, his non-inheritance. He paced from one room to another until he stopped in his studio where he nestled a fresh canvas on the easel. He thought he'd try a new portrait of Angelica, one from early memory, like the first summer she came to Dawn's Hope. Instead, an insolent red-head's face loomed in his visions. She'd left in a hurry, too repulsed to let him kiss her again.

She'd accused him of using Angelica's death as self-recrimination, a malignant tether to keep him from leaving Dawn's Hope, Angelica's wooing a figment keeping him moored to Mirror Lake. Angelica was dead. How could she hold him here against his will? Something else, something hidden from himself kept him in this limbo—a detached lily pad tangled in rooted vines, unable to float free.

Go or stay? A simple choice wasn't it? Father would say, "Make a list of the pros and cons, and let the longest list help you decide."

Where's the heart in formulas, facts, and figures?

Jonathan picked up a charcoal and spotted the canvas. A shape took form, then a face. Not Angelica. Not Sam. He reshaped the eyes, more oval, and then drew a hyacinth in the long tresses. He smoothed the nose in a slight upward angle.

Mother.

Jonathan thrashed the canvas to the floor and stormed from his studio, a gale of confusion, knocking over lamps and pushing furniture out of his way. Where to go in this mausoleum of remorse to escape Mother's memory? He paced the hall from the studio to the kitchen and poured a cup of coffee.

Returning to his studio, he picked up the damaged canvas, the remains of a delayed temper tantrum, his fume, latent, but now expressed, more powerful, more pervasive, cloudier than Angelica's memory. He forced himself to recall Mother's last day.

"Your mother's asking for you," Father said. Father had found him in the sitting room practicing his scales.

A young Jonathan stomped his feet. "No, I don't want to go to her." If he didn't she couldn't say goodbye. She wouldn't die until she said goodbye…she'd promised.

"That's enough, Jonathan. Be a man. Buck up. You need to face the facts. Your mother is dying. Nothing can keep her with us."

"You're wrong!" Jonathan ran from the house down the paths, and didn't stop running until he reached Triune Point, and hid behind the largest stone, gazing into the glassy water. No angel for Jonathan. Father found him four hours later. "She's gone, Jonathan. You should have talked to her when she asked for you." Father turned and left, perhaps assuming that the son would follow a father's footsteps, as every Gladstone before followed their father.

But Jonathan didn't. Not then, and he never would. He remained at the inlet and shook a fist at

Emmanuel's monument.

As dawn came, Jonathan still had not settled the matter with God. Instead, he picked up his grief and carried it like a banner over his soul. To make room for it, he had pushed Mother's memory aside.

For generations, the sons of Dawn's Hope hung their mothers' portraits in the gala room, a ritual of honor, even stone-hearted Father who'd hung dour Grandmother Gladstone's portrait the day after she died. Every son fulfilled his duty—except for Jonathan, who defied heritage even in this simple act. He'd hung Angelica's since there would be no heir to honor her. And of all the mistresses of Dawn's Hope, he believed she had loved the estate the most, understood the echoes of the ancestors, and deserved to be among the matrons.

But Mother loved Dawn's Hope with the same passion as Angelica.

He strained to remember the long walks with Mother along the lake's perimeter. She often snapped pictures of the flowers, studying their cycles from bud to decay. Sometimes, she'd pick a hyacinth and place it in her long black tresses. They'd stop for a picnic lunch at Triune Point, and Mother would entertain him for hours with her stories from Emmanuel's journals.

Jonathan gritted his teeth. Was this, then his sin? That he had failed a loving mother? Was her voice the other, stronger call to remain at Dawn's Hope? His unfinished business?

He resumed pacing, at first aimlessly, then, as if pulled by an unseen force, he ended up in Father's personal study, a small alcove off the former master bedroom, untouched since Father last frequented the room. The last time Jonathan came into Father's presence there, the air had been so frigid, Jonathan could see the mists of their breaths.

Though the air now stank from years of disuse, this time Jonathan felt strangely warm, as if a different Presence invited him to stay. Not Father, a holier Spirit. Something significant waited for him here.

24

Harlan Styles stood over Sam with a knife poised to plunge. Her own scream yanked her from deep slumber. A voice that seemed both near and far called to her. "Sam! Wake up. It's only a dream." Someone shoved her. She rubbed her eyes. Where was she? If it wasn't Harlan Styles standing over her, who was it? She squinted. "Leon?"

A fresh floral scent filled the room. Not quite like hyacinths, less intense, but similar. She stared at Sadie's wall mural of Queen Guinevere, holding a bouquet of wildflowers, her billowy gown like angels' wings, her eyes, sad and woeful, yet strong and beautiful, staring back at Sam. Then she remembered she was in her temporary room, in Haven. She saw the candles she'd bought from Sadie's shop—no hallucinatory scent. She felt her cheeks, wet with sweat.

Leon's face tightened with concern. "Sam? Are you all right? You were screaming again."

She glanced at the clock radio. Nearly six. She'd only been asleep for an hour. "Leon? You came up here to tell me something. What?"

"Darnell Washington is back, and asked to see you."

"Well, *I* don't want to see *him*."

"I think you might want to reconsider. The news broke while you were asleep."

"News?"

"That Harlan guy you put away? He's getting out tomorrow."

A rushed gasp escaped her. For Leon's sake, she sloughed it off, playing the hardened prosecutor. "What can I say? Justice isn't always blind. And sometimes the guilty manipulate her. What does Mr. Washington want with me?"

"He said he had to see you on urgent business."

"If it was so urgent, he should have called. If he could take a leisurely drive up here, then I'm taking the time for a shower. Maybe he can take advantage of Sadie's pork roast while waiting. And if Sadie puts a little something special on his plate, mind you only a tease, nothing lethal or sickening, I'll pretend it was an accident." Sadie would call it harmless revenge.

Leon laughed, shook his head, and turned to go. "I guess you do have a mean streak. OK. I'll tell Sadie to give Darnell *the special treatment*. Don't tell her I said so, but she can get a little mean herself, sometimes. I'll keep him occupied 'til you get downstairs."

When Sam came out from the bathroom, a pungent floral aroma filled the room. Not the candles as before, but the ever-present aroma that found its way to her in troubling moments. How long did olfactory hallucinations linger? She glanced toward Zack's bouquet, already withered. She sniffed their rancid decay to be certain, then tossed them in the waste basket. The phantom essence remained, and in its waft, she found confidence to battle the dragon one more time.

She threw on her armor—the black dress slacks, tailored green silk blouse, and black blazer she miraculously found at Bianca's Boutique along with a pair of black pumps and a gold necklace to accessorize. Quasi-professional. Fear edged her confidence. She hadn't thought to bring a weapon. She visualized the revolver locked away in a safety box in her closet, the bullets stored in a separate drawer in the kitchen. Abe insisted she get one for her protection. She hadn't argued, never confessed her aversion to owning one. She'd hidden it away, vowing she'd never touch it.

Not until Darnell Washington showed up did she wish she'd brought hers. Something about cold metal boosted a person's confidence. Sadly, she'd have to face Washington armed with little more than her wits.

And Me, child.

"And you, Lord."

She squared her shoulders, rehearsed her walk, and plunked downstairs. Washington sat at the table conversing with Sadie, listening more than anything else, to her excited summaries of how she and Aaron moved to Haven and started this food ministry, and Washington drinking a half glass of water with every bite.

Her legs stiffened with determination. Taking three deep breaths, she boldly walked toward his table. Sadie stood and wiped her glasses on her apron as Sam approached. "Oh, here's Sam. Nice chatting with you, Mr. Washington. I hope you'll stop by again, sometime. I'm sorry the pork roast tasted a bit salty and didn't measure up to your expectations." She stacked Washington's plates on a tray, gifting Sam with a smile and a wink. "I'll take this into the kitchen and let the two of you talk."

Sam initiated a handshake and used her practiced congeniality. "Good evening, Darnell. Sorry to keep you waiting. I hope you enjoyed Sadie's cooking."

Washington craftily avoided an answer, busily scanning the room—judging by his squinty eyes, with a glint of distrust. "Interesting place. I still don't see a license or a seating capacity certificate from the code inspector."

Sam came to Sadie's defense. "This isn't a restaurant in that respect. She doesn't even advertise. Do you see a cash register? She truly does cook enough to feed an army and likes to share. Nothing illegal about that."

"Yes, well, I still wonder what the Board of Health might have to say about all this *company*—"

"What do you want, Darnell. I told you not to come here again."

He motioned toward Aaron's office. "I don't think we should talk here."

The last time they'd talked in private, Sam had been at a disadvantage. Her strength rested in an audience, the courtroom her podium. She took a quick scan and counted ten guests besides the regulars. Zack, her protector, sat alone near the bar, his eyes locked on Washington.

"I've nothing to hide—nothing at all. But it might be a little more private by the bar."

He followed her, braced his hand on the counter and whispered as he leaned forward. "As I'm sure you know by now, my client will be released tomorrow morning…"

Justice couldn't seem to budge for Kiley, but, for Styles, the scales tipped swiftly. Why did a loving God allow the innocent to suffer and men like Styles to prosper? "House arrest is still imprisonment. Styles isn't exactly free."

"True, but a much better arrangement for my

client. Now we can focus on proving his innocence. He *is* innocent, Miss Knowles."

"As innocent as Satan."

"You'll see."

Her case was solid. How could he be vindicated? "You didn't come up here to tell me something that's pasted all over the front page."

"I won't mince words. We wanted you off the case. You wouldn't budge so we got what we wanted from your boss."

Nausea hit like a bullet. Why did Abe go behind her back? He could have at least consulted her before taking over completely and letting this scum get off so easily.

"We tried to find the least damaging avenue—"

"Damaging to whom?"

"To you, of course, but your insistence has left me with few options, Miss Knowles. I brought the affidavit before the new judge who agreed your conduct was prejudicial. He dismissed you from the case."

"What happened to Normandy?"

"Removed."

"What do you mean? From the bench?"

"No, only from the case. Seems he spread prejudicial gossip about my client in front of a juror. As for you—"

"Are you saying *I've* been fired?"

Washington leered, a vile, violent veneer covering his smile. "I suggest you take that up with your boss…excuse me, former boss."

Sam willed herself to stay standing. "Abe wouldn't fire me—he's my friend…like a father to me. You have no right to come barging in here to tell me these ridiculous lies. You're trying to distract me. It won't work."

"On the contrary, Miss Knowles. I came here by helicopter, at my own expense. I advise you to stay away from this case. I know your reputation, and I suspect that you won't let go. I'm warning you—"

"A threat? Not a wise place to do that." Sam looked around to see if anyone overheard. Zack stood poised to come to her honor—so cute when he acted gallant, yet irritating. Sam Knowles could take care of herself.

"I hope you get the paper here. Check the want ads. I'm sorry to be the one to tell you this bad news. I assumed Mr. Hilderman would have told you, by now."

Judge Normandy prejudicial? Of all the lies spread in the last few days, that was the worst. Who did Washington bribe to make this all happen, and so quickly? Her knees wobbled as reality hit. The courts *never* moved that quickly, never engineered so radical a sentence reduction with the speed of lightening. Abe must have been working behind the scenes the whole time, maybe even during the trial...way before she took a vacation. So clear now—his insistence—a ruse to distract her while he put his plan into action. Abe was the one man in this world she thought she could trust. Why had he betrayed her?

The room spun as her knees buckled even more, Washington's face contorting into a grotesque mask. She gripped an empty bar stool for support. Clarity came like a whiff of heavy perfume. But, of course...Abe's prize, The Ingram Family—Styles's connection to them. No wonder Abe never truly supported Sam's fight...tried to convince her to lighten up—worked a deal that he knew Sam would never sanction. Abe wanted to shut down Ingram for good—Styles his ticket—wanted it so much, he'd throw Sam under a dozen buses. It must be true what they say: every man has a price. For Abe, it was Ingram.

Washington tugged on his suit coat then picked up his briefcase. "You have no more legal right to pursue this case, Miss Knowles. I wish the best as you reshape your career. I understand you're taking an interest in estate management these days—very lucrative."

Sam met his gaze and spoke as she poked his chest. "You listen to me, Darnell. You might represent Lucifer, but God is my Advocate."

He brushed her hand aside as if dismissing the Almighty Himself. "I warn you, Miss Knowles, if you so much as follow this case, I'm prepared to tell the world how your father died and how those unfortunate childhood experiences have narrowed your objectivity. Furthermore, I'll see to it you're declared psychologically unfit to practice law—at all."

In her heart, she shouted to the rooftops, *you have no right to those records. They are sealed*. But she herself had invaded the privacy of many, including Harlan Styles. Although not permissible in court, she knew at age fifteen, he'd been involved in a gang that murdered a police officer, that he had not fired the shot, but was part of the altercation that led to the cop's death, that the charges had been reduced to probation by a gutless prosecutor.

Stunned to silence, she glared at Washington. Courage, minute but present, rose anew. She would not, could not play Abe's game. "Goodbye, Darnell. I *will* see you in court."

Washington offered a handshake, but she refused.

Instead, he waved a farewell with his briefcase.

"Goodbye, Miss Knowles. I do hope you'll use discretion. I would hate to interfere with Miss Sadie's hobby." She followed Washington's swagger, until the door slammed on Sam's career.

Zack came to her side. "How did you find the restraint not to haul off and smack him one? I wish you would've let me do it for you."

"Last thing Sadie needs right now is a brawl. Washington will shut her down for sure."

"Is Sadie in trouble?"

"No. He's after me, not Sadie, and he's emptied his quiver to get me off this case. Now do you understand why I have to go back to Manhattan?"

Zack resisted trailing Washington to give him a taste of his own blood. Sam was right—a brawl was the last thing Sadie needed right now—the last thing Sam needed, too. He wanted to hold her, protect her, to love her. She stood so close to him he could smell the raspberry shampoo that Tracey had given her, yet, she might as well be a mile away. Why wouldn't she let him in? Too strong…too independent…

"I'm warning you, son. Independent women will vex you into tomorrow," Dad once said after he and Mom had an argument. In all likelihood, a relationship with Sam would lead to more pain. Yet, if she were the least bit encouraging, he'd say, "Bring it on." Here was a girl in need of a lifeline, inside a woman who refused to take it.

He inched closer to a trembling Sam. For the first time she returned his gaze with a flicker of promise. In that instant, he saw a small house surrounded by beds of spring flowers. A carrot-topped toddler sat between him and Sam while they took turns reading fairytales.

Sam's eyes welled with tears. Unexpectedly, she squeezed Zack's hand and leaned into him.

"Come with me," he said and led her to the rear exit, down an ivy-bordered path. When he stopped, she rested against the stone wall, her eyes hungry. He kissed her, and she returned his want with a certainty Zack could not misconstrue. As he released his hold, he kept one arm against the wall and made his pitch. "Stay in Haven, or nearby, at least. You'll find something to do here. I'll help you look."

She ducked underneath his arm, already pulling away. "I have to go. I have to see that Styles gets what's coming to him."

"Then what just happened between us?"

"I don't know. I like you Zack."

He smiled. "Something more than like in that kiss, Sam."

"Let's say for argument sake, I *am* attracted to you. I can't afford that complication right now."

"Is that what I am to you? A complication?"

Footsteps neared. Sadie approached wearing a knowing, broad smile. "You two gonna stay out here all night, or have some supper?"

Zack would have preferred to stay outside, but she answered for them. "We'll be right in."

At least for now, she let him hold her hand until they entered the lounge. "We need to talk about this," he whispered.

"There's nothing to talk about. I'm going home."

He wanted more than a fleeting kiss from a distracted female. He wanted an *us*. If she wouldn't stay here, why couldn't he go there? He was riding the town's outer rim as it was. "You know what they say about Mohammed and the mountain?"

"No, Zack. There is no mountain to come to. It was a kiss. That's all."

She turned and headed for the stairs.

They'll vex you into tomorrow.

Sam fell to the bed, and sighed, starving, but too proud to go back downstairs and face Zack again.

What was wrong with her? She'd kissed two men today, and neither kiss should have happened. Maybe she should stay in Haven and date Zack. If the romance worked out, she could give up her career and be a homemaker, an honorable profession. She could learn to cook and clean, take golf lessons and join the ladies Thursday night league. Zack meant a quiet, simple life on the hillsides of paradise.

When she locked glances with him, the desire billowed, like echoes from a childhood fantasy, a prince charming who would take her safely from the beast's lair to an ivory castle. No more pain. Prince Zack saw her naked soul and loved her, anyway.

What if Zack turned out to be like Daddy? What if her prince was really a crocodile? Or what if he abandoned her like Johnny Miller did after graduation? She had to douse this spark now before it consumed her. Zack would find someone else, someone better suited for him. Sam wasn't born to small town life. Her mission was to keep garbage like Harlan Styles from contaminating more innocents. If she stayed in Haven, she'd never get her job back.

If she could get through tomorrow, then Thursday, she and Lucille II would be tooling home.

25

The morning sun blasted into the room, owning the day. She checked the clock. Eight thirty. She shook her head in disbelief that she'd slept so soundly, especially given last night's trauma. She scurried out of bed, jumped in the shower, and threw on black slacks, a thin white sweater, and a black blazer, the second of the two outfits she'd bought yesterday. She whipped her purse from the armoire and opened the door to a beaming Leon about to knock.

"You OK, Sam? Never heard a peep out of you last night. Not even a whimper. Must be you didn't have a nightmare."

She felt rested and strong and confident. "Nope. Fell asleep and next thing I knew, it was morning."

"Your guests are here. Justine and your boss."

And Abe was about to get an earful.

"Thanks. I was on my way down."

"Sadie's serving them breakfast."

If it wouldn't make Sam look like a psycho, she'd ask Sadie to give Abe *the special treatment*.

As she took the steps to the lounge she prayed for wisdom, for patience, for an ounce of comprehension—her true desire, though? To heap coals on Abe's head. Did God answer prayers with warped motives? Probably not.

Justine bulldozed toward Sam with outstretched arms. One might think they hadn't seen each other in five years instead of five days. Five days. That's all it had been? How can a life get so messed up in five days?

Abe waved and stayed seated as Sadie plopped two plates of scrambled eggs onto their table. "Yours is coming right up, Sam."

"Don't bother—"

"Now, you didn't eat any supper. No use arguing."

Sam shrugged helpless shoulders and winked at Justine. "See what I'm up against?" She led Justine to where Abe sat, and gave him a frosty greeting, surprised at her ability to grace him with even that much. "Hello, Abe."

"Now you folks dig in," Sadie said when no one touched their eggs. "If you don't, I'm apt to stand right here and spoon feed the three of you."

"She means it, too." Sam pulled up a chair and sat at their table while Justine and Abe eyed Sadie with suspicion and picked up their forks.

"*Phsaw,*" Sadie said, and zipped into the kitchen.

Sam studied Abe for any truth to Washington's allegations. If so, Abe camouflaged his intentions, as congenial as always. Waiting wouldn't make her feel any less angry. Sam plunged into the topic. "Darnell Washington paid me another visit, yesterday."

Abe dropped his fork and took a sip of water, still too placid. "No end to that man's crassness. And what did he say?"

"That I've been fired. Is he right?"

Abe set the glass down and leaned back in his chair. "I don't think this is the time or place to discuss—"

Sam laughed, her hysteria reverberating in the

near empty lounge. "Nothing stays secret in this place, and Justine is family. Go ahead. Give it to me straight."

Justine hurled an accusatory glare at Abe. "How could you take me for a four hour ride and not say a word about this to me?"

Readying for a verbal duel, Sam let her mind roll off from her tongue. "I don't believe *you* could do this to me, Abe. How could you wimp out like that, reduce a life sentence to house arrest and get me canned in the process."

"You're not fired, Sam. Not exactly."

"What does that mean?"

Abe averted Sam's glare. "I never meant for you to get hurt. I swear. The plan was to get you temporarily out of the picture so I could override your case and set Styles up to deliver the goods."

"I figured that much out."

"We've been negotiating with Washington for months, even before the trial, trying to get Harlan to roll."

"I figured that out too, but why…" Sam slammed the table. "I see it, now. You used me, you and the DA. You knew I wouldn't rest until I won a murder conviction. You pretended to be supportive when all the while you were making deals with Washington. Once the life sentence became fact, you pushed Styles into a vice."

Abe's stare, cold. "I told you, Sam. Sometimes you have to dance with the devil."

"So you've said, but I never thought that meant betraying a friend. I trusted you."

"It was a rotten thing to do to you. I admit it. Believe me when I say I had second thoughts. When Washington delivered that affidavit to us, he forced our hand with a lawsuit we couldn't win. Not to mention ruin any chance we had of getting Ingram. If we'd known about your history, there's no way I'd have assigned you the Styles case. You should have told me a long time ago. You don't belong in Special Victims, Sam."

She growled. "You think I'm a whack job, too!"

"I wouldn't go that far...I don't think you're crazy, but—"

"But you think I asked for the case to get back at my dead father."

"I don't know, Sam...yeah...subconsciously, maybe. Look, I care what happens to you. Granted, I took advantage of your zeal for my benefit—"

She stood. "You snake."

Other patrons...no she couldn't call them that...company...turned and stared.

Abe set his napkin on the table. "Sit down, Sam, you're making a scene. I'm sorry I tricked you. But you have to believe me—if I thought for one second your career would be damaged in any way, I'd have never gone the route I did. I'll leave you gals to look at the church and go over the reception details with Sadie, and I'll wander around town. When you're done, I'll take Justine home. You won't have to talk to me at all." He stood to leave.

Justine's tears spilled. She grabbed them both by the shirt sleeves. "Sit down, both of you."

They sat, and Justine turned toward Abe first, but by the steam in Justine's eyes, Sam knew her sermon was on deck.

"You'll do no such thing, Abe. I'm not too happy with you right now, maybe even furious with you, but I still want you to give me away, and I want you to see the church with Sam and me." Abe sat back down, and Justine turned to Sam, her eyes pleading. "You have to find it in your heart to call a truce. Please. For my sake? You'll be able to forgive him…" Justine glared back at Abe. "Eventually."

Abe shook his head. "I can see I'm in for a long car ride back to the city."

Reaching across the table, Justine grabbed Sam's hand. "I don't like the way things turned out any more than you do. You've known Abe for a long time. You know he connives, likes to juggle the knives, but I believe him when he says he never meant for you to get hurt."

Sam leaned back in her seat. She had to calm, had to muster civility toward Abe or ruin Justine's wedding. That didn't mean she had to forgive him. "Abe, you're the one who taught me justice shouldn't come with a price tag. What about Kiley? Who spoke for her?"

He raised his napkin like a pointy finger. "See? This is what I'm talking about. You're obsessed. It clouds your judgment. I also taught you that sometimes you've got to put the little fish back in the pond in order to get the big fish."

"You think the death of a two-year-old is a little fish?"

Abe leaned forward. "You had a solid case, but it unraveled. It happens sometimes. So, you make the best of the bad situation. In this case, Ingram's the big fish."

"But Styles killed Kiley, even if it *was* an accident…"

Justine's eyes bugged. "Do you hear yourself, Sam? I agree you're obsessed. I see it, Abe sees it. Why can't you see it? Obsession can't bring true justice. Think of it, Sam...*Ingram*. Think of how many Kileys will be better off if Abe busts this ring."

She withered, too exhausted from anger to argue any longer. She'd have to surmount this hurdle somehow, find a way to move forward, in spite of Abe's delusion that his actions were justifiable. The damage was done...irreversible. She was out of a job. *God, help me.*

Abe searched her face. "If it helps any, Sam, you're not fired, you're suspended. You can thank me later."

"I don't know if I can ever forgive you, Abe, not in the sense I'll ever agree you did the right thing. But, for Justine's sake, we'll put this matter on hold—make a truce at least. "

Abe cracked a smile.

"It might be a setback to my career, more like an amputation, but I'm sure there's some temporary job I can find in the city...work for a non-profit, maybe."

"Sam..."

There was more—much more—more than Abe wanted to share. "Spit it out, Abe." She looked at her watch. "We don't want Justine to be late for her appointment with Reverend Gottlieb."

"You can't go back to Manhattan. Not yet."

Sam glanced around the lounge. Empty, except for them. "Out with it."

"The only way we got Washington to back down on the civil suit was assurance you'd be taken off the case. The DA knows how doggedly determined you are. He wanted to fire you, even move towards disbarment on ethical misconduct, withholding information critical to prosecutorial proceedings. I used every argument I could, trying to convince him not to go to that extreme. He wouldn't budge. Then I made the suggestion for you to take an extended leave of absence…away from the city…until the dust settled. He said if you agreed, he would conditionally suspend you."

"Why not transfer me?"

"Would you have agreed to stay away from the case?"

"Probably not, but the DA can't dictate where I live."

"No, he can't. You have every right to live where you choose. But convincing the DA you'd be miles away from the case, professionally and geographically, was the only way I could keep your job."

Banishment went out with middle ages. The whole unfairness irked, riled, steamed her to buck like an unbroken stallion. "If I agree to this, how long am I banished, excuse me, *suspended* for?"

"As long as it takes to get Ingram behind bars."

"That could be years, not months, Abe. How do you expect me to agree to something like that? Manhattan is my home." She leaned back against the chair, unable to breathe, the emotional punch in the stomach worse than any beating Daddy ever gave her. She was Humpty Dumpty, broken by a great fall, and all the king's men had given up on her. Somehow, she'd piece herself back together and climb right back on that wall. Justice demanded it. "How can they take my home away from me, Abe?"

"It's not like that. Keep your apartment, Sam. I'll get you reinstated, soon, I promise. You're a great prosecutor. Once the DA's calmed down a bit, and can be assured you'll not interfere with the Ingram proceedings, including Harlan Styles, I'm sure he'll want you back on the team."

"But not in Special Victims."

"I doubt it."

"What will you do, Sam?" Justine asked, through heavy sobs. She'd often preached that a smidgeon of faith could move a mountain. Sam had a whole range to face. To keep her job meant leaving everything familiar behind for God only knew how long. If she agreed to assuage the DA's wrath, she'd be caught in a paradox: in order to keep the job she had craved since the first day of law school, she had to give it up, indefinitely, a vagabond existence with no immediate end in sight. Could she trust Abe to negotiate lifting her suspension as he promised?

Lean not on your own understanding, my child. Delight in Me, and I will give you peace.

"God and I will figure something out."

Sadie peeked through the door again, and Sam waved her in. "For now, we'll finish our breakfast, and go see the church, then come back here and talk to Sadie as planned. I might be temporarily unemployed, but life goes on. Worst case scenario, I'll stay in Haven a little longer."

Abe met Sam's stare. "You're not letting go. Are you?"

"I'm still a lawyer, aren't I?"

"You're too calm—"

"Nonsense. No use crying over something I can't control." Sadie placed a plate of eggs and toast in front of her. "You do owe me a huge favor, though."

"What?"

"I'll call you with a list of things I'll need as soon as I figure out where I'm going to hang my hat for the next few months. Since you got me into this mess and I can't go to where my things are, I'll expect you to bring my things to me."

"Fair enough."

"You do what you have to do, Abe, and so will I."

26

Sam hadn't set foot in a church in three years. What had happened to that hallelujah girl who waved her hands in praises during the worship choruses? Of all her sins, forgetting God's love for her had to be at the top of the list. *Lord, I've missed you. If I stay, I promise to go to church, maybe here.*

Sam snatched a couple of brochures off a table by the entrance. Tom Bordeaux had given her a crash course on this particular church's history, but remembering it all would be a trick. In all probability, though, Justine had done enough research to write her own pamphlet. Sam returned the brochures to the table, then joined Justine, who stood by the baptismal font. Abe wasted no time in investigating the alcoves and corners, giving Sam her space, the tension between them still too raw to carry on any conversation.

"The original church was founded by Emmanuel Gladstone after The Revolutionary War." Sam oozed with pride for remembering a fact or two from Tom's mini-course.

"I feel as if I'm walking through the portals of time," Justine said.

"During tourist season, Reverend Gottlieb conducts special Sunday services as reenactments of colonial times. He wears the clerical garb of the day, and the congregation uses replicated psalm books. Sadie thought you might like to theme your wedding after a colonial model."

"Robert will love that! I'm so glad you thought of this place."

While Sam and Justine talked, Abe sidled up. Sam cringed to be so close and not whack him once or twice. Her rage hadn't come close to simmering.

"The architecture looks like a Peter Harrison design," he said, staring at the etched ceilings and columns.

Sam grimaced, as much venom as she could display in a holy place. "All right, show off, I'll bite. Who's Peter Harrison?"

"He was the first professional architect in the colonies."

Justine snapped a few dozen pictures of the interior. "To send to Robert," she said. "I read on the Internet that the church was an army hospital during The War of 1812. Probably because of the Great War Path, the intricate waterways—"

"Between the Hudson River and Lake Champlain." Sam beamed.

"Sam…I'm impressed," Justine said.

"Aaron Golden and Tom Bordeaux are good teachers."

Justine squealed. "No way! Tom Bordeaux, as in Professor Bordeaux? You should have mentioned him sooner. You know what a fan I am. I've read every one of his books."

"He's Zack's father. His wife, Lillian is the librarian. If there's time, I'll take you by the library. He's substituting today so won't be there until about three o'clock."

Justine turned to Abe. "Do you mind leaving a little later than planned?"

Abe stared at Sam. He probably wanted to keep his distance as much as Sam did. "I suppose."

Sam shrugged off the tension for the moment, letting herself enjoy the walk through living history. She rubbed one of the white box pews that lined the wall near the front. The balcony intrigued her, too, similar to the Old North Church in Boston. Tom said that colonial architecture focused on practicality, not art, yet, Christ Church of Haven was surprisingly ornate.

Justine sat in the foremost box pew. "I read somewhere that in colonial churches prominent families owned these boxes and the common people filled the smaller pews in the rear."

A tallish, older man, perhaps late fifties or early sixties, approached, his clerical collar a giveaway. "Hello. Right on time." The man offered a handshake. "I'm Reverend Gustov Gottlieb, Pastor Gus for short. Although when I'm in colonial costume, I go by Vicar Gottlieb."

Sam smiled. "Thank you for seeing us on short notice."

"Normally, our secretary interviews applicants for our wedding packages. We've already filled the available slots for this year, but Sadie is a dear acquaintance. I agreed to consider your request as a favor to her."

"I'm—"

"No need for an introduction, Miss Knowles. You're a celebrity of sorts. We don't have many moose killers among us."

Let it slide, Sam. "I don't suppose you do. This is Justine Rivers, the bride. And this gawking man is Abe Hilderman, my bo…err…Justine's boss." Her eyes moistened. Of all the losses heaped on her in the last five days, this rift with Abe was the most bitter.

Justine turned her attention to Pastor Gus. "My fiancé is Captain Robert Ferrari." She waited for the usual giggle, and Pastor Gus supplied it on cue. "We hoped to be married the first weekend in June when Robert comes home on leave. We had made arrangements at my home church in Manhattan, but the reception plans fell apart."

"Sadie filled me in on your unfortunate circumstances, Miss Rivers. I fully understand why you don't want to wait another year with your young man going off to war again."

"This church is perfect. Both Robert and I love history."

Pastor Gus took out a calendar from his inside coat pocket. "Our wedding packages normally start in late June. Since your date is earlier, I think we can make an exception and pray it isn't too cold. Of course, we have heat, but we run the furnace sparingly…to preserve the original fixtures. I'll have to add an extra fee if the weather doesn't cooperate."

"That's fine. Will you be able to officiate as Vicar Gottlieb?"

"I'd be honored. If you follow me I'll give you the spiel."

Pastor Gus led the trio through the sanctuary, adding a few more tidbits to Tom Bordeaux's crash course. While Pastor Gus played tour guide, Abe fell behind, headed toward the entrance, then disappeared, presumably to explore on his own. "Even though Emmanuel Gladstone donated the money to build the church, he and his family never sat in preferential seating, but used one of the common pews instead.

After church, Emmanuel usually invited a local family of low means to his home for Sunday dinner. Legend says that Emmanuel paid for the advanced education of twelve local children besides his own, although I can find only one reference to this in the volumes at the House of History—a journal entry by one of his beneficiaries. Apparently, Emmanuel kept his generosity low-key. I did find a bank transaction to match the sum mentioned in the boy's journal. Seems, though, subsequent generations were much more vocal about their philanthropy. Emmanuel's grandson, Henry, was the first Gladstone to occupy the Gladstone box during worship services."

Sam had to know. "Did all the Gladstones attend here?"

"Most were church goers. Some, I'm afraid, more for the political advantages than the call to worship."

"What about Jonathan Gladstone?"

"He used to attend regularly, first with his mother, then with his wife. He stopped coming after his wife died, but he still sends sizeable contributions for our renovations."

Justine asked more questions, interspersed with her accounts of what a wonderful man her Robert was. She rambled on about her home church ministries and that she'd be sure to let her friends know about Haven, and particularly Christ Church.

Sam's attention zoomed in and out, although she caught Justine's question about decorations. "I live four hours away. Are there any bridal consultants in Haven?"

"Sadie Golden is the best caterer around here," Pastor Gus said. "She'll handle everything from decorations to flowers and even your wedding cake.

You won't have to worry about anything except showing up for your wedding."

While Justine talked with Pastor Gus about her esteemed guest list, Sam took a turn in the box pew, imagining each Gladstone ancestor from Emmanuel to Jonathan, parading with their families, Angelica holding on to Jonathan's arm and wearing the gown in her portrait.

Justine's elbow brought Sam back to the present. "Where's Abe?"

"I think I saw him go downstairs."

Justine laughed and faced Pastor Gus. "We promise not to leave without him."

They took the steps, and Pastor Gus continued the tour. "The downstairs has been renovated into Sunday School classrooms. In the early years, the basement would have been a storm cellar. During the days of slavery, because of the water routes, Haven served as part of the Underground Railroad, particularly Christ Church."

A thump then a muffled, "Get me out of here."

Pastor Gus shook an amused head and removed a nearby section of floor. Abe crawled out, a spider hanging from his head. Justine flicked it off. "I don't believe you actually hid in there."

Pastor Gus pointed to the grave-like opening in the floor. "These cells were used to hide the slaves. The last person I pulled out of there was an eight-year-old boy. Normally adults don't see if they fit in these tiny places."

Abe brushed off the moist, clay dirt from his dress slacks and oxford shirt. "Sorry. I saw an odd alignment in the floor. Curiosity got ahead of my better judgment. I wanted to know if a person could hide themselves, or if someone had to do it for them. When I slid the flooring back in place it stuck. I can't imagine people being cramped in one of these cells for hours on end."

Pastor Gus rocked on his heels. "Some slaves actually suffocated while they waited. If you're interested, Tom Bordeaux has written two books on the influence of African-Americans on Washington County."

Justine glowed. "Yes, I've read them. Fascinating." She slapped Abe's shoulder. "No more hiding. Please." She turned to Pastor Gus. "Thanks, again. I'm sold on the church. You can ink in the date."

Pastor Gus stretched his brows as he took out his calendar and put the date in. "If you'll excuse, me, I really should make a visit at the hospital. I look forward to your wedding, Miss Rivers."

The three went back to the lounge. On the way, Justine spurted ideas she planned to discuss with Sadie.

Sam smiled at the thought, the sheer inanity lifted her spirits: Justine and Sadie—together they would be lethal—death by ambiance. "Why don't you throw a masquerade ball for the reception?"

Sam had meant it as a jibe, not a real suggestion, but Justine screamed with excitement. "That's a marvelous idea."

"I *was* kidding, but if that's what you want, I'm sure Sadie can make it happen."

The lounge was empty, with the exception of the shuffleboard and bridge players. Sadie rushed up and ushered them all to a table. "I'll be right back." Before they could sit, she returned carrying an album, flipping to pictures of flower arrangements and cakes. "These are a few of the parties I helped plan. Might give you some ideas. Now mind you, I don't run a restaurant, and I don't have a consulting business. I don't give you a bill, not even for the food. You'll pay the vendors directly. The vendors and I work out an informal deal amongst ourselves. One hand washes the other I always say. I give them business. They send business to my store."

Justine surveyed the lounge once again, her eyes popping with enthusiasm. "I love this place. But how do I pay *you*?"

Sadie sloughed off the question with a wave of her open hand. "If you want to reimburse me, well, that's between friends. Right, Sam?"

Abe and Justine hopefully would stretch their imaginations and give Sadie the benefit of the doubt. As for Sam, she was no longer a public servant.

27

Sam stifled the yawn begging to escape. For three hours, Justine pored over pictures and scenarios and Abe wandered the lounge, counting the lanterns, reading the scripture verses on the crossbeams, and talking with Aaron. Sam, on the other hand, felt drained, wanting a nap in the worse way, resentful of the constant tiredness since her accident, glad when Justine announced the end to deliberations. "Looks like we're all set, Sadie."

Sadie closed her notebook and engulfed Justine with as much tenderness as she would Tracey. "Don't worry about a thing, dear. You leave everything to Sadie."

The door burst open like the SWAT team on a raid. Jonathan entered and all eyes except the shuffleboard and bridge players turned in his direction.

Justine's jaw dropped.

If his baggy eyes were any indication, he hadn't slept all night. He came up to Sam, ignoring Justine and Abe, rudeness as natural to him as his talent. "Sam, I've decided to fight, and stay at Dawn's Hope. Will you represent me?"

To think she had kissed him, the rudest man in the world. "Jonathan, these are my friends, Justine Rivers and Abe Hilderman. They're here to make arrangements for Justine's wedding."

Jonathan raked his hair. Something in his

mannerism endeared, in spite of his forwardness, pulling Sam in when she wanted out. He offered Abe a handshake and bent his head in an aristocratic bow to Justine. For Sam, Jonathan's brusqueness was as brisk as a cold fall day, but Justine ogled him like a Madame Tussaud wax exhibit.

"My apologies. I shouldn't have barged in like this." Jonathan said.

You're right. Then why am I glad to see you?

Scanning his height, Justine gulped. "No need for apologies, Mr. Gladstone. If you want to talk to Sam privately, Abe and I will check out Sadie's store."

Sadie took Justine by the hand and motioned for Abe to follow. "I'm going over now. Did you need anything, Jonathan?"

"No."

Abe rose reluctantly and followed the women, his face furrowed, probably not overjoyed to spend another hour in girl-land while Justine gushed over every one of Sadie's displays, especially the landscapes. Served him right.

Jonathan cast his gaze to the floor. "Sam, can we step outside a moment?"

Stay inside. You shouldn't be alone with any man right now. "Sure."

She took two steps with every one of Jonathan's and still fell behind his pace. He stopped on the other side of Sadie's enterprises, sufficiently out of earshot of any lounge guests.

Sam leaned against the wall, partially for support and partially to distance herself from coconut eyes, a hyacinth-scented coat, and pine-scented cologne, the scents ordinarily incompatible, but on this mountain man, tantalizing. "What do you want from me,

Jonathan?"

"I want to contest my father's will. Can we, after so many years?"

"There are always contingencies, especially if it was an informal probate."

"How's that?"

"How the will was registered."

"I don't recall ever signing off, or agreeing to the terms in any formal situation."

Like Sadie who couldn't take the caterer out of the woman, Sam energized with a legal challenge. "We might have a case, then."

"I want the land for my own. Name your price. I'll even throw in free rent at the cabin."

Sam bristled to her full height and glared. "Look, Mr. Gladstone. For your information, I don't need a job, and what makes you think I need housing?"

"Zack called me this morning and told me about your predicament."

Sam seethed. "For your information, I'm merely taking an extended leave. There is no predicament. If I remain in Haven, which I have not made a decision about one way, or the other, I already have a room. I won't take this case based on your outlandish belief I'm in need of charity."

Jonathan's windblown lips slanted upward. "I'm not offering charity. I'm impressed by your diligence with the Styles case. I want that kind of determination on my side. And as for the cabin, I thought you'd enjoy the view."

Sam shifted her posture to a practiced legal stance. "We can file a petition, but I must warn you, the process might be a lengthy one."

"But winnable, right?"

"I can't make any promises, but I believe so. I *am* curious, though. Yesterday you were ready to give the estate away to the town of Haven. What changed your mind?"

His lips moved into a full smile. "Your tirade, for one. People generally tell wealthy people what they think that person wants to hear. Except for you and Zack, I rarely get an honest opinion. That's why I like you—you speak your mind."

Far from it. Especially now.

"I don't think I was that persuasive. What else happened?"

"You are good, Miss Knowles." He hesitated. "After you left, I couldn't shake free of what you said. You are rather blunt."

So she'd been told.

"I suppose that directness makes you good at what you do."

"Maybe not. I'm unemployed. Go on."

"I couldn't sleep last night and paced the house. For some reason, I ended up in my father's study. Not a place I frequented. Father summoned me to his study only three times. Once when he told me Grandmother died. The second time was after Mother died. He told me he'd be spending time away from Dawn's Hope and that he'd hired a nanny to take care of me. The last time was when he told me he'd changed his will, making my son the heir to Dawn's Hope."

Jonathan looked away, as if fighting a memory. "Out of curiosity, I tried to open his file cabinet, maybe find some kind of clue as to why my Father hated me so much. But, the drawer was stuck. I managed to pry it open and found Father's journals. One of the journals had been tipped up, causing the jam."

Jonathan reached inside his coat and handed Sam a yellowed letter, tucked inside a gold embossed envelope. "When I opened the journal to read it, this fell out."

Sam studied the envelope addressed to Estelle Gordon. "There's no stamp on it. I don't think this letter was ever mailed."

Sam examined the handwriting, hasty and scrawling, possibly written during a time of emotional stress. "Your father's last wife was named Estelle. Is this the same woman?"

"Yes, but this letter was written years before Father and Estelle married, before my mother died. If you check the date at the top, you'll see that when Father wrote this letter, Estelle was married to Senator Gordon and lived in New York City."

The more Sam learned about Richard Gladstone, the more reasons she found to hate a man she'd never met. "Were they having an affair?"

"Estelle is a good woman. I don't think they ever had an affair, although they were close friends since childhood. My grandparents were frequent visitors to her parents' estate in Greece. Go ahead, Read it."

She slipped the letter from its entombment.

Dearest Estelle,

I thought you should know that my father passed away last week. I am left with an odd feeling I cannot explain. I find myself as indifferent to my father in death as he was to me in life.

I'm reminded of what you said the day you refused my offer of marriage. You called me a heartless man, just like my father. You were right to say so. Never has emotion been so absent in me as when I watched my father take his last breath.

Yet, through this week of formality, my heart aches for Jonathan. Will history repeat itself when my time comes? Will my son be as unmoved in my death as I was at my father's? I am, however, comforted in this, that at the last my father and I shared one mutual love—Dawn's Hope.

What saddens me most is that Jonathan and I lack even that bond. Jonathan, I fear, is not cast from the Gladstone mold. He takes after his mother in his love of the arts. I doubt he will ever grasp the magnitude of his heritage, though I've all but beaten it into him. I must conclude that he will never love the land he is to inherit.

I find myself offering up a desperate plea to the Almighty for favors I do not deserve. If Dawn's Hope is to be preserved, it will be by God's grace alone. Sadly, my biggest failure in this life is that I produced no appreciative heir.

You have been much on my mind of late, and I am filled with regret. I cannot say which pains me more. Knowing I will never gain a son's affection or having suffocated your love for me. Should our paths cross again, I pray I'll be a better man than when you last saw me.

I remain forever,

Your Ricky

Sam folded the letter and returned it to its crypt. "Of course, your stepmother's claim may be another factor to consider if we contest."

"She doesn't want Dawn's Hope. She moved out two weeks after Father died. But, I do think she would testify on our behalf."

"This letter might prove helpful."

Jonathan turned and gazed toward his mountain. "I know childhood memories are usually blurred, but honestly Sam, I don't remember Grandfather at all. He died when I was ten. I remember Grandmother, probably because she lived with us, although I didn't like her very much. At every dinner, she scolded me to sit up straight and to remember I was a Gladstone. Odd, I remember her so well, but not my grandfather. The only thing I know about Oswald Gladstone is that he was an ambassador, primarily to Greece."

Sam followed Jonathan's gaze. Dawn's Hope no longer loomed as a mystery, like Rochester's gothic mansion, but a home barren of love. "Geesh, Jonathan. What a horrible way to grow up."

Jonathan veered his gaze and met hers. "I have known love, Sam. Mother…Angelica. But, I never thought Father cared for me much…until I read that letter. Father pushed Gladstone duty on me like a daily vitamin, and I resented him for it. After Mother died, I think resentment turned to hatred. If only he could have told me his true feelings…"

Sam's throat tightened, Jonathan's childhood was as marred as hers had been. "Believe me Jonathan, regrets are poison. Your life was what it was…you can't change the past, but you can go forward. And that's what we'll do by contesting the will."

"I think all these years I tried to hate Dawn's Hope because Father loved it. If I hadn't married Angelica, I would have left Haven and never returned."

"And now?"

"Father loved the legacy, the power, the prestige it gave him, but not the land. I realize now, the ghosts that haunt me are not Angelica, or Mother. They come from within. I *am* bound to Dawn's Hope—my heritage is not in power or prestige, but as Emmanuel's seed. I am bound to his vision, not his empire. Does any of that make sense?"

"On some level, I think it does." Her gaze shifted from Jonathan's adolescent eyes, confused, frightened eyes, to his lips—dry, caked, and so appealing.

And what about Zack? What was wrong with her? How could she be so equally attracted to two men at the same time—men as different from one another as day and night?

Her thoughts raced. She pretended to re-read the letter while Jonathan impatiently tapped his feet. She wanted to accept the case, the cabin called to her, the frosting on Jonathan's tempting cake. Haven had given her new friends, but Dawn's Hope offered serenity. She couldn't ignore the risks. Could she maintain her professionalism in close proximity to the most alluring puzzle of a man she'd ever known?

She resealed the letter and handed it back to Jonathan. "I will represent you. I'm not so sure the cabin is a good idea, although, the offer intrigues me. You like to paint there. Wouldn't I be in the way?"

"I've used the barn near Triune Point as a studio in the past. I can paint there while you have use of the cabin. I promise I won't knock on your door without an invitation."

Something in the reassurance disappointed.

The lake flashed before her eyes. The hyacinths blooms would fade, all too soon. Still…

"The cabin is unlocked."

"Small detail. I'll have one of the groundskeepers put a lock on both doors."

"It's rather isolated."

"You needn't worry about unwelcomed guests. I have security cameras all over the estate. There's an intercom and panic button in the cabin. As for your car, the road where you hit the moose is actually an access road to the cabin. Granted, it's a bit rough in places, but usable by car. And I'll loan you the Max II so you can roam the property at will, ride on the lake if you want."

He'd answered every objection except the one she couldn't voice. *What do I do if you try to kiss me again*?

Jonathan cracked another lopsided smile at her hesitancy. "Sam, are you afraid I'll take advantage of you?"

On some level, she wished he would.

"You needn't worry. I might wear jeans, flannel shirts, and sport a beard, but underneath beats the heart of a well-bred gentleman. And while you are a very attractive woman, I am no more interested in pursuing a relationship than you are."

Her cheeks warmed to think she'd fantasized his interest, their kiss nothing more than a heated moment. "Well, then. I guess I can't come up with any more objections." She extended her hand, and they pumped the air like two farmers swapping the back forty. "We've got a deal. You have a lawyer, and I have a client and a place to live. I'll write up a retainer agreement. Then I'll move in."

He leaned in; a whiff of hyacinths encircled him, a scented halo, strangely arousing her senses. "When?"

She traced his lips with her imagination, remembering their kiss. "Tomorrow."

28

Justine rushed at Sam the second she came into Sadie's store. "Whoa. You didn't tell me how cute he was!"

"Cute?"

"A mountain man with talent. Rich, too. Don't let that one get away."

"Are you kidding? The man's carrying around too much emotional baggage."

Justine huffed. "Like you're not?"

True enough. Sam had her own truckload to deal with—all the more reason not to get involved with Jonathan, although he did dangle sensuality like Aaron sank a lure. Only, Jonathan had no desire to reel Sam in—baited with no hope of being caught.

Not Zack. Zack wouldn't toy with her emotions. He embodied purity and kindness—and easy to look at, too. Where Jonathan both repulsed and magnetized her, Zack held her admiration, a much better proposition in Sam's book of *The Ten Most Desirable Traits in a Man,* and the clincher—Zack wanted her.

"I'm interested in someone else, Justine. Since I'm going to be stuck in Haven for awhile, maybe I'll pursue a relationship with him. He seems to like me at least as much as I like him. Jonathan Gladstone is a client, nothing more. Oh, and my landlord. I'm moving into his cabin tomorrow."

Abe frowned. "You know better than to mix your

practice and personal life. This can't end well."

The days of feasting on Abe Hilderman's legal genius were over. Who was he to give Sam advice? Traitor. "I wouldn't have to if someone I know hadn't fed me to the wolves."

Abe shrugged and previewed a set of *Little House on the Prairie* books. "My niece loves these."

"Abe, while I appreciate your concern, there is nothing personal between Jonathan and me. The cabin is part of my fees—his idea, not mine. Besides, the arrangement is temporary. You did promise me, you'd get me reinstated, didn't you?"

Abe peered at her over his glasses. "Sam, I know what I promised, and I intend to keep that promise. But, there are alternatives to returning to Center Street. Maybe all this trouble will give you a chance to explore those options. Maybe start over somewhere else...like Haven. You seem happy here."

Dead moose eyes haunted her. "I'm a city girl, Abe."

Justine pushed Abe aside. "Enough, you two. I want to hear more about Sam's intended love interest. Lots more. Let's pay for our stuff and go someplace where we can chat."

Abe waved them on ahead. "Give me your selections, Justine. You and Sam go on, and I'll meet you outside."

Sam picked up three legal pads and a leather binder then shoved them at Abe. "While you're at it, you can pay for these, too."

She huffed her way outside with Justine close behind. "When do we meet Zack?"

"I could call and ask him to stop at the library with his father. In the meantime, we can take a walk around town."

"Sounds like a plan." Justine glanced toward the row of parked cars. "We brought up those things you asked for, including your spare laptop and Satellite Internet card. I know you, Sam, and I know you're up to something. You're too calm. The Sam I know would have told Abe to get out of her sight, my wedding or not."

Sam puffed her cheeks in denial. "I don't know what you mean."

"You're not going to let go, are you?"

"How do you know that I'm not taking Abe's advice to heart—starting over?"

"Like I said, I know you. Let the case go, Sam. Lie the helm."

"Excuse me?"

"Heave to and ride out the storm."

Sam chewed her lip. "I can't, Justine."

"Fine. I'll feed the info to you…but if I lose my job—"

"I don't want you to get in trouble…but I could use an insider."

Abe rejoined them with their purchases. "Justine, you owe me ten dollars and thirty-two cents. Sam, consider yours a gift."

Sam laughed in spite of her grim mood. She was still angry enough to hang Abe in effigy and not feel the least remorse, but Abe was Abe, a man defined by his desires, not much different than Harlan's girlfriend. Brenda Smith's loyalties depended upon whose wallet was the heaviest. Abe's allegiance bent according to his definition of justice. Perhaps every son and daughter of Adam drummed their existence according to what defined them. If so, to what beat did Sam Knowles dance?

Sam walked Justine and Abe to the parking lot to retrieve her belongings. "You two go ahead and explore Main Street, and I'll catch up after I dump these things in my room."

Abe dropped his double chin to his chest and looked up. "Remember, Sam. Let the case go."

Sam turned and gave Abe a shrug.

Abe shook his head. If he knew her as Sam thought he did, he knew distance would never stop her from stalking the Styles case, and this time he could not look the other way, widening the wedge between them, perhaps so deep it could never be healed.

A whisper in her soul argued against interfering, a warning Sam chose to ignore. She set her computer on her bed, plugged in her wireless connection, booted up her accounts then transferred more assets to the Haven bank.

"Desperate times called for desperate measures," Great Aunt Susie often quipped. If these desperate times meant Sam had to deplete all her resources, then so be it. No better way to spend Daddy's money. She closed her laptop, slid it under her bed and traipsed down the steps and out the door.

Zack came in at the same second Sam started out. He pulled her into him to avoid a collision, holding her a few seconds more than necessary, searching her eyes, and this time she initiated a kiss. "Well, Mr. Bordeaux. We have to stop meeting like this. People will talk." She played her eyes, hoping he'd read her intent. Zack pulled her closer and kissed her. She put everything she had into her return kiss.

By the look in Zack's eyes, he got her message. "Tonight? Maybe a movie?"

"Yeah. Sure."

"Do you need help moving tomorrow?"

"You know already?"

"Jonathan called me."

These two men had their own grapevine, faster than any ten women Sam knew. "Thanks for the offer. Maybe. Right now, come with me to the library. Justine wants to meet you, that is, if I can pry her away from your father."

29

Harlan eased himself into Reg's lumpy recliner, the entire apartment not even as big as Brenda's closet. "Thanks for letting me bunk with you, Reg. Made it quicker to get out if I didn't have to wait for the social worker to find me a place. I knew I could count on you."

"What's a brother for, Harlan? Still can't get over how quick you got this deal. It took my friend Earl six months to negotiate house arrest."

"I've wondered about that myself. Washington and Hilderman had a few confabs even before I went to prison. I finally figured it out. I was set up, Reg…by Jay."

"Why?"

Harlan squeezed his head. He should have seen it coming, should have guessed. He would have if Brenda hadn't distracted him. Then again, this whole mess had been Brenda's fault. He'd crossed Jay because of her. He took Brenda to bed with both eyes opened, knowing this day would come, the only mystery…how it would unfold.

"Circle of life, Reg."

"I don't get what you mean, Harlan. Course, you're the one that got yourself that fancy education."

"Let me connect the dots for you. I crossed Jay when I got tangled up with Brenda. Now why on earth would Jay send me his highest paid attorney, pretend like all was forgiven? Who does Jay want to see out of the picture more than me?"

"Ingram."

"Who does Hilderman want to see out of the picture more than Jay?"

"Ingram."

"Bingo."

Reg whistled. "You mean you ratted on Ingram? What'd you do a thing like that for, Harlan? If you knew the score, why did you fall into Jay's trap?"

Harlan took a long drag on his cigarette. "Only way I could get out. I'm dead no matter what, even if I zippered shut. Ingram won't take the chance now that a deal's been offered. Jay knew that, too. But before I leave this earth, I've got me a score to settle." He leaned back, the weight of the ankle bracelet, a reminder of all he'd lost, Brenda, his money, his cars, his life—all because of Knowles. At least if he ran, Ingram would have a harder time finding him, buy a few extra days of breathing. Time enough.

Harlan bit his lip, afraid to ask but he had to know. "Where is she, Reg? Brenda, I mean."

"I told you, I don't know."

Harlan shot out of his chair and put Reg in a strangle hold until he gurgled, close to his last breath. "Tell me, Reg, or I swear I'll finish you off right now."

Reg squeaked out an OK, and Harlan let go. "Geez, Harlan. Take it easy. I hear she's living with Ingram."

"Ingram?" So, Jay would get rid of all his headaches at once.

"She ain't worth it, Harlan. Look what that broad's done to you. She's the one you should kill, not Knowles."

Harlan sat back and buried his head in his hands. "Brenda's who she is. This time the viper bit herself."

"You always talk riddles, Harlan." Reg sat on his urine soaked couch, the stench alone enough to suffocate a man.

"Where's the revolver, Reg?"

"In my gym bag. Washington said he got you some privileges, shopping, doctor's office—didn't know you had a heart condition—Bally's and church. Church, Harlan? Since when did you get religion?"

"Shut up, Reg."

"See, Harlan? House arrest ain't so bad. Why you want to mess it up?"

"I had to sing a whole movie scroll to get those privileges."

"Figured something like that. Hilderman's no dummy."

"Washington managed to convince Hilderman that I wanted to make things right, make up for Kiley's accident. Hilderman wants that promotion so bad he'd take a rain check on the Rapture to get Ingram. Don't know if he bought my sudden conversion or not. I had to go to a bunch of Bible meetings to look convincing."

"Don't seem right, Harlan, you taking the rap for Brenda like you did and her goin' off with those hoodlums. You treated her right and look what she done—you with your life tickin' away and her sipping champagne by Ingram's indoor pool."

Let her sip while she had breath. Who would Ingram slice first? Brenda? Harlan closed his eyes again, imagined Brenda in her bikini stretched out in the blood-stained water, the scent of blood mingled with her expensive perfume. The ankle bracelet pinched, idiot monitors got it too tight. Didn't matter, he wouldn't be alive more than another few days. If he had to die, so would Knowles. A life for a life.

Reg wrung his hands. "You mean to do it, then. Kill Knowles? You're insane. If you stayed put, a year can go by pretty fast."

Harlan leaned back and closed his eyes. "I have to. My kind of justice."

"You won't get very far before the cops find you. You'll go back to the slammer. Ain't killin' an ADA like killing a cop? Ingram won't be the only one after you, then."

"Don't matter, Reg. I told you, I'm a dead man no matter what."

"You don't know that for sure. I thought Hilderman promised protection."

Harlan pushed out a laugh and lit another cigarette. "Do you think that's going to bother Ingram? If I can figure out a way past those goons outside, don't you think Ingram will, too? You don't get it, Reg. I spilled it *all*. Jay, too. Question is, who's going to find me first?"

Reg squeaked, like he had when they were kids and he was scared. "You *are* dead, man. Say…what if Ingram or Jay comes looking for you tonight? If you wanna get yourself killed, there ain't nothin' I can do about it, but why you getting' me in the middle of it? Want to get me killed, too?"

Harlan blew out three rings, and took another drag. Reg's reasoning capacity was as cramped as his apartment. "Don't worry. Neither one of us will be here, tonight."

"What's the plan, Harlan?"

"We're going to the gym and you're getting your bag out of your locker, then I'm having a heart attack.

You're calling an ambulance and notifying my case manager that I'm being taken to the hospital. Only, the ambulance won't get out of the gym parking lot. Make sure you slip me the revolver and the keys to your jalopy."

"And the goons?"

"That girl at the counter, Roxanne, she owes me a few favors. She'll keep them occupied."

Reg smiled. "Clever. Might even work, though these newfangled devices are pretty hard to fool. They'll be after you soon enough."

"I only need a head start. You got those directions?"

Reg threw him a scrawled map. "Managed to find as many cow paths as I could."

"And do me one more favor."

"Sure, anything, bro."

"Make sure they play the bagpipes at my funeral. I'm partial to bagpipes—*Danny Boy*—not *Amazing Grace*. No grace where I'm headed."

Reg's smile disappeared, replaced by concern. "Don't like it when you talk that way, Harlan. You should have something to eat before we go to Bally's."

"Absolutely...Mexican?"

"Got all kinds of stuff...but...oh, I get it...indigestion, heh?"

Harlan put out his cigarette, lit another one, and sucked in a long drag. Reg busied himself in the kitchen, making extra spicy tacos. Reg couldn't get more than one down, and Harlan forced himself to eat six.

Complicated plan, but it had to work. He deserved this one slice of satisfaction before he died. He'd make Knowles sweat it out an hour or so, treat her like the animal she thought he was, satisfy himself with her, then like a sick dog, put her out of her misery.

He'd never taken a life before, not on purpose—that cop fiasco wasn't his fault—he didn't pull the trigger, though he gave Damien the gun. Hell's gate swung open ready to welcome Harlan Styles. Might as well rack up a few extra points for the devil to congratulate him on.

The added spice on his tacos did the trick. His stomach soured like never before. He tucked his pack of Camels into his shirt pocket. "You know, Reg, they say the Adirondacks are real pretty this time of year."

30

Zack let go of Sam's hand while she said goodbye to her friends and imagined how the night might go, still reeling at Sam's sudden passion toward him.

Justine ducked into the car, extending her thumb and pinky as she spoke. "Call me."

Sam smiled. "I'll email you after I move into the cabin tomorrow."

Abe adjusted the rearview mirror. "One last warning, Sam. Stay clear of the Styles case." He revved the engine as he shook his head. "Keep an eye on her, Zack."

Wrapping one arm around Sam's waist, Zack shook hands with Abe. "I'll do my best." As Abe's Cadillac pulled away, Justine gave a papal-like wave from the passenger side.

"Is that some sort of secret signal between you two?" Zack asked.

"That's her blessing. She likes you."

He leaned in, hoping for another kiss, but Sam tugged at his sleeve. "Come on. Let's eat. I thought I smelled spaghetti sauce cooking when we left. "

Oregano and onion aromas vied for dominance and guests dug into steaming plates of pasta lathered in Aunt Hilda's Ancestral Sauce—according to Aunt Sadie, a recipe handed down over past generations.

Zack and Sam sat by the fireplace, her gaze waltzing in rhythm with his hopes. His palms sweated.

Yesterday, he'd assumed the door had closed where Sam was concerned. Something changed her mind. Maybe he shouldn't dig too deep and accept his good fortune. "So…uh… what movie did you want to see later?"

"Is there a theater in town?"

"No. Generally I go into Albany or Glens Falls if I want to see a new movie. Most of the time, I settle for rental. "

Sam gazed away, a far off look, her mind seemingly in some distant place.

"There's the library, too…if you don't mind watching something as old as my grandmother."

Her face lit up like a kid on Christmas morning. She must have returned from wherever the momentary detour had taken her. "Happens I like old movies." Something not right…her changing her mind so fast, this euphoria, not natural for a person who'd lost as much as she had. A lot of people in Sam's situation struggled with denial. This was deeper…more like escapism.

"There's a thirty-two inch, state-of-the-art television in my mother's office she uses for conferences. We can bring it into the VIP lounge on the third floor or bring it into the large meeting room where there's a fireplace. Gas fired, though, but still pretty to look at. We can pick up soda and popcorn at the pharmacy on the way."

Her gaze didn't seem normal, either—too intense…too inviting. "I'd like that."

"So…um…what movie would you like to see? *Twelve Angry Men*?"

Sam closed her eyes and groaned.

"Sorry. I figured you'd like courtroom dramas."

Sam pushed half her spaghetti to one side. "My life is drama enough right now. I was thinking more along the lines of *The Wizard of Oz.* I feel a little like Dorothy Gale right now."

"What does that make me, the scarecrow, or the cowardly lion?"

"I'm thinking Tin Man. You're all heart, Zack."

Sadie brought in two long-stemmed goblets and sparkling grape juice. Zack answered Sam's puzzled look. "I asked her to bring us something sparkly…to commemorate our first date." He opened the bottle, filled the goblets, and raised his for a toast. "To your new life in Haven."

Sam managed to finish a quarter of her plate before surrendering. The spaghetti did taste other-worldly—better than any she had eaten in Manhattan, even Regaldi's, a five-star Italian restaurant—the kind of place that had so many eating utensils, royalty wouldn't know which fork was used for what.

Sadie wheeled up a dessert cart. "What'll it be? I got strawberry cheesecake, spumoni, lady fingers, or black forest cake."

"I'm sorry, Sadie. I couldn't force another bite if you put a gun to my head."

"You didn't eat a thing, Sam." By Sadie's standards, if you didn't go for seconds you hardly touched your plate, and a quarter-portion meant you were starving to death. "I probably ate more tonight than I've eaten all week. Delicious. Are you sure you don't want to open up a real restaurant? I'd back you."

Sadie's brows furrowed. "Now don't go tempting

me, Sam."

"What'll you have, Zack?"

He squeezed Sam's hand and sighed. "Not tonight, Aunt Sadie. Sam and I are taking in a movie, complete with popcorn and soda."

She bristled. "You're passing on my homemade delicacies for store-bought popcorn?"

She turned on her heels, wheeling the cart to the next table.

Apparently, for Sadie, an empty plate and two desserts was the only satisfactory proof of a satisfied customer. "Did we just hurt her feelings?"

"Maybe we can request black forest cake to go." Zack went over to Sadie's cart, kissed her on the cheek and returned with two wrapped pieces of cake. "Aunt Sadie's happy now."

She turned and waved at Sam.

They walked from the lounge toward the pharmacy, swinging hands like long-time lovers, exchanging tidbits about their favorite stars. After purchasing a package of movie popcorn and a six-pack of root beer, they continued on their way to the library while singing the theme to *The Wizard of Oz.* She mused at the spring in her step and the warm flush in her cheeks as they hip-hopped their way down their own yellow-brick road of waiting romance. Would it be as sweet as its anticipation?

Within minutes, Zack had the lounge resembling a private theater, complete with soft lighting and a warm glow from the fireplace. The hyacinths in the Gladstone mural over the mantel danced in rhythm to the crackling flames. Sam sat on the settee, sinking deep in its luxury, and Zack slipped in the disc then joined her, flipping up his foot rest. "There's one on your side, too. Now what movie theater would give you this much comfort and privacy?"

They exchanged laughter, trading trivia until the flying monkeys zoomed toward the unsuspecting Dorothy. "This part always gives me the willies," she said.

He put his right arm around her shoulders. "Don't worry. I won't let anything hurt you." No doubt, he could banish celluloid threats, but there was no heart big enough to deflect the knives thrown at her today. No home. No job. No purpose. No reason to keep on living.

The heat from the fire and the subdued lights made her drowsy. She yawned and rested her head on Zack's shoulder, and he brought her in tight against him. She wanted, needed to be cradled, to feel loved, secure, and Zack seemed more than willing to be her rock, her rest. His eyes said permanency, something she could count on. Could she put her life-long ambition aside, start fresh as Abe suggested?

Zack nudged her. "Hey, sleeping beauty, the movie's almost over."

"There's no place like home," Glenda said, and Sam rubbed the back of her neck, warm and knotted. Tomorrow's reality loomed too near. No matter how many times she clicked ruby red slippers, she could never return to Kansas. Even if by some miracle, Abe managed to get her reinstated, nothing would ever be as it was.

"I enjoyed the evening Zack, but it's time to call it a night. I'm exhausted."

His smile shredded with his sigh.

How patient could she expect him to be? She'd toyed with his affection, using him to fill her need, selfishly ignoring his.

"What can I do to help with the big move?"

"I have one smelly pilot case, a tote, an armful of hang up clothes, a purse, and a laptop. Hardly a monumental task."

"I hoped to see you. Let me do something."

Time to be the woman, Sam, and let Zack be the man. "I thought I'd go to Glens Falls in the morning and pick up a few supplies. I could use some muscle to move furniture around if you don't mind coming over after work tomorrow. Jonathan might be an artist, but his sense of interior design is the pits."

"Consider it a date."

"Some date, but I did have a good time tonight, Zack."

He kissed her. "It doesn't have to end."

No, it didn't. Nor did she truly want it to. She returned his kiss, then backed away. "Yes, it does."

He searched her eyes, probably looking for solid ground between them, and she couldn't even offer him a shoal. "Zack, I like being with you, but—"

"I sense an awfully big but coming."

"I'm still not sure what all of this means."

"All?"

"You and me."

"We don't have to have it figured out ahead of time, Sam. We can just let it unfold as we go along."

She kissed him lightly on the lips. He returned her kiss with far more passion than she could sort out at this late hour. "Let's take this slow."

He lifted her chin and stared into her eyes. "I think you know how I feel about you, Sam, but take all the time you need. I'm not going anywhere."

"Apparently, neither am I."

"I imagine at this point, you feel a little trapped in Oz, with no Glenda to help you get home. You're smart, Sam, and tough. You'll figure it out."

Would she? Right now her future was as uncertain as Dorothy's dark forest. Lions and tigers and bears threatened Sam at every turn. "Until I do, I don't want us to get someplace we can't get back from. Does that make any sense?"

"No. I think that's tired, talking. Don't analyze your feelings too much. Sometimes, you just have to trust them. Come on. I'll straighten up later. Let's get you to the Lighthouse. You look beat."

They strolled hand in hand underneath a playful moon and a cascade of smoky clouds. When they reached the Lighthouse, Zack kissed her on the forehead, and she felt his awkwardness, his uncertainty. If this thing between them, whatever it was, didn't work the way he hoped, what then? He stepped into her path like that moose, out of nowhere, lethally innocent.

"Good night, Zack." She rushed up the steps. There. They'd had a date. Did she want another?

Yes.

She booted her laptop to check for messages.

Two.

She clicked on the one from Justine: *How did the date go? Details.*

The second from HSenterprises. Sam's stomach rose to her throat as she read the message. *Leave your light on.*

Scare tactics.

Sam shook off the uneasiness and turned on the television, channel surfing for a comedy re-run or something mild to keep her mind off Styles. She chided herself for letting Styles's threats get to her, and surfed a little more, stopping when she heard the news bulletin: *Two ambulance drivers killed during a convicted felon's escape…"*

31

Sam trembled, the phone's *ring,* as ominous as Styles's email. Should she answer it? What if it were Styles? Ridiculous, the ring tone was merely an echo of her fear. She gathered her courage and picked it up on the fifth ring. Abe's shaky, rushed voice alarmed her even more, the last person she wanted to have a midnight chat with.

"Sam, sorry to call at this hour, but I thought you should know that Styles is on the lam."

Anger regurgitated with her half-digested popcorn and soda. "I saw the news alert, but isn't he *your* problem, now?"

"I deserve that. We have reason to believe he's heading toward Haven. Every cop in the area is looking for him. I called to see if you wanted protection."

"From what? He's all hot air. He's probably in Canada by now."

"His hot air got two ambulance drivers killed."

"I hope you're satisfied. Shortcuts never work, Abe, and you're the one who taught me that."

"Now's not the time for a debate over our philosophical differences."

Her body shook with rage. If Styles was after her, it was Abe's fault. He should have left that piece of crap in jail where he belonged. "I'll be fine. If it makes you happy, I'll look both ways before I cross the street.

Besides, if he's going after anyone, it'd be Brenda. I heard she ran out on him as soon as his cell door slammed."

Abe hesitated. "A plausible theory, Counselor, but we have Reginald Styles in custody, and he told us Harlan blamed you for Brenda leaving him."

The weak always blamed the strong for their troubles. "You're making too much of this, Abe. Brenda's going to camp where she can find the most *bling*. Styles might be trying to find her and convince her to skip the country with him."

"Sam, I know you're still mad at me," his voice mellow, weak, thin, as if he'd aged ten years since this afternoon, "but don't let your anger affect your judgment. I can have a cop at your door in fifteen minutes."

"You'll do no such thing. You've done enough to ruin my life. I won't be coddled. If I hid under the covers over every threat, I'd never get out of bed." She hung up, but the disconnect did little to satiate her rage.

She put on her night clothes then turned on every light. She sniffed the vase of fresh hyacinths. Underneath was a note from Sadie: *Jonathan brought these by after you left with Zack and said he'd see you tomorrow.*

Sam played a few games of solitaire on her computer then rechecked her email, one from Justine: *I need to know how many columns and pews there are in that church so I can figure out how many bows I'll need. I know Sadie could do the decorating, but Mother wants to at least decorate the church. Be a doll and find out for me?*

Like that's all Sam had to do with her time, count pews and columns. In truth, the diversion might be helpful, but Justine didn't need to know that. Sam hit reply: *I'll check it out tomorrow. BTW, I do have a life here, you know.*

She turned on the television, and settled for a marathon of *I Love Lucy*—Lucy stomping the grapes in her anger at the master stomper…Lucy punch-drunk on a vitamin elixir…Lucy, the redhead...

In the dream, Harlan Styles stood next to her bed, wielding a knife. Then Daddy joined Styles. "I'm in hell, and it's your fault."

She sat up with loud moans, drenched in sweat while tears streamed down her face, staring at Guinevere, who laughed from her spot on the wall. Wildflowers waved with the rippling curtains. Sam rose and closed the window, and the shadows behaved.

A knock and a worried inquiry. "Sam. Sam. Are you all right?"

She opened the door. Flannel striped pajamas, blended with an opened, blue terry-cloth robe and moccasins, glided toward her like Glenda in the bubble. Leon held a bouquet of fresh hyacinths. "Maybe these will help. Oh, I see you already have some. Zack dropped this bouquet off late last night after you had already gone to bed, so I promised to give these to you at breakfast. When I heard you crying, I got worried."

She buried her face in their scent, then stuffed them into the vase with Jonathan's. "Another bad dream."

"You seem to have a lot of them. You should talk

to Doc Hensen."

"No. It's just that I have a lot on my mind."

"It's six o'clock. Want to go down for an early breakfast?"

"But it's too cold to traipse around in Tracey's baby-doll pajamas."

Leon dashed to his room and came back with a brown terry robe. "It's not pretty, but it'll keep you warm. You're trembling."

"Thanks." She wrapped herself in Leon's offering, its hem encircling her ankles.

"I don't have an extra set of slippers, but you can't go around barefoot in this cold, either. Follow me." Leon led her to his room and fished out a pair of navy blue argyle socks.

"And they match!" Sam put on the socks and stretched her toes. "Thanks. Very comfortable."

They paraded downstairs, Leon's borrowed robe trailing behind, a king and a princess in terrycloth and argyle. The clamor of pots and pans echoed through the lounge. Sadie came in from the kitchen, wiping her hands on a polka-dotted apron. "Poor Sam. Couldn't sleep, again? Coffee?"

Leon and Sam both nodded. Sadie disappeared into the kitchen and returned with three mugs and an urn. "Just finished brewing. Muffins are still in the oven. If you're hungry, I can make some toast."

Leon shook his head. "Coffee's fine. I'd rather you sit a spell with us. I worry about you, Sadie. You do too much."

She waved an objection. "Keeps me out of mischief, don't you know. Besides, Aaron's already gone fishing. Doc picked him up about an hour ago." Sadie poured the coffee and handed Sam and Leon their mugs. "So, Sam, today's a big day for you. Is that why you couldn't sleep?"

"Could be."

Sadie winked. "And Zack Bordeaux, too?"

Sam blushed.

"Nicest boy in Washington County, if you want my opinion, even if he is a relative by marriage."

Sadie passed Leon the milk and sugar then she rested her elbows on the table and took a sip before tilting her head to one side, peering at Sam. "I think it's great you're representing Jonathan Gladstone and that he's staying in Haven. Can't find answers to your problems by running away from them. Right, Leon?"

He took a sip and waved his cup in the air. "Got that right, Sadie."

Sam ignored the indictment. "Jonathan has the guesthouse stocked, but mostly for the fishermen. I plan to go to Glens Falls this morning and purchase a few things to hold me over until I can figure out what to do next."

Sadie put her mug on the table, her gaze motherly. "Should you be running around on your own with that Styles's feller on the loose? Maybe you should wait until school is out. Zack would be happy to take you."

"Thanks for your concern, but I don't think Styles is after me. If he's out to get anybody, it'd be his former girlfriend."

Sadie took another sip and clicked like Justine when she was about to rip a sermon. "I hear a bit of anger in your voice, dear. If you don't mind my saying so, sometimes when things go other than the way we planned, we get mad at everybody in the world except where most of the blame sets…right inside ourselves."

Not like Sadie to point a finger.

"I suppose it's more my fault than anyone else's. If I'd been in Manhattan, hadn't handed the case over, maybe those ambulance drivers would still be alive."

"I can't read your boss's mind, but I'm sure he did what he thought best for everybody. I know you don't agree with his actions, but putting yourself at risk to get even don't make no sense. It's not a sign of weakness to accept a little help now and again."

Nor was it like Sadie to preach. Yet, Sadie's counsel, laced with love, was easier to digest than Justine's condemnations.

Sam stood. "Thanks for the advice, but please don't worry. I'm sure they'll catch Styles before the sun rises. I think I'll go up to my room and pack up what belongings I have. When I get back from shopping, I need to stop at the church. Justine wants to know how many columns and pews there are. Do you know, Sadie?"

She squeezed one eye shut as if calculating. "Well now, I never counted them before."

Sam started toward the steps. "Are you coming up now, Leon?"

"Think I'll stay here a mite and finish this good coffee. You can keep the robe, if you want. Don't need it, and it gets mighty cold in that cabin, so Aaron says."

"Thanks. I'll do that."

"You sure you want to be there all by yourself?"

"I'll be fine, Leon, don't worry."

"Who's going to rescue you from your nightmares?"

Yes, who? "My father died when I was twelve—my mother a few months after my father. I went to live with a great aunt who slept away most of her days. She died during my freshman year at Columbia. I'm used to being on my own."

Leon squished his eyebrows together, forming one straight line across his brow. "If you say so, but you seem to shake a whole, big bunch after one of those nightmares. No wonder you sleep with a light on."

"Leon, I'm not afraid of anything. Least of all the dark." She lied. "I slept with a light on when I was a kid. Guess the habit carried through into adulthood."

Leon arched an eyebrow. "I suppose that's one explanation."

Sam was not about to give him the other one. "Sadie, I'd like to settle up my accounts before I leave this morning. How much do I owe you?"

"Can't say off the top of my head. I'll have to send you a bill since I haven't figured it out, yet."

Sam took the steps heavily, her sadness deepening with each stair. She turned on the television, flipping from one news channel to another and booted her laptop, surfing through news feeds and reading anything she could about Styles. She opened her email and noticed she'd overlooked one from Justine sent last night before her errand request.

As we were leaving Haven, a van followed us. Abe managed to double back and got the license plate number. It's registered to Montel Atkins, a private detective on Darnell Washington's payroll. Abe's trying to figure out what business Montel has in Haven. In the meantime, please be careful.

32

Sam switched on the air conditioner as she pulled out of the discount store's parking lot, the noon-day air thick with moisture, like the day Daddy died. She glanced at her watch, she'd be cutting it close, but she could still stop at the church and be on time for her date with Aaron, then on to the cabin and start settling in while she waited for Zack.

She pushed aside her worries about Harlan Styles, entertaining the idea of her temporary life in Haven and looking forward to the tranquility she'd find at Dawn's Hope. Would she finally find that peace that passes understanding—a peace other Christians claimed, but that eluded her? Maybe Sam Knowles didn't deserve peace. In one of Justine's mini-sermons, she'd said, "If you want to float down God's peaceful river, you have to drop your oars and let God do the rowing."

Sam tightened her grip on the steering wheel. Easy enough for Justine to say; her life was the stuff of magazines—beauty, brains, boyfriends and bounce. Why wouldn't she feel peace when everything in her life turned out to be as perfect as a Jonathan Gladstone landscape? At this moment, right or wrong, Sam's hands were glued to the oars and she couldn't drop them unless God performed an amputation.

She pulled up in front of Christ Church and rushed up the steps, hopeful Pastor Gus would be in his study so she wouldn't have the onerous task of counting every pew and every column. She picked up a brochure on her way in. There should be something in there about the layout and structure. However, the subdued natural light made the church too dark for her to read the black print against the blue background. She couldn't find the light switches, or maybe they didn't use artificial light in keeping with colonial times. If she could find him, Pastor Gus would probably know how many columns and pews there were. She knocked on the office door, but no answer. Should she wait or start counting? She moved to the front. *One—two—*

Heavy steps—quick, decisive steps like Harlan Styles made when he entered the courtroom—came towards her from the curtained area behind the pulpit. Sam retreated to the entrance and ran downstairs, the footsteps following her picking up their pace. She kicked up the loose board in the basement, crawled into the box grave, and slipped the heavy covering in place, listening to the approaching clods, first over her head, then on either side of the cell. A thud, like heavy doors closing, then quiet. *Elvis has left the building…now, how do I get out?*

Something crawled over her pant leg. She pushed, but the covering wouldn't budge, leaving her sealed in a spider-infested casket. *Great.* "Is this what you've got in mind for me, Lord? Save me from a moose and a stalker only to bring me to eternity via suffocation?"

A prism of light sneaked through the cracks, followed by a group of footsteps and a husky voice. "Because of its proximity to Lake Champlain, this church was part of the famous Underground Railroad. We saved this hiding cell during our renovations to remind us of man's inhumanity to man, a stain on our American history—"

Sorry I doubted you, Lord. Sam pounded against her coffin lid. "Pastor Gus. Help! Get me out."

The covering lifted, and a surly-faced clergyman hauled Sam up. A young couple and presumably a set of confused parents stood bug-eyed in disbelief. "I can explain," Sam said.

"Don't tell me. You're as much a history buff as your friend's boss, trying it out for size."

"Not like that. I thought someone followed me, so I hid. I'm sorry if I've interrupted something with my foolish fears."

"These nice folks are here to look at the church for their wedding next year." Pastor Gus introduced the group. "I hope we didn't alarm you."

"These were different steps."

"No one else is in here except for us…although, I did see a stranger, a dark complexioned man, walking north on Main street as we came into the church. We get a lot of people who pop in out of curiosity…maybe that's what you heard, a passerby."

With heated cheeks, Sam dusted a spider web off her slacks. "Yes. Probably."

"Was there something I could help you with, Sam?"

"My friend Justine wanted to know how many columns and how many pews there were in the church."

Pastor Gus pointed at the brochure. "It's all in there."

Of course.

Outside, Sam drank the air for reassurance, but her spaghetti-legs still wobbled. There was a fine line between bravery and stupidity. After she settled into the cabin, she'd call Abe and take him up on his offer for security.

Sam tapped impatient feet while Aaron perused the trooper's statement. "Speed imprudent? How fast do you think you were going?"

Sam struck her practiced be-serious-in-front-of-Judge Normandy stance. "It was raining. I'm sure I slowed down. Besides, I was looking for a place to eat, not searching for game."

"I take it you're representing yourself?"

"I *am* an attorney." *At the moment, anyway.*

Aaron dropped his jaw and stroked his cheeks. "Trooper Mitchell does make a good case about the unwise speed given the sleet and subsequent dangerous conditions. The mangled remains and degree of damage done to the vehicle estimates your speed at fifty miles per hour."

"In a fifty-five-mile-per-hour speed zone."

Aaron smiled, and a chortle escaped. "Good point. But that speed may still have been too fast to maintain proper control of your vehicle given the road conditions."

"And what speed would have been prudent according to Trooper Mitchell?"

Aaron offered another smile, his court demeanor unlike Judge Normandy's. "Another point well taken, Counselor. Trooper Mitchell was simply doing her job, and I'm trying to do mine. Let's say we reduce the charge to a non-moving violation?"

She studied Aaron's determination—reduced

violation would be the best she could hope for. She could cry unfair until doomsday, the outcome wouldn't change. "I might have been distracted."

"Well, now that would be one explanation. Do you think you skidded because of a balding tire? When did you replace them last?"

Like, never. She used public transportation the majority of the time. "Very possible, Your Honor."

"Well then—two hundred and fifty-dollar fine, and we're done here."

Sam took out her temporary debit card and paid the fine, grinding her teeth with the unfairness of it all. "Don't expect me to say thank you."

Aaron signed the documents and handed her a receipt. "I hear you're moving into the cabin this afternoon."

"That's the plan."

"Do you think you should be out there, alone?"

Why did everyone assume Sam incapable of protecting herself?

"Pastor Gus called me about your scare at the church. You wear a brave face, but this isn't a game. Could be Styles isn't anywhere near here, but should you take the chance?"

"I'll be careful, but with Jonathan's security array, I'm as safe there as here. ADAs get threats all the time. I can't hide with every squeak." Now if she could only convince herself she'd be safe, maybe she could sleep. "Quiet and solitude is the best medicine for me, right now. You're not worried about the fishing, are you?"

Aaron laughed. "That's the least of my worries, Sam."

"The fishermen are still welcome. But they'll have to knock. I sometimes forget to put a robe on."

Sam started for the door and Aaron stood like an old world gentleman. "Still, living in Jonathan's cabin might be construed by an estate judge as a conflict of interest."

"I don't plan to make it a permanent residence."

"Consider yourself advised as a professional courtesy."

If she compiled all the professional courtesies she'd been afforded, she'd have a tome. Let the anthems ring. Sam Knowles beat her own drum.

"Jonathan told me that you were Richard Gladstone's attorney?"

"I was and I continue to manage the trust fund for the estate."

"What can you tell me about him?"

"Richard was…a complicated man."

As were all the other residents of Haven. "Can you tell me why Richard drew up the will the way he did? At least give me a hint."

"Can I speak off the record?" Aaron sighed.

"Of course. As far as I'm concerned, we're two friends sharing a bit of Haven history."

"Jonathan's disregard for Dawn's Hope pained Richard greatly. They drifted apart and that rift intensified after Jonathan's mother died. Richard thought if he could tie Jonathan to the land long enough, maybe he'd grow to appreciate his heritage."

Sam smiled. "Maybe that day has come."

33

Harlan flicked his cigarette butt to the ground, his ears tuned for any snap of a twig.

A car pulled up and Harlan ducked into the trees. He waited until the driver got out then walked a little closer to the edge of the road, careful to remain cloistered until he was sure it was Montel. "About time you showed up. I'm chewed up alive from these bugs."

"I can't stay here long, Harlan. Whitehall might be a small town, but the cops are everywhere. Might be looking for my van, too. I think Hilderman spotted me when he was in Haven yesterday. What did you do with Reg's car?"

"It's in the canal."

Montel paced and looked over his shoulder every two seconds, so nervous he'd make a dead mule buck. "Washington hopes I can talk you out of this. I don't know that I can."

Harlan sneered. "Not likely. I don't trust Washington, and frankly I don't trust you. Give me your keys."

"You're insane, but here." The keys whizzed past Harlan's head, landing on the ground five feet behind him. Harlan gripped the revolver in his pocket, but he needed Montel, needed more information. *Patience.* Harlan scooped up the keys, keeping one eye peeled on Montel.

He leaned against his truck, his head moving

every which way, but towards Harlan. "Why did you go and kill those ambulance drivers? Of all the stupid things you've ever done, killing those drivers tops the list."

"I didn't kill those men…exactly."

"Exactly?"

"The plan was to sneak the gym bag into the ambulance. Reg was going to ride in the bus with me, get the ambulance drivers to stop, short out this ankle bracelet, and run. For some reason, Reg pulled out the revolver while they were loading me. The one guy got mouthy, so Reg hit him on the head with the gun…too hard. The other guy fought to get the gun away from Reg and it went off. We high-tailed it out of there."

"Not how I heard it. I heard you hung Reg out to dry, left him to take the whole rap."

Harlan shrugged. "He killed those men. I didn't."

Montel lit a cigarette, shaking with every drag. "If you're telling me the truth, Washington might still be able to get you a deal with Hilderman. But you've got to forget this notion of revenge. It's suicide. You're not a killer, why go after her?"

"Didn't your Mama ever take you to church? Like it says in the Bible, an eye for an eye, a tooth for a tooth, a life for a life. I'm as good as dead because of her, no matter what I do. Where is she, Montel, still at that place they call the Lighthouse?"

"I followed her into Glens Falls. She loaded up her car with a bunch of stuff. Looks like she's moving somewhere. When she stopped at this church, I followed her in, but I think she heard me and hid. I quit after that. I can't see the sense in all this. They'll figure out I helped you and every cop will be gunning for me." Montel threw the cigarette butt to the ground and squished it. "You can't pay me enough to warrant that kind of risk. Take my van, but that's it. From here on out, you're on your own. You want to end up in the cemetery, be my guest. But I'm not about to join you there."

Montel swaggered toward the road, still looking to the right and to the left, but not behind him. Harlan pulled out the revolver, sweat pouring from his face. Could he do it? He slowly cocked the trigger then fired, the bullet striking Montel in the head.

Harlan leaned over Montel's body. *I killed a man…just like that…with a quick click of a revolver.* Harlan did an instant replay. *Bam. So easy.*

In his mind, he saw his gas-bag foster mother pointing a knotty finger at him, telling him how evil he was and that he'd let Satan possess him. Maybe she had it right all along…knew he was a killer at heart. She was right about one thing. Harlan Styles was going to hell.

Now he knew without a doubt he could kill Knowles when he found her. He wouldn't even think twice. He'd changed in that instant—no longer afraid. He felt…powerful. He kissed the revolver, the talisman that gave him authority over life and death. Exhilarating, like being reborn. Death would claim him soon enough; the how and when didn't matter as long as Knowles died first. Then let the Almighty curse him for all eternity.

34

Sam whooshed relief when she saw the landmark, the barn with the blue rooftop, where tarmac ended and the gravel road began. Sam slowed, keeping her eyes peeled in case the moose's relatives were lurking about. The entrance to the cabin should be about a quarter mile from here.

Jonathan said the driveway might be hard to spot from the road. No markers or even a mailbox. *Rats.* She should have set up a post office box today. So many things to think of.

"Aha. There it is." Hearing her own voice made her less nervous. She hit her signal light, realizing the stupidity…that no one would even see it on this private road. Lucille II ran smoothly over the crushed stone surface, surprisingly quiet. Sam calculated the distance from the road to the cabin—a quarter mile, a good ways in. Jonathan sat on an ATV loaded to the hilt with art supplies.

When she parked, he dismounted—his stare unreadable. "You're late. I've been waiting over an hour. Even artists have things to do, you know."

A joke? Hopefully. "I ran into construction on the way to Glens Falls and court took a little longer than expected."

"Need help unloading?"

"I thought you had things to do?"

Now he grinned. His bronze cheeks wrinkled with

the effort. "There's nothing on my agenda at the moment."

Sam glanced toward the mound of canvases. "You said you wouldn't paint in the cabin."

"And I won't." He pointed at another gravel drive. "That leads to the barn near Triune Point. I thought I'd paint in the loft."

Sam hauled out the suitcase she'd borrowed from Sadie and her laptop. "Suit yourself. But I should warn you, I know how to use a gun. I noticed the rifle when I was here before. So don't pull any funny stuff."

"Doesn't work."

"What doesn't?"

"The rifle. It's only a decoration. The trigger's busted."

"Well, I can still use a frying pan."

Jonathan smiled again. Twice within five minutes…maybe he could be pleasant company, after all. Sam handed him the suitcase, then pulled out the two bags of purchases. "There's a huge box of food in the trunk that Sadie packed. That's it."

She followed Jonathan to the door. He set down the suitcase and held out a keychain. "As I promised." He showcased each key. "This one's for the front padlock…this one's for the back."

"What about the ATV?"

"ATVs…plural. The Max II is good for both land and water, but you're going to want a smaller one for the trails. The keys are kept in the ignition."

He opened the front padlock, tossed her the keys and went inside ahead of her. "I restocked the cupboards and fridge to get you started. Milk, eggs, bread, sandwich meat, peanut butter, and jelly."

"Thanks Jonathan. You didn't have to go to all that

trouble. Sadie packed enough food for a month."

"Need help arranging anything?"

Why the gushing helpfulness? The Jonathan she met the other day could barely muster a civil word. "Zack's coming after school to help me set things up. I hope you don't mind if I girlify the place a little."

Jonathan's face returned to its taut familiarity. "Knock yourself out. When do you want to get to work on my petition?"

"Tomorrow soon enough?"

"I hoped we'd start on it today, but I guess I can wait."

"I'll meet you at the main house tomorrow at nine."

"Do you know how to get there from here with the ATV?"

By road, yes…trails via ATV? Sam shook her head.

"Let me drop off these supplies to the shed, then I'll show you. I can come back for you, or you can follow me, get a little better idea of the lay of the land. It's up to you."

"Well…I—"

"I'll meet you out back." He went out the door, mounted his ATV and spun around the cabin.

She supposed he meant she'd have to go outside, relock the front padlock then walk to the rear of the cabin since she couldn't open it from inside if it were padlocked. She couldn't imagine herself driving a four-wheeled motorcycle. What other challenges would rural life bring her? She longed for the familiar and secure. Harlan might as well take her life; because of him, she'd lost everything else that mattered. "God, I've lost everything."

I have come that you may have life, life more abundant.

"Then why is Styles free and I'm a prisoner? He murdered a child and two innocent men. He deserves to die. Not me."

Did your father deserve to die?

"Yes. He chose to drink. Are you saying I'm supposed to forgive both my father and Styles?" Sam whipped out her ATV keys. "You're asking too much, God. There's no comparison. Daddy's death was an accident. The judge said so."

Are you sure?

God was too big to fight. She'd argue her case another day. Jonathan had parked his ATV parallel to two others. "Which one should I take?"

He patted the smaller, but still monstrous ATV, which was bigger than Jonathan's. "Use the Max II for water travel. This baby will get you wherever else you want to go. Climb on."

Sam mounted and glanced at the buttons and metal. "You'll have to give me a crash course." She laughed. "Not literally, of course."

"Like driving a car."

"Easy for you to say." She snapped the helmet in place. "Now how do I start this thing? I was riding before and didn't pay any attention to what you were doing. Riding and driving are two different matters."

Jonathan leaned over and pushed the start button, his pine cologne demanded even more attention than cinnamon.

"What are the levers for?"

"Brakes. Like a ten-speed. Or you can use the one on the floorboard."

For the next five minutes, Jonathan pushed buttons and shifted gears and rambled on about drive-trains and amphibious ATVs and how they were different from trail blazers. He spouted trivia like a Jeopardy contestant, ending each bit of knowledge in the form of a question. "OK?"

"Yeah, sure." Sam engaged the ignition, applied the brake and slipped into reverse. She purred to herself as the engine revved, giddy with the power beneath her, something Lucille II could never give her. Between this ground ATV and the amphibian she could go anywhere on the estate she desired. She flicked the headlights on then off. Day or night. "Let's go."

35

Jonathan led the way towards Emmanuel's barn, glancing back every few minutes on Sam's progress. Amazingly, she'd taken to the ATV as if she'd ridden for years. A ten-point buck appeared at the edge of the stream paralleling the path to the lake. The deer lifted his head as if granting permission to enter his domain, not the least disturbed by motors. Few humans, except Jonathan, came this deep into Dawn's Hope territory. The buck reared in recognition.

Jonathan stopped at the barn's entrance, and Sam pulled up next to him, sitting straight and tall like a bronco rider. She took off her helmet, shaking her red tresses over her shoulders, then slid the helmet onto the handle bar. "Is this where it goes? That's what they do in the movies."

Jonathan put his on the back grid. "Fine, for now."

Sam's eyes widened as she took in the barn's enormous height and width, half as large as the mansion. "It's huge. I was expecting something like a closet."

"The colonists built small houses, but huge barns. Tom Bordeaux says that they wanted to make a statement. 'We're here to stay.' Follow me." He opened the front doors, revealing the expanse of stalls. "Grandmother kept prized race horses, but my father sold them after she passed away. Be careful, some of the beams and floorboards are loose."

After unloading his supplies, Jonathan directed Sam down a steep trail toward the lake. When they reached the bottom of the hill, he waited to see if she needed help before offering his hand. The woman was too independent for her own good. She used whatever branches she could find to keep herself upright and finally accepted his help at the last drop. He lifted her to level ground. Not a word of complaint.

At Emmanuel's inlet, Sam walked brazenly toward the boulders at the water's edge. "Triune Point. An interesting name."

He should warn her to be careful, that the ground could easily give way, and that the water was alarmingly deep, a dangerous place for someone who couldn't swim. Seemed, though, she scowled with every comment he made. Best to stay in tour guide mode. Lord Protector only brought the ire out of her. "Do you notice anything peculiar about the three boulders next to you?"

"They resemble a miniature Stonehenge."

"Now look into the water."

Sam gasped at her reflection. "It *is* like a mirror, exactly the way you paint it, so clear I can see the scar underneath my chin from when…" she trailed off.

"Most of the lake is pristine, but this is the purest spot."

Jonathan avoided the reflection pool, fearing what he might see. Memories flashed in spite of his resistance.

Sam gazed at the spot, transfixed, the silence actually awkward. He felt relieved when she finally spoke. "So, this is where Emmanuel struggled with the angel. You told me the story, but I suspect there's more."

"The king's relative Emmanuel saved might have been an illegitimate son, and that's why there is no written record of Emmanuel's heroism. Supposedly, Emmanuel slit the throat of an Iroquois warrior who was about to scalp the lad."

"War is hell, they say."

Sam's sarcasm, like a spicy gourmet dinner, soured his stomach. Yet, he hungered for the punishment. "A grateful king knighted Emmanuel, and the rest is history. The irony is that Emmanuel was the son of a merchant, not a very successful one at that, and, as family lore goes, Emmanuel was a bit of a drunkard, too. Some say he killed a man in a barroom brawl, then stowed away on a ship heading towards America."

Sam teetered slightly.

"We should start making our way back to the barn, now."

Sam followed Jonathan's lead.

"Then Emmanuel wasn't born a nobleman?"

"Hardly. Some of the crew wanted to throw him overboard, or hang him from the mainsail when they discovered him. Fortunately, the captain, a God-fearing man, spared Emmanuel's life and they became friends."

"Is that how Emmanuel became a Christian?"

"No. When Emmanuel arrived in the New World, the captain gave Emmanuel a letter of recommendation for a commission in the King's army at Ft. Ticonderoga. That much is documented. After The French and Indian War, Emmanuel left military service, built a barn and stocked it with goats and sheep, an inept shepherd according to his journals. One day a ram chased him to this inlet."

Sam laughed, and the sound of it filled a hollow. "You're joking, right?"

Jonathan held his right arm up. "So help me, Counselor. The ram took off, but Emmanuel saw a reflection that glowed like the morning sun. The clouds were thick overhead. Suddenly, he felt as if arms compressed him and threw him to the ground. He wrestled with whatever had captured him until the moon rose. Then he heard a voice slide over the water. 'How long will you spurn My love for you? As I saved you from the noose, I want to save your soul. If you will follow Me, I will increase you in this land.'"

Jonathan stopped. "Going up is tougher than going down. Why don't we rest a moment?"

"No argument from me." Sam leaned against a tree. "Did Emmanuel obey the Voice?"

"He struggled with the angel until sunrise, finally surrendering, and the angel departed. After that, he named the estate Dawn's Hope."

"Is that when he joined the colonists?"

She soaked up the story like a child, like he had, at Mother's knee. "According to family history, Emmanuel felt divided in his heart, loyal to the king, yet understanding of the colonists' position. Eventually, the crown pressed him into service. During the Battle of Saratoga, he jumped off his horse and ran into the woods. He wrote in his journal that he saw the angel again and followed it. 'I shed the last of King George's hold, my uniform.' He offered himself up to the renegade general, Benedict Arnold, who decided to put Emmanuel's military expertise to good use."

Sam smiled, so much like Mother's. Memories returned—walks with her along the perimeter and stories she passed on, embellished for a child's fantasy, perhaps. "After the Battle of Saratoga, Emmanuel returned to Dawn's Hope. He spread word that any British soldier who joined the colonist cause would be granted a tract of land to farm when the war ended."

Sam gazed at her reflection. "And that's how he founded Haven?"

Jonathan felt the disbelief in Sam's gaze. "A lot to swallow, I know. Some details are probably romanticized. More than likely, Emmanuel realized the colonists fought for land, for the right to be self-governing, unlike the British who had no ties to America. I think he sensed which way the wind would blow, and he wanted to be on the winning side. As for the angel? Who knows? The whole experience could have been a hallucination. I'd like to believe Emmanuel's account actually happened. Wouldn't we all like to see an angel? Something changed Emmanuel that night. And there is no medical explanation for his limp."

Sam tripped on a jutted rut, and he caught her in his arms, reluctant to let go once she regained her balance. Jonathan looked up at the thickening clouds. "We'd better make a quick run to the house to show you the trail, and then get you to the cabin before it rains. Zack might be worried if you're not there when he comes."

Sam's gaze met his, her intent confusing. "Yes. We should go. Or not."

36

Zack closed his office door, guzzled a bottle of water then rubbed his cheeks to revitalize his sagging energy. What a day. He had no idea politics could be so exhausting. The school board and the kids he could handle. But the parents…that was a whole different matter. He expected to be a negotiator with the school board, but never in his wildest dreams did he see himself as a complaint department. Maybe he'd misjudged Frank, expected more from him than regulations, parents, and social systems would let him do.

He thumbed through his stack of phone messages, lining them up like batters.

Most of them could be deferred to other departments, an overdue library book and a lunch tab that would make the local bar cringe. However, fifteen-year-old Jimmy Hodgekin's second fight this week could not be ignored. Zack had no choice but to report the kid this time. But what if Jimmy were thrown out of his new foster home, the third in two years? If the trend continued, the kid would graduate from foster care to a division of youth facility, or in another year be sent to an adult prison.

Zack lifted his eyes toward heaven. Why had God put him here if he could do nothing for the Jimmy Hodgekins of the world, except report his escalating criminal activity? Zack thought he wanted Frank's job, got it, and now that he had it, he couldn't wait for Frank to return. Hopefully, Frank would be on the mend soon and behind his desk before graduation

Zack put on his boulder cap, locked the door, and shuffled to the parking lot, exhausted and not looking forward to primping a cabin to a woman's specifications, an indecent thing to do to a fisherman's lair. But, this would be Sam's home for awhile, and he didn't blame her for wanting it to be a little more feminine. He'd rather move furniture around all night and be with Sam, than go home and take a nap and miss an opportunity to spend time with her.

Zack started his engine ,then turned it off, remembering Frank might be transferred to Albany medical center today. Zack walked back to his office and called Tracey. "I'm sorry, Zack," she said in near sobs. "Frank coded. He passed away an hour ago."

She'd almost let Jonathan kiss her again.

While Jonathan drove his ATV to the rear of the cabin, Sam parked hers in the front. She opened the padlock, stormed into the cabin and stomped with agitation. Why did she always go headlong into trouble against the good advice of so many? Staying at the cabin felt wrong from the start, yet whatever pulled her here was stronger than good sense.

She kicked the door with muted frustration. Why have padlocks on the doors but no interior bolt? Everything seemed upside down in this town. Sadie had bolts to her rooms, but no means to lock the doors while a person went out. Now she had a padlock, but no way to secure the cabin while she was in it. She'd set Jonathan straight…insist he provide her with better locks.

Sam went into the bedroom and changed out of her dusty clothes into the pair of jeans and sneakers she bought at the mall. She rarely wore them in Manhattan, but somehow life in the cabin called for a change of modus operandi. She came out of the bedroom, eyes to the floor. The soft swoosh startled her at first, then she laughed to see Jonathan sweeping.

He stopped and held the broom like brandishing a weapon. "Afraid of a little broom?"

"I'm tired. Sorry."

Jonathan resumed his housekeeping. "I thought maybe I could help until Zack gets here."

"I *can* sweep, you know."

He bulleted the broom back and forth, a juxtaposition of mountain manliness and homey homemaker, his fitted tee outlining every chest muscle. "I managed to wash the cabinets and clean out the refrigerator. You don't want to know what I found in there. If you need help with the work, my housekeeper's great."

"I do know how to keep house, Jonathan."

He shook his head. "Not what I was implying. I thought you might still be sore from your accident."

"I'm fine, but thanks for the offer. I thought I'd take another run to Glens Falls tomorrow. I started a list. A vacuum cleaner and mop are at the top."

Now he used the broom like a cane, leaning against it. "Why don't I make a pot of coffee?"

Jonathan should leave…why was he trying to find things to do? Not that she minded watching him work, but her mind couldn't handle the image right now. Way too confusing. "That's all right, I'm sure you've got things to do. I'll start putting these purchases away until Zack gets here."

Jonathan stared, his face taut with indecision. "OK. I'll be honest. Aaron said you shouldn't be left alone with Styles on the loose. He asked me to keep an eye on you. I said I would and that I'd have the groundskeeper post a vigil while you're asleep. I didn't want to tell you because I know how independent you are—"

"You know nothing about me, Jonathan. I prefer you go on about your business." Why did everyone in Haven think of her as a damsel in distress, like one of Sadie's Arthurian women? Even the surly Jonathan Gladstone felt a need to protect her. She preferred the insolent, rude Jonathan over this broom-wielding patsy who hovered over her like a bodyguard. She had thought about calling Abe. But if she asked Jonathan to use the phone now, she would look like a coward, fall right into his superiority.

He tossed her the broom. "Put it where you want." This Jonathan she recognized.

Sam closeted the broom in the cubby by the rear exit. "I'm sorry. It seems no one in this town believes I can take care of myself. Please, forgive my rudeness, and let me make the coffee."

"Do you know how?"

Urgh!

"There's a muffin with your name on it if you move that recliner." She lifted her head towards the fireplace. "Too cramped over there."

"I tried to arrange this for optimum viewing of the lake, but if—"

She scoured the cupboards for mugs that weren't chipped. Finding none, she opted for the least damaged ones, filled them to the rim, wrote *dishes* on her list, then, after setting Sadie's muffins on the counter, she handed a filled mug to Jonathan. Sam pointed towards the far opposite corner. "I'd like the chair over there."

Jonathan put down his coffee mug and with a half grunt, saluted, then inched the monstrosity across the room, sweat dripping from his biceps. He stood and stretched, his smile belying his protest. "I thought Zack agreed to help you move things around. That's all the slave work I'm doing, your highness."

Jonathan gulped the rest of his coffee, put on his flannel shirt, jacket and cap and grabbed a cinnamon bun. As he nibbled, he picked up her list. "A lot of stuff for someone who's determined not to stay here."

"For your information, Mr. Gladstone, this cabin could use a makeover."

Jonathan grabbed the pencil. "Well, in that case, I have ideas I'd like to add—"

"That's my list." She snatched it away.

Like a tug of war, they pulled at the paper, until Sam let go and squeezed Jonathan's side.

"Cut that out, I'm ticklish."

She didn't expect his giggle, and her gaze fell to his mouth. Before she could object, his lips found hers. Cinnamon melded with hyacinths, a dizzying, confusing mixture. Against what she desired, she pushed herself away, but Jonathan pulled her in again.

"Don't, Sam. We both knew this would happen, both wanted it to." He smothered her cheeks, lips, and neck with fevered lips and this time she surrendered fully to his passion, returning his kisses, her lips opening hungrily in search of his.

A thud erupted like a fist against the door, then

footsteps moving away from them.

Sam pushed Jonathan aside as Zack's fleeting form ran outside. "Jonathan, I have to go to him."

She called to Zack as he opened his car door. He stopped, but refused to turn around. "Don't try to explain. It's pretty evident you've changed your mind about us. I'm not surprised."

"I'm sorry. I never meant to…I don't know what happened in there with Jonathan—"

"You don't know? Looked pretty clear to me—"

"I mean…yeah, I'm attrac…but I didn't think I…well…what you saw…"

Zack opened his car door, still refusing to look at Sam, and slammed a fist on the hood. "You made no promise to me…I foolishly thought you…liked me a little—"

"I like you a lot. This with Jonathan…took me by surprise. I'm…sorry."

He turned toward her. "It's obvious you don't know what you want, Sam, and frankly, I don't want to be your pin cushion while you're trying to figure it out." He got into the car and slammed the door. Tires spit gravel as he sped toward the road.

Sam choked in the dust of his heated retreat.

Jonathan leaned against the counter, wallowing in self-loathing. Jonathan Gladstone lived by no rules but his own, yet, he'd broken some kind of code—unstated expectations between friends.

Sam returned, her eyes red and her cheeks wet. "I think you'd better go, Jonathan."

"I won't apologize for my attraction to you, Sam.

I'm only sorry Zack came in when he did."

"I need to think. I shouldn't have agreed to stay here. I can't kiss you and then represent you. I'm moving back to Aaron's tomorrow." Jonathan caressed a stray strand of tear-soaked hair stuck to her cheek. She shoved his hand away. "Jonathan, I can't."

He turned and left, letting the door slam on his way out. He pushed the ATV as fast it would go, gravel, twigs, and stray stones buffeting his legs, yet, not one jolt compensation enough for the wrong he had done, knowing he'd kiss Sam again if he had another opportunity, and that she'd let him, of that he was certain.

Were there two different Sam's, the one Zack thought he loved and the one Jonathan desired? Zack described a paper doll, vulnerable, in need of protection. Not this spitfire Jonathan had spent the afternoon with. She reveled in his stories about Emmanuel, placed herself inside the drama, and her joy had teased his ego.

A prayer found its way to heaven. "How do I make this right?"

37

Harlan Styles lit a cigarette and drew one long intensified puff, then pulled Montel's cap over his eyes. If he stayed parked here much longer, he'd draw attention to himself. He'd counted twenty people going in and out of the Lighthouse Lounge. No sign of Knowles, but maybe someone in there knew where he could find her.

They might recognize him, though—even country bumpkins watched television. Drops of rain hit the windshield, a misty, hesitant rain that matched his uncertainty. A fat man came out of the Lighthouse and tapped on his window. "Excuse, me. You can't park here." He pointed toward the lined patch of tarmac underneath the truck. "Fire code."

"What's it to you?"Harlan gripped the gear shift, but the man pounded harder on the window and took a peek at the license plate. Harlan let go of the gear shift and fondled Reg's revolver. The longer he hesitated, the longer he argued with this idiot, the longer before he'd find that self-righteous Knowles. But, killing a man on Main Street wouldn't serve his purpose. *Keep your eyes on the prize, Harlan.*

He used to be a patient man; falsifying prescriptions was a tedious job. He played patient with the cops, with Brenda's habit, with Dr. Jay and even Ingram. Survival depended on patience. Until he met Brenda, until her brat got into his drugs, until Knowles thought she had to do God's work, until he'd killed a man, Harlan Styles had the patience of Job.

He rolled down his window…trying to remember what patience felt like. "Sorry, mister, I'm still making up my mind if I should go in and grab a bite to eat. I hear the lady who runs the place is a good cook, though she seems to like to salt things up a bit."

"No food I've ever had was salty, best in the world as far as I'm concerned."

Harlan accepted the man's handshake.

"Name's Rusty Whalen."

The man looked like he expected a name in return. "Montel Atkins. Where can I park?"

Whalen pointed down the road. "There's a small lot down yonder. They don't start serving until five, but you can go on in and rest 'til then. Tell Sadie, Rusty sent you, and she'll fix you up proper. Only, she's not there. She and Aaron had some errands to do in Whitehall." The man sauntered off in the other direction, oblivious to how close he'd come to dying.

Harlan turned on the ignition and parked in the designated area. He needed a more thorough disguise. In the storage compartment between the seats, he found chewing gum, a pack of Marlboros and sunglasses. He put on the shades and stuffed the gum and cigarettes into his pocket then headed towards the Lighthouse.

So close now. He'd not be deprived. He could see her on her knees begging. He'd tell her if she gave herself to him, he'd spare her life, then when he'd had his taste of her, he'd put a bullet between her eyes. He should turn the gun on himself and rob Ingram of the pleasure, choose his own time and place.

The lounge smelled like Thanksgiving dinner. A

group of old codgers surrounded the shuffleboard, and a lanky man with a portable oxygen tank danced in circles when he pushed off another old goat's disc.

One of the shuffleboard players walked towards Harlan, the guy so frail a gust of wind would blow him into tomorrow. "Can I help you, sir?"

"I'm an ADA from Manhattan–looking for a friend of mine. I heard she was staying here."

"I stay here. I think there was a nice girl who had the room next to me. She's gone now."

"Samantha Knowles?"

"Mighta been her name. Lovely girl."

"Do you know where she is?"

"Not exactly."

"Look, mister—"

The old man stood back.

Patience. Harlan forced a smile.

"The name's Leon." The codger proffered a hand.

Harlan played polite, shaking it like a politician, though he'd like to choke the loony tunes right out the guy. "Nathaniel Shuster. I have a gift for Sam, a going-away present."

"Now that's right nice of you. Sorry, I didn't catch your name?"

This conversation was about as useful as a snot-filled tissue. "Nathaniel Shuster. I worked with Sam in the narcotics unit before she transferred to Special Victims."

Leon scratched his head. "You look familiar. Sure you haven't been here before?"

"No I haven't. I'm kinda in a hurry."

"Who did you say you were looking for?"

Harlan growled. Not even Job would last with this group. "Samantha Knowles."

"No. Don't know anyone by that name."

An ancient hag ambled up next to Leon and grabbed his hand. "Who's your friend?"

"Says his name is Shuster."

"That's right. Nathaniel Shuster."

"Says he works with the DA in Manhattan."

"Narcotics unit." Harlan flashed every one of his costly crowns. "I'm looking for Samantha Knowles, Miss—"

The old man put an arm around the wrinkled broad. "Her name's Mazie, but she doesn't remember, so no use asking her."

Two more shuffleboard players sauntered up. The one with the oxygen tank wheezed something that sounded like Sam had moved out. This bunch was about as clear as Brenda after a snort. Brain dead, the lot of them. "Can anyone tell me where she's moved to?"

A khaki clad fisherman came out from the restroom and joined the group. "Leon, anything wrong?"

The two huddled, but Harlan overheard Leon's whispers, about as mute as a television in a nursing home. "This fellow says he's looking for a gal used to live here. Do you know where she went to?"

"It's OK, Leon. He looks harmless enough."

So Leon wasn't crazy, he was playing a game. Harlan hated being played as much as he hated being poor. When he finished off Knowles, maybe he'd come back and do a mercy killing on this bunch.

Leon and the guy he called Doc came back. "Who did you say you were, again?"

"Shuster."

Leon nodded his head. "Right. Nathaniel Shuster.

Says he works with Sam. Or did, anyway."

The fisherman offered a handshake. "Name's Doc Hensen. I'm a friend of Aaron Golden's. I'm expecting him here shortly for a game of rook. Aaron and Sadie ran up to Whitehall for a quick errand. Turkey dinner with all the trimmings tonight, if you've a mind to stay. Sam moved into the cabin on the Gladstone estate. There's no direct line, you'll have to call the main house. Want the number?"

At last. Something useful. "That's all right. I'd like to surprise her. Would you mind writing down the directions?"

"Don't mind at all. Soon as I get a piece of paper—"

"I'm in a hurry, why don't you just tell me."

Doc pulled out a prescription pad from his shirt pocket. "Guess no harm in writing directions on this…you aren't going to forge my name on any scripts, now are you?" He laughed.

"No."

"Getting a bit blustery out there. Be careful on those gravel roads. There's been some moose sightings lately."

Harlan faked a laugh, a pretty good imitation, too. "I heard Sam met one face to face."

Doc scribbled down a paragraph of directions, and acted out every twist and turn in the road.

Patience. "I've got a GPS, I'll be fine."

"Cabin doesn't have an address. Only the house."

"Thanks. I'm sure I'll find it."

"Hope you do. Poor Sam could use some good news for a change."

38

Her stomach growled from hunger. How could she think of food? She'd pierced a kind heart and a vulnerable soul. Worse than that, she'd sabotaged a friendship—a strange one, to be sure—but, a friendship, nevertheless.

These men were as different as fresh popcorn and cinnamon buns, yet both irresistible. Emotions she thought she could do without now clawed at her—disparate emotions that had no business occupying the same psyche.

Jonathan's raw masculinity and ruggedness was certainly attractive, yet something else drew her to him…open wounds…as deep as hers. Foolishness. How could she wrap her broken spirit around his? She'd plunged into the water to save a drowning man when she couldn't even swim.

Zack was her grownup Johnny Miller: handsome, intelligent, athletic and willing to carry her books home after school, a sure prom date. Zack was simplicity, serenity, safety—Sir Galahad in an orange vest—while Jonathan, Fay Ray's King Kong.

She couldn't trust either attraction.

A streak of jagged light ripped the sky, an exclamation point to her summation.

A gust of wind blew the door open. Great. A flimsy door and a storm. She propped a chair against the knob then stood in front of the picture window. In the growing gray, budding trees danced in the wind, their long branches flailing—the twigs like accusing fingers, the clouds blocking the descending sun.

The wind banged against the cabin walls, rattling the windows. She rummaged the cupboards in search of a radio. Finding none, she clicked on her laptop, and a low-battery warning flashed on the screen. Probably enough juice to at least check her email, then she'd plug it in while she repacked everything.

The first email was from Justine: *Tried to call you but Sadie said you'd already left for the cabin. The police found Montel Atkins's body in the woods near Whitehall, and they suspect Harlan Styles. He's over the edge crazy. Be careful.*

Sam hit reply: *I'll explain later, but leaving the cabin tomorrow. Hope they find Styles soon so we can put an end to this nightmare.*

A second message from HSenterprises.

You've ruined my life. You'll pay. H.S.

The screen went black. As she reached to plug in her laptop, the lights flickered and died. She could use a protector or a mountain man, now, and a feeling of vulnerability seized her as never before. Neither Zack nor Jonathan would return any time soon, if ever—Jonathan would probably fire her, and Zack would never speak to her again. She paced the kitchen. The only available light filtered through the picture window.

"Think, Sam. You've got no one else to rely on but yourself."

You are not alone, My child. Trust Me.

She should. She wanted to. "I don't know how."

She'd get through the night and hope in dawn's clarity. Certainly, Aaron could help Jonathan find another lawyer. She'd learned a few things about impetuosity, and that it had its advantages as well as its pitfalls. Why not throw whatever she could in the car, drive through the storm, and see where she and Lucille II ended up, out west, maybe, the farther away from Haven and Manhattan the better.

To a city, though.

Rain, white with tiny hail, pounded against the window, like the night Daddy died. Flashes of that horrible evening came with every lightning burst.

Mama had been to court earlier that morning. When she came home, she told Sam the judge issued an Order of Protection—that meant Daddy had to move out. In the afternoon, she changed the locks. "We'll be safe from now on, Samantha," she'd said, and almost smiled.

A few hours later, the awful storm hit, toppling power and phone lines. Twelve-year old Sam shivered in the darkness. "I'm scared, Mama. What if Daddy comes home?"

Mama lit candles and gave one for Sam to take to her bedroom. "Daddy won't hurt us anymore. Now go to your room."

Sam obeyed but couldn't sleep.

Loud bangs.

"Open this door, woman. Now."

"Go away. Come back when you're sober," Mama yelled.

A loud crash…Mama screamed…Daddy cursed…claps of thunder and bangs from the kitchen. Sam covered her ears.

Lightning flashed…Mama screamed again…Sam jumped out of bed. Mama needed her.

Through flickering candlelight, Sam saw Mama on

the kitchen floor moaning, blood on the floor, Daddy standing over her. He turned and came towards Sam. "What's your problem, girl?"

She ran to her parents' bedroom and snatched the revolver from the nightstand. Heavy steps came nearer…grunts and foul-mouthed threats thundered through the storm. "You're dead, Samantha. I'm going to kill you, and then finish off your mother."

She trembled…trapped…alone in the dark. The bolt of lightning outlined Daddy's form in the doorway. "There you are. Did you say your prayers?"

The scent of hyacinths filled the room and gave her courage. She stood and aimed the revolver. "Don't, Daddy."

He laughed. "You don't have the guts."

She fired and missed. He took two steps…she aimed again. "Go away, Daddy. I won't miss this time."

He stopped. "You really do mean to kill me. Don't you?"

She squeezed the trigger. "Get out."

Daddy laughed and ran into the storm. A truck's horn blasted in harmony with the thunder clap.

Screeching breaks…a man's curdling yell…Sam ran into the night…Daddy's mangled body on the road. Neighbors spilled from their houses—awakened, they said, not by screams, or a gunshot, but by a loud horn.

Although the judge seemed understanding of Sam's plight, a gun had been discharged and an investigation required. Months of drilling, months of psychoanalysis, recounting Daddy's abuse, recounting the number of times Daddy had hit her and Mama. "You acted in self defense, Sam," the psychologists kept saying. Even after the court seemed satisfied, the nagging doubt continued, Sam pushed another truth deeper into her soul, a truth to be reconciled, not with an earthly court, but with God.

Perhaps she'd acted in self defense as the judge ruled. But long before that night, she'd wanted Daddy dead. She wanted him dead when he squeezed her arms and dared her to stop him. Every time Daddy hit her or Mama, she saw him in his coffin and smiled. She imagined how she might kill Daddy some day. She read about poison. Sometimes she dreamt she'd cut Daddy's heart out while he slept. The truck killed Daddy before she could. She was angry that the truck robbed her of revenge.

Vengeance is mine, child.

A sudden cold filled the cabin as Sam shut out the memories, yet a verse she'd learned in Sunday School rushed through her mind—*For out of the heart come evil thoughts, murder, adultery, sexual immorality, theft, false testimony, slander*. Justine said if you entertained an evil thought, sooner or later, you would act on it.

She'd never given that part of her guilt, her anger that a truck killed Daddy before she could, over to God. "Life and death are God's domain," Justine had said. The question burst open on her heart. Had she sought revenge against Styles to get even with a dead father?

What if Daddy hadn't died? What if she'd come into adolescence with even more hate bottled up, like Harlan Styles had done? Would she have become just like him? If the truck hadn't killed Daddy…if God had not intervened…Sam shuddered with the realization. There, but for God's mercy…she might have traveled the same road as Styles.

Zack drove for an hour, thoughts swirling in his head like the dust blowing around him, his anger as wild as the wind. Maybe all women played with their catch, reeled them in, then tossed their broken hearts back into the water like undersized bass.

So Sam preferred Jonathan's caviar to Zack's peanut butter. No way could he compete.

Sleet beat against his windshield as he turned onto Main Street. If Aunt Sadie wasn't too busy tonight, maybe she could help him figure out what to do. If she didn't have any advice, at the least, she'd talk a blue streak and get his mind off Sam for a few minutes. Besides, he was getting hungry.

Hang Sam. Hang all women. He'd have an extra large portion of Aunt Sadie's turkey dinner, fill his belly, then, buy a sympathy card for Frank's wife. Tomorrow he'd start a collection for flowers from the faculty. Time to put plan *A* in place. He'd finish the school year, and after commencement, move to New York City. He'd join the police force as soon as his residency was completed…become a juvenile officer…help the Jimmy Hodgekins of the world.

The lights flickered as he entered the lounge. Zack shook off the excess water from his coat and flung it over the chair. Eerily quiet. Where was everyone? "Hello? Anyone here?"

"That you Zack?" Leon popped his head into the lounge "I was on my way upstairs."

"Kind of quiet."

"Doc's gone home early. Cynthia gets riled when it storms this bad. Aaron and Sadie had gone to

Whitehall, but then Tracey called…a tree fell through her roof. So they went to go get her. Temperatures are dropping fast and a cold front's moving in behind the storm. Took Mazie with them. Sadie closed the lounge for supper tonight, but must be you didn't see the sign outside. Storm's playing havoc with the power and phone lines. Thought I might dig out some candles and hunker down with a book. Where's Sam? I thought you went to help her settle in."

"Turns out she doesn't want my help. Looks like I'm alone tonight."

"I could rustle us up some cold turkey and coffee. You don't have to be alone."

"I'd like that."

Leon disappeared into the kitchen and returned with a couple of drumsticks but no mugs.

"Coffee, Leon?"

"Oh, that's what I forgot. He went back into the kitchen, carrying a tray with cups, pointing to it with bright eyes. "Remembered the urn this time, too." He poured the coffee into the mugs, handing Zack his. "Say, did Sam's friend make it up there?"

"What friend?"

"Sam's attorney friend, from where she works."

"Abe?"

"No, some handsome fellow who stopped by. Least wise, I think he was handsome, hard to tell with those dark shades on. Never saw a man wear shades in a storm. But city folks can be awful weird, sometimes. Anyway, the man said his name, but I don't recall it. Said he worked with Sam at the DA's office. Doc gave him directions to the cabin. That was about an hour ago. I figure he must have come while you were there."

"Someone showed up all right, but it wasn't any of

Sam's friends from work." Zack devoured half the drumstick in three quick bites. "I found her with Jonathan. I think she likes him more than she likes me."

"You don't say."

"I don't know what to do, Leon. I have feelings for Sam. Sometimes, I think she has feelings for me, too. Other times, she shuts me out and shoos me away like an annoying fly. It drives me crazy."

Leon smiled. "Sounds like Sam's confused. Believe me, I know how painful it is to be confused. Know what I think?" Leon had better get the notion out before it ran away from him.

"Tell me."

"I think you're rushing her, Zack. For crying out loud, you've known the girl less than a week. Give her time."

Zack gulped the lukewarm coffee. "I lose no matter what. She's determined to leave Haven. If she does, I'll never see her again. If she stays, well…I can't compete with Jonathan. Look at him. The man could model for a lumberjack catalogue. He has talent coming out the wazoo. On top of all that, he's rich."

"Have you talked to God about Sam?"

No he hadn't, afraid of what God would tell him to do, and if Sam turned to God, she might not want Zack around. "I should have."

"You and that Gladstone boy are squeezing her, like she's some kind of new toy you both want to play with. The way I see it, Sam's come up against a brick wall. One God put in her way. One she and the Lord have to climb together. Ever occur to you that you and Jonathan are getting in Sam's way of conquering that wall?"

Wise words. Pity that in an hour or less, Leon wouldn't remember he'd given Zack exactly the sermon he needed to hear. Zack finished his coffee, took one last bite out of his drumstick, then grabbed his coat off the chair.

"Now where are you going in such an all-fired hurry?"

"To the cabin. I've gotta talk to Sam—apologize for acting like a jerk when she most needed a friend. You're right, Leon. I've been riding the coattails of her need."

"Right about what?"

The cabin walls seemed to close in on her, heaving accusations as lights flickered on and off.

Hang the storm. She searched the drawers and found a flashlight, then grabbed the padlock keys. Why bother locking the house? She had about as much security with a bull in the bedroom. She threw the keys on the counter, removed the blockade from the door and rushed to the parked ATVs, laughing hysterically at Haven mindset. Unlocked doors, leaving keys in vehicles, people traipsing into her room willy-nilly. Some harbor Haven turned out to be. She felt safer in her Manhattan apartment.

She pushed the helmet aside, revved the motor, backed out and put the ATV in high gear—gravel and sticks flew in every direction. The hard rain blurred her vision and slashed at her bare arms like razors. Let it. She switched on the headlights, the creeping dusk throwing shadows around the trees and boulders. An impulse greater than anything she knew propelled her toward the lake, toward Triune Point. She recognized the markers, parked the ATV and galloped towards the trail, sliding on wet leaves. She lost her balance and rolled down the rest of the hill. She freed her tears when she came to the boulders. The rain had stopped, and the fading sun split the horizon, a trail of orange and gold beams splayed across the lake.

A light shone far behind her and reflected off the water. Emmanuel's angel? She fell to her knees, lifting her heart towards heaven. "God, I don't know what to do. I've made a mess of things here. I'm sorry for the trouble I've caused. I don't know where to go, or what to do. I can't stay here, and I can't go home. I need a Guide. Not Zack. Not Jonathan. Not Leon. Not Sadie. Not Justine. I need you, Lord. I'm giving You my oars."

Tears flowed and she prayed until the last flicker of daylight escaped across the lake. No voice, no angelic forms, not even the familiar comforting scent of hyacinths. Strangely, though, she felt at peace, the peace she'd searched for since Daddy died.

When you would not call on Me, I sent you hyacinths. I will never leave you or forsake you.

"What do I do about Zack and Jonathan, Lord? I didn't mean to hurt either one of them. Will they ever forgive me?"

I will work all things together for good.

A new emotion replaced her hatred, her anger at God for thwarting her chance for revenge. Not just against Daddy, but against Styles, too. It was not hers to mete out. Pity mingled with compassionate sorrow. Daddy tragically thwarted God's mercy even with his dying breath. Would Styles do the same?

"I forgive you, Daddy."

When she'd prayed until she could pray no more she looked up. Night had fallen with only the crescent moon in the sky.

She'd left the flashlight on the ATV. How would she find her way back?

The glow behind her reappeared, closer this time. Moving towards her. She squinted at the brilliance aimed directly in her face, but recognized the shadowy figure in front of her, holding a gun.

"Harlan."

"Hello. Miss Knowles. Done praying? It's time we had a chat."

39

Jonathan paced the whole of his mansion for two hours, not certain if he should go back to the cabin or leave bad enough alone. Sam had asked him to leave—no, ordered him out—minutes after the most passionate kiss he'd known in his life.

Anger filled him. He paced the whole of the mansion, the only witness to his moans. He stopped at the portraits. Heritage. What a laugh. Only two generations separated Emmanuel and Henry, the forebear of the Gladstone curse, and from Henry on, each Gladstone lived a miserable imitation of Emmanuel's greatness. They pranced and paraded their phony aristocracy, a banner of privilege no more deserved than a day in the sun. Neither wealth, nor dominion conceived, or owned the stars—they remained in the heavens only by the will of the Creator.

What irony. The legacy he fought against proved to be the very essence of who he had become—the worst of all Gladstone men—arrogant to the core.

Jonathan knelt before Emmanuel's portrait—to be half the man he was, to be half as passionate, to know half his purpose. Then again, even Emmanuel knew a poverty of spirit, an emptiness that made him wrestle with something until dawn brought new hope. Jonathan strained to recall Emmanuel's scribbled confession, dated the day after his ordeal. "I was the worst of sinners..."

Jonathan raised his heart toward heaven. "I, too, have sinned in your sight, Lord."

You are forgiven.

"What am I supposed to do now?"

Trust.

"And Sam?"

She belongs to no one, but Me.

The doorbell's chimes broke into his prayer. He checked the security camera. Zack. Had he come to take a swing at his rival? Zack paced while he rang the bell like a stuck computer key, more agitated than angry. Zack raised his head in full view of the camera, an image of a man possessed by fear, not anger.

Jonathan raced to the door. "Zack? What's wrong?"

"Is Sam here?"

"Look—Zack—I'm sorry—Sam's sorry. We didn't mean for that kiss—"

"Is she here?"

"No. She told me to leave."

"She's not in the cabin. Her car is in the drive and *both* ATVs are gone. I thought you'd gone for a ride together or maybe she came here..." His voice trailed off. "To be with you."

Jonathan laughed. "Fat chance. She gave me the brush off right after you left."

Now Zack paced. "Maybe she took that friend of hers for a ride to the lake."

"What friend?"

"Some guy from the DA's office in Manhattan. Leon couldn't remember his name. He said the guy wanted to surprise Sam with a gift. Something seems wrong, Jonathan. Sam never mentioned any friends other than Justine and Abe, and Leon said he wore sunglasses during the storm. What normal person does that?"

Jonathan felt Zack's alarm. "Just because somebody wears shades indoors doesn't make them crazy. Besides, Sam can take care of herself, she's told both of us a hundred times. But if it makes you feel better, I'll run the security tapes. Though, if anyone bothered her at the cabin, she could press the panic button…"

"What?"

"I forgot to show her where it is."

Jonathan scanned the tape from the time he left the cabin. "There's Sam leaving on the Max II. She's alone, and she looks upset. Maybe she took a spin on the lake to calm down."

Zack leaned over Jonathan's shoulder, his face ashen. "Then who took the other ATV?"

"I'll switch to the front scans." Jonathan halted the tape. "Look. There. Behind the trees. If that man is a friend, why is he trying to hide?" He advanced the tape at slow speed. The man in the shadows mounted the ATV and sped off in the same direction as Sam.

Zack gulped. "Can you zoom in?"

"Yeah. It was still daylight when Sam left." Jonathan froze the frame, clicked on the man, and highlighted his face. "Looks familiar…I've seen him someplace before…"

Zack rushed toward the door. "Call the police and get your ATV. That's Harlan Styles."

Sam had always feared death, until now, as it

stared her in face. If God brought her home today, she knew she'd been forgiven, had forgiven Daddy. And strangely, she felt sudden compassion for the man who determined to take her life. Why did he hesitate? "You won't get away with this Harlan. It won't take a rocket scientist to tie you to my murder."

He squeezed his head, and Sam started towards him. Not quickly enough, and he struck her with the end of the revolver; something warm trickled down her cheek.

"Don't try it again. You underestimate me, Miss Knowles."

Over the edge crazy, for sure. She'd keep him talking as long as she could. "Before you kill me, at least tell me why you feel you have to do this. You got the deal of the century from Abe Hilderman, and I'm not a threat to you, anymore. I don't have a job, and I'm homeless. If you wanted me to suffer, then I have. If you kill me, you'll be doing me a favor, ending my misery. Is that what you want?"

"You've wanted me dead all along, Miss Knowles. Admit it. Your boss wanted to make a deal, but that wasn't good enough for you. You scraped me like scum off a pond."

Scum who'd murdered an innocent child. "I only wanted justice for Kiley."

"I didn't kill Kiley. Maybe if you'd let up on me, the other three people would still be alive."

"You can't blame me for the deaths of the others. You've always had a choice, Harlan." With the statement, Sam felt suddenly free from the burden of Daddy's death. Daddy always had a choice, too. His choice caused his death, not Sam.

Styles laughed…maniacal…deep. "I didn't kill

those ambulance drivers, either. But, I did kill Montel Atkins. I liked it. And I'm going to like killing you."

"Then do it. What are you waiting for?"

"Not yet." Harlan inched closer and pushed the revolver hard against her abdomen, lifting her sweater slightly. "Maybe I don't want to kill you…maybe we could go into that barn and you can make it all up to me. If I like what you do, I'll let you live."

She felt sickened, yet knew she had to distract him, keep him talking. "If you didn't kill Kiley, did Brenda do it? Were you covering up for her?"

Styles pulled her arm, twisting it, forcing Sam to her knees. The jutted rocks tore through her slacks—blood oozed from her knees. He twisted her arm even more. "Kiley's death was an accident."

She wanted to scream for the pain, the nausea begging release, but she refused to give Styles the satisfaction. Her eyes filled with unwanted tears. "You want me to believe Kiley fell down the steps like you said? Her head was bashed in. How do you call that an accident?"

"She did fall. But not the way I said."

Styles let go of Sam's arm then squeezed his head again, the man no longer on the edge, but falling into an abyss.

Lord, help me. "There are no such things as accidents, Harlan."

His hand shook. "Any other ADA would have gotten tired spending every night over law books, and worked a deal for a misdemeanor. Washington thought I'd only get probation. Hilderman warned you to ease up. Why didn't you listen to him? You hounded us, me and Brenda, manipulated the evidence, and got the jury and Normandy to believe I was worse than Al

Capone, never stopping one minute to consider that Kiley's death was a mistake."

No matter how he spun the details, Kiley's death had not been a mistake, rather the result of a felony, a felony he committed, and regardless of Brenda's culpability, Harlan Styles deserved more than a slap on the wrist. Yet, as he stood broken before her, irreparably damaged, for that split second, she saw him as God saw him, a creature to be pitied. "Then tell me, now. What really happened?"

"Kiley had a tea party with my coke. That part is true. Brenda had been drinking, and I blamed her for not watching Kiley better. Brenda pushed me, and I grabbed a board, not to hit her with it, more like to scare her into thinking I might. Brenda grabbed the other end of the board, and I pulled to get it away from her. All of sudden, she let go. Kiley must have come between us while we fought and neither one of us noticed. Next thing we knew, Kiley fell down the steps and blood streaked the board."

"Harlan, put the gun away. Let me try to help you."

Harlan snarled. "Too late, now. I'll die soon enough. If not by a cop, then Ingram's hit man. At least, I'll have the satisfaction of seeing you die before I get mine."

"You don't have to do this. There are ways, witness protection."

"Come to the barn with me, now."

"No."

Harlan hit himself in the head with a rolled fist, and pushed the revolver against her forehead. "I have the power to let you live, but you refuse the chance? And people call me crazy? I could take you by force, but I'd probably be disappointed." He cocked the trigger.

"Father, into Your hands I commit my spirit."

Bright headlights loomed on the far side of the lake near the cabin. Styles veered his gaze toward the light, his attention broken. Sam pushed him with all the strength she had left. Styles slipped on the moss…his head cracked against a jutted rock…the revolver discharged. From the searing pain in her hip, she knew she'd been hit. She stumbled, slid and fell half in and half out of the water, managing to grasp one of the boulders to keep from falling into the deep collection pool. Style's moans stopped.

In the dark silence, Sam clung to the boulder. She prayed for God's help as she pulled herself out of the water to a stand, then leaned against a boulder. Her side oozed; the warmth of the blood misted the cold air. The white glow along the trail behind the inlet brightened as her knees buckled, and she fell against Styles prone body. Emmanuel's angel had come to take her home.

40

From somewhere in a dark well, Sam rose to consciousness, focusing on a wall clock. Twelve. Noon, since light shone through the window. Apparently, she wasn't dead. She tried to raise her head, but the room swirled. "Stay still, Sam. I don't want you to pull out your IV." The disembodied voice came into view, and Tracey Golden leaned over the bedrail. "Glad to see you awake."

"What happened?"

"You don't know?"

"I mean, after I passed out? I was shot—"

"In the hip. We operated last night."

Machines beeped and a blood pressure cuff tightened on Sam's other arm as Dennis Faubert came into the room.

"So…what's the verdict, Doc? Give it to me straight…in English, not that medical lingo."

Dennis smiled. "The good news is you'll walk again."

"Then there's some bad news?"

"You'll need physical therapy for a couple of months. The bullet fractured your hip bone. Once you've healed from the surgery, we'll make a referral to a bone specialist, but I'm afraid you'll always have a slight limp."

Sam gulped…Emmanuel's angel had fought her and won. "So, I won't run a marathon…otherwise…I'll be normal?"

Dennis patted her hand. "As normal as you ever were."

She'd laugh if she weren't in so much pain. Normal? There was no defining normal as it related to Samantha Knowles, never had been, and certainly less so than a week ago.

Tracey smoothed her covers. "Trooper Mitchell is waiting in the hall to talk to you."

"Maybe she wants to give me another ticket."

The sour-faced trooper walked in. "I heard that." There had to be something muscularly wrong with a face that never smiled.

"What happened to Styles?"

"You tackled him pretty good. He had a slight concussion. He'll live, unfortunately. He's been released into our custody and being held for questioning, probably extradition."

Good. He wouldn't be coming to finish what he botched. Although she'd never underestimate him again. He'd managed to escape a pretty tough house arrest program.

Trooper Mitchell took out a notepad. "What happened out there, Miss Knowles?"

"Styles found me at the lake, threatened to shoot me, so I pushed him down and the gun went off. That's about it." Sam left out Emmanuel's angel. "I'd like to know how I ended up at the hospital."

"Mr. Bordeaux states he went looking for you at the cabin. When he couldn't find you, he went to Mr. Gladstone's house. Mr. Bordeaux and Mr. Gladstone became suspicious that both ATVs were gone from your cabin. Mr. Gladstone checked his security cameras and spotted Mr. Styles watching you leave the cabin and mounting the second ATV. They called 911 and left immediately to assist you. They found both you and Mr. Styles unconscious, you with a bullet wound and Mr. Styles holding a revolver. Mr. Gladstone took possession of the weapon, and secured the suspect while Mr. Bordeaux administered first aid to your wound. We arrived on the scene soon after."

So, Zack saved her life again, this time with Jonathan's help. Her life in ironies.

Trooper Mitchell tapped her notebook with her pencil. "Mr. Gladstone and Mr. Bordeaux have given us their statements. Mr. Styles is not very forthcoming with information. Lawyered up. Anything you can add would be helpful."

The walls heaved, and her stomach flip-flopped. "He did confess to killing Montel Atkins. Otherwise, you've pretty much covered it."

Trooper Mitchell closed her notepad. "We'd appreciate you sticking around until we've completed our investigation."

Sam glanced at the array of machines and tubes. "Doesn't look like I'm leaving Haven any time soon." Where would she go after the hospital? Certainly not to the cabin. "Am I a suspect?"

"No ma'am. But the circumstances are a bit peculiar. Why did you go to the lake in the pouring rain?"

"Looking for an angel."

"What's that?"

"I wanted to clear my head a little."

"We'll be in touch, if we have any more questions."

Trooper Mitchell left, and Sam closed her eyes. When she opened them again, it was two o'clock. Two vases of hyacinths sat on her nightstand.

"Hello, there." Zack's voice startled her. How long had he been sitting in that chair?

Jonathan came in and handed Zack a cup of coffee. "Tracey said to give you this. Hello, Sam. About time you woke up. How're you feeling?"

"Like I've been shot. What are you two doing here?"

Zack spoke first. "We feel responsible, Sam. If we hadn't argued…"

"Enough with the guilt trip…both of you. A man as crazy as Harlan Styles would have found a way to get to me even if you guarded both doors. Maybe killed you in the process. I'm alive, thanks to your quick thinking."

Jonathan and Zack locked glances. "Do you want to tell her, or should I?"

Who served as a bouncer in a hospital? She'd ring for Tracey to boot these two out, but Zack had inside privileges. "I don't care who talks first, just spit it out."

"Go ahead, Zack," Jonathan said.

Zack put his coffee down on Sam's nightstand. "The Lighthouse doesn't have an elevator, and it might be awhile before you can manage steps. Pastor Gus said you could stay at the parsonage while you recover and sort things out. You won't have to deal with either one of us for awhile."

"What's to sort out? When I'm well enough, I'm going home. After what Styles pulled, all deals are off the table. There's nothing to keep me here." At it again…the two of them trying to arrange her life, when neither of them had done a very good job in managing their own.

Jonathan inched toward the bed. "What Zack is

not saying is that...well... he and I have talked. We want to help you."

"By dictating how I should live my life?"

"Not at all," Zack said. "We don't want you to leave Haven because of either one of us. The people in this town hope you'll stay. Uncle Aaron's taking full retirement as soon as his term is up, so another lawyer in town would be handy."

Jonathan cleared his throat. "Aaron said he'd help me get the will revoked. After that, I'm going to Paris for awhile. While I'm away, Dawn's Hope will be in need of a caretaker. I can't think of anyone better for the job than you."

Would Dawn's Hope be the same without Jonathan, it's Rochester?

Epilogue

Three months later

Sam hauled the labeled box off the trailer and dragged it up the steps to her new office, the first floor of the old Beacon House in the middle of Main Street. She stopped at the top and gazed at the mountains, their circus of colors heralding a new season of life coinciding with Sam's.

Her limp was barely noticeable now. Three months of therapy had done wonders. Two weeks with Pastor Gus, then a move into Dawn's Hope—the fresh air and walks along the beach as good as any medicine.

Sam brought the box inside and set it on the oak table, a gift from Abe, a thoughtful gesture. She'd forgiven him, but restoring their relationship would take months more, perhaps years.

Justine emptied boxes on her side of the office, her wedding picture displayed prominently on her desk.

"You're certain Robert doesn't mind you working for me during his tour?"

Justine smiled. "He likes the idea. He said he's hanging up his uniform when he finishes this gig and would like to settle in Haven…thinks it's a great place to raise a family. So, guess you're stuck with me for a long time."

Sam smiled. "Best way I can get back at Abe…steal his assistant."

The phone rang. "That's your line, Justine."

"Probably my mother. She calls me every day about this time since I moved up here."

While Justine chatted, Sam started unloading law books and stacking them on her shelves. Doc Henson peeked in. "Where should we take this armchair?"

"That's Justine's. Sadie's remodeling the two upstairs apartments. We're storing Justine's furniture in mine until hers is ready. In the meantime, she'll stay with me at Dawn's Hope. Sadie has a lot of projects going on at the moment. She won't be able to start on this building until after Christmas."

Doc shook his head. "I know…Zack's wedding is around the corner. I hear our boy is going into the police academy in a month or two. Who'd have thought? Still can't picture him a New York City cop. His fiancée is going into the force same time as he is."

Justine ended her phone call and continued unloading boxes. "Sam, where should we put this big old clock?"

"You decide. Of course, Sadie will probably want me to throw it out once we set her loose on the office."

"Wonder what kind of theme she'll come up with?"

"We'll see. The house was built in 1859…maybe antebellum?"

Sam took out the photo of her, Zack and Jonathan, taken on the day she moved into Dawn's Hope. She placed it on the shelf next to her desk.

Justine glanced at the photo. "Have you heard from Jonathan since he went to Paris?"

"No."

Not that Sam expected to, he owed her nothing, a long-distance attorney-client relationship. When Jonathan returned, she'd move into the other upstairs apartment above her law office. Much more convenient—especially the commute. She'd be right across from the Lighthouse and near the church, her own Triune Point. Still, she'd like to know if Paris was as romantic in the fall as it reportedly was in the spring.

Sam considered herself blessed, confident this decision had been the right one. Haven had given her so much, friends, affection, shelter, and now a purpose. From now on, she would defend the innocent, rather than attack the guilty.

The phone rang and she answered it, taking the handset into the other room as her helpers buzzed with excitement. "Sam Knowles's office." She liked the sound of that, and beamed, even though no one could see her pleasure but the Lord.

"Sam, it's Abe. I don't know if you heard, yet. I know you're busy with the big move, today."

"Heard what?"

"Harlan Styles is dead. Brenda, too."

Three months ago, Sam might have felt cold satisfaction with the news, a sense they both got exactly what they deserved. Amazing how much a person can change in that amount of time. Rather than rejoice, Sam pained for their tragic ends. "I hoped they might turn around."

"Who knows what their last thoughts might have been."

Only God knew for sure. "What happened?"

"They found Styles's body in the prison laundry room—strangled. They found Brenda floating in Ingram's pool—her throat slashed."

Tears formed as Sam counted the losses surrounding this case…so many. Could any of them have been avoided? "Thanks for letting me know, Abe."

"Are you happy, Sam? I mean, with your decision to stay in Haven? Your old job's yours if you want it."

It felt good to hear Abe's voice. Why waste her life being angry? Besides, in a way, Abe had been responsible for her new life in Haven. "I hope you will come to Dawn's Hope for a visit, sometime?"

"Thanks, Sam. I think I'd like that."

Sam brought the handset back into the front room as Rusty came in with the last box. "Thank you everyone," Sam said. "You've done enough."

Justine slung her purse over her shoulder. "We're all going over to the Lighthouse. Spaghetti tonight. Are you coming?"

"In a few minutes. Go ahead. I'll meet you there."

As Justine crossed the street, Tracey Golden came up the steps. "I'm on my way over to my parents' but wanted to drop this off, a little office-warming present." She handed Sam a satin-wrapped soap dispenser. "Sadie's invention."

"Is there anything she can't do?"

"Probably not."

"Thanks for your thoughtfulness. I'll put this in the bathroom." Sam grabbed her purse. "I'll walk over to the Lighthouse with you."

"Don't tell Sadie I warned you, but she's cooked up a special party for you. Everyone's waiting."

Sam spotted Sadie as she clipped across the street, agitation with every step.

"Speaking of Sadie…maybe she's come to drag me over herself."

Sadie shoved a citation in Sam's hand. "You've got to do something about this. The Board of Health's trying to shut me down…claiming I got too many people in my lounge while I'm serving food. Now that's ridiculous. What's America coming to if a body can't have friends over for supper?"

"Of course, I'll represent you, Sadie. I'm sure it'll be fine."

"Good. Now you hurry it up, supper's waiting."

"Yes, ma'am."

Sadie grabbed Tracey's hand. "You come with me. I need your help." Sam watched the pair cross the street and disappear into the Lighthouse, like any mother and daughter who loved one another.

Sam closed the door as a delivery truck pulled up to the curb. The driver emerged with a small box and clipboard. "Are you Samantha Knowles?"

"Guilty."

No smile.

"Special delivery from Paris."

Her hands trembled as she opened the box. She gasped at the ivory statue perched on top of a small music box. Etched at its base was the inscription, "Emmanuel's Angel." A note was attached.

Sam,

I wanted this angel to keep you company until I return.

Affectionately,

Jonathan Gladstone

She returned to her office, to set the angel on her desk. She turned the key and wept as it twirled to the familiar chorus of hope:

I've anchored my soul in the "Haven of Rest,"
I'll sail the wide seas no more;
The tempest may sweep over wild, stormy, deep,
In Jesus I'm safe evermore.

Sam sang as it played, unconcerned about her

pitch. Her heart, in tune with God, swelled with gratitude for He had taken her to the other side of darkness, a place where hope dwelled.

Harbourlight Books
The Beacon in Christian Fiction™
www.HarbourlightBooks.com
an imprint of Pelican Ventures Book Group
www.pelicanbookgroup.com

May God's glory shine through
this inspirational work of fiction.

AMDG